Published in English in Canada and the USA in 2022 by
Groundwood Books
Text copyright © 2021 by Fanny Britt
Illustrations copyright © 2021 by Isabelle Arsenault
Translation copyright © 2022 by Susan Ouriou
First published in French as *Truffe* by Les Éditions de la
Pastèque, Montreal (2021)
Published in agreement with Koja Agency

Groundwood Books / House of Anansi Press
groundwoodbooks.com

We gratefully acknowledge for their financial support of
our publishing program the Canada Council for the Arts, the
Ontario Arts Council and the Government of Canada.

Canada Council   Conseil des Arts
for the Arts   du Canada

ONTARIO ARTS COUNCIL
CONSEIL DES ARTS DE L'ONTARIO
an Ontario government agency
un organisme du gouvernement de l'Ontario

With the participation of the Government of Canada | Canadä
Avec la participation du gouvernement du Canada

Library and Archives Canada Cataloguing in Publication
Title: Forever Truffle / three stories by Fanny Britt ; illustrations
by Isabelle Arsenault ; translated by Susan Ouriou.
Other titles: Truffe. English
Names: Britt, Fanny, author. | Arsenault, Isabelle, illustrator. |
Ouriou, Susan, translator.
Description: Translation of: Truffe.
Identifiers: Canadiana (print) 20210335505 | Canadiana
(ebook) 20210335548 | ISBN 9781773060705
(hardcover) | ISBN 9781773065830 (EPUB) | ISBN
9781773065847 (Kindle)
Subjects: LCGFT: Comics (Graphic works)
Classification: LCC PN6733.B75 T7813 2022 | DDC
j741.5/971—dc23

The illustrations were rendered in pencil, ink and collage.
Printed and bound in South Korea

MIX
Paper from
responsible sources
FSC® C013572

FOREVER
TRUFFLE

Thank you to Flavie, Rafaël and Darius for breathing life and humor into Flo, Riad and Louis. Thank you to Margot for the cake that made you so happy you were a little sad. Above all, thank you to Hippolyte for embodying — like a true Funghetto since the day you were born — joie de vivre, curiosity and a love of music — FB

For Fred and Fanny, indispensable members of our killer trio — IA

For Ben and Amélie, who dare to dream big — SO

FOREVER TRUFFLE

Three Stories by
Fanny Britt

Illustrations by
Isabelle Arsenault

Translated by
Susan Ouriou

GROUNDWOOD BOOKS
HOUSE OF ANANSI PRESS
TORONTO / BERKELEY

TRUFFLE THE ROCK STAR

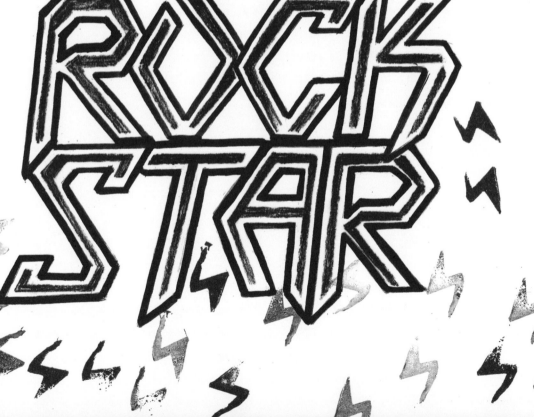

Truffle has always loved music.

When I was a baby, I never stopped crying,
except when my parents played Verdi's
songs extra loud in the kitchen.

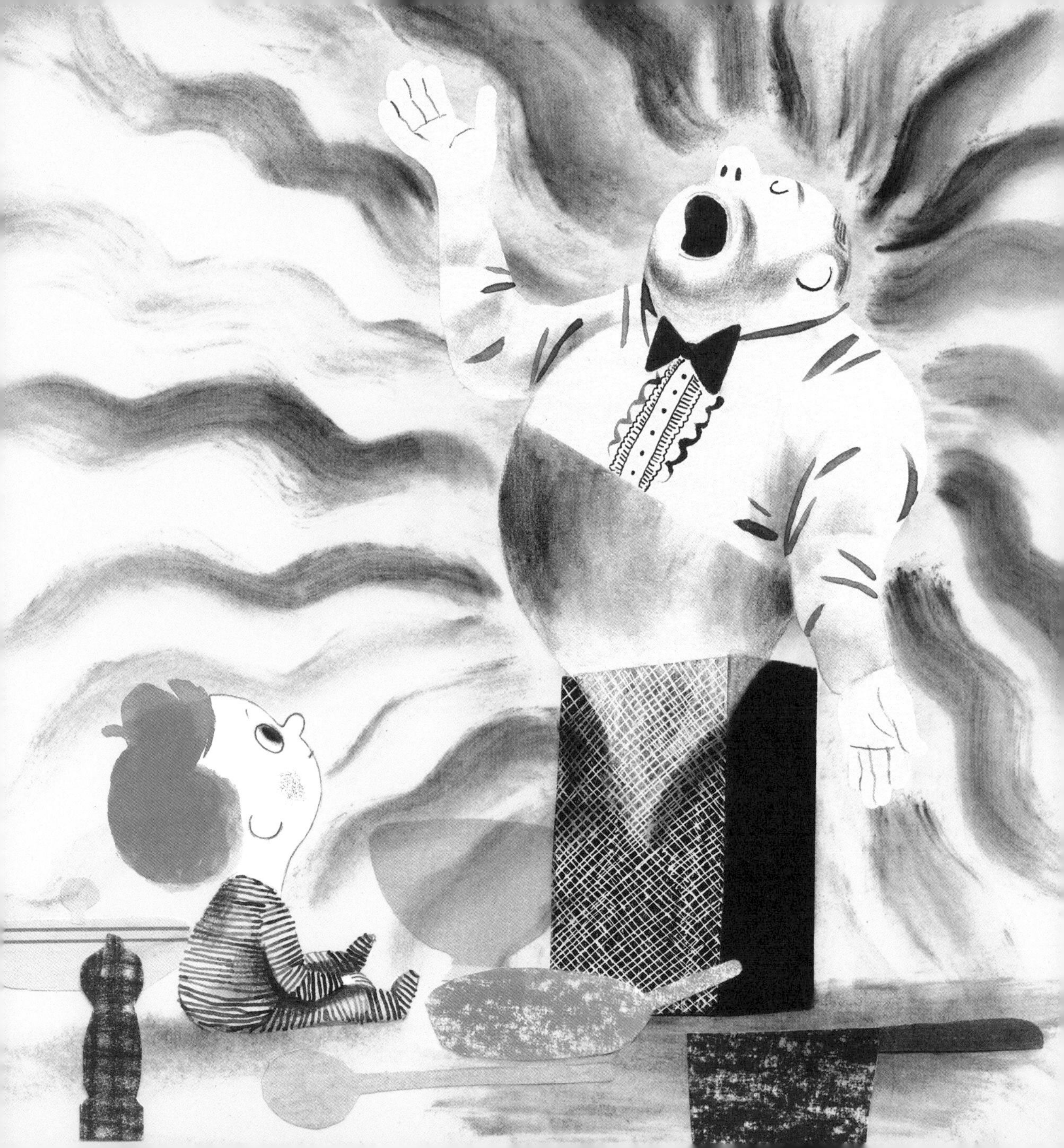

For his birthday, Truffle asked for a biker jacket.

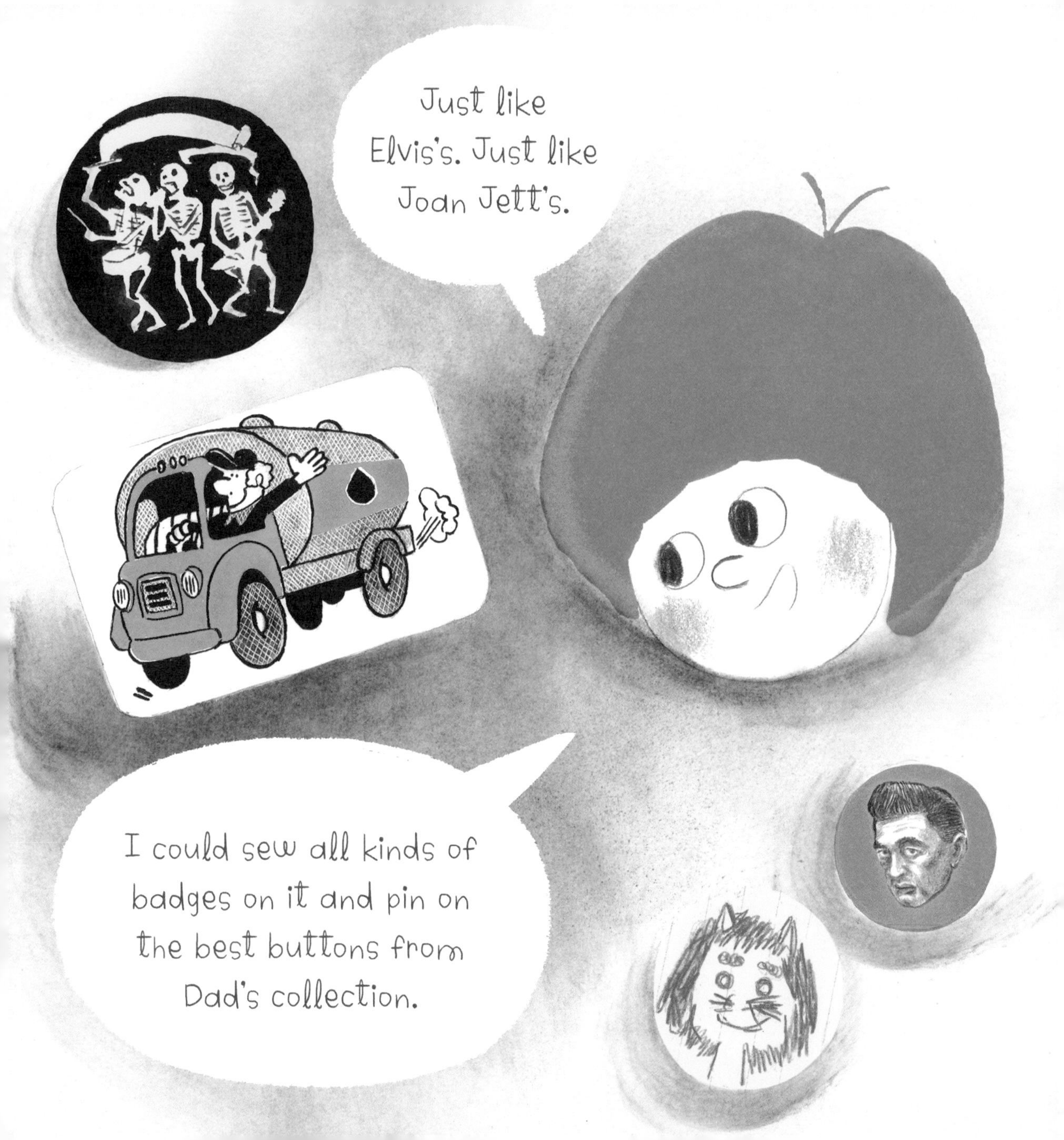
Just like Elvis's. Just like Joan Jett's.
I could sew all kinds of badges on it and pin on the best buttons from Dad's collection.

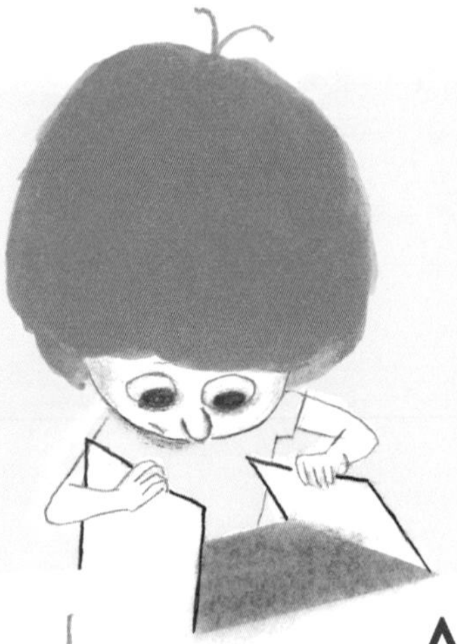

After he unwrapped his present,

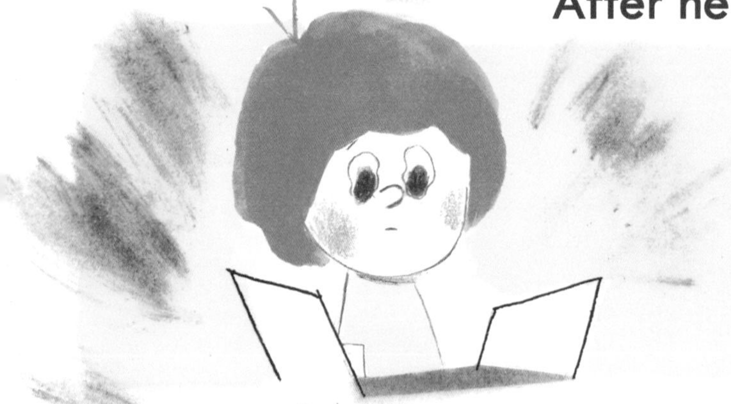

Truffle shed a tear.

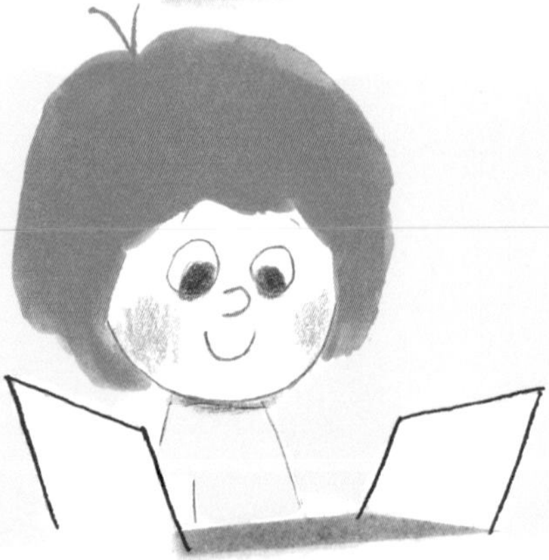

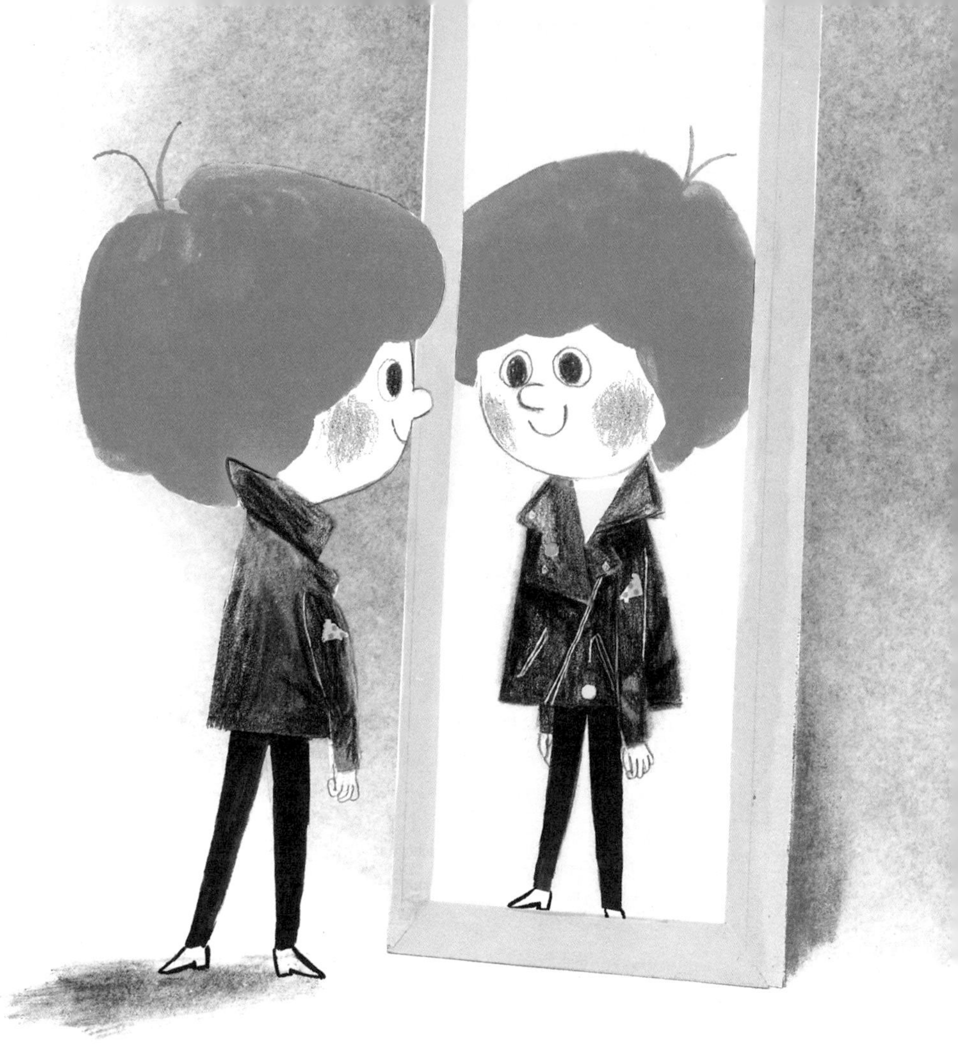

He swore to himself he'd wear the jacket every day of his life, even when it got too small.

A band is the only thing missing for you to be a real rocker.

ME, a real rocker?

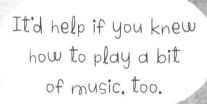

It'd help if you knew how to play a bit of music, too.

You're being sarcastic, aren't you?

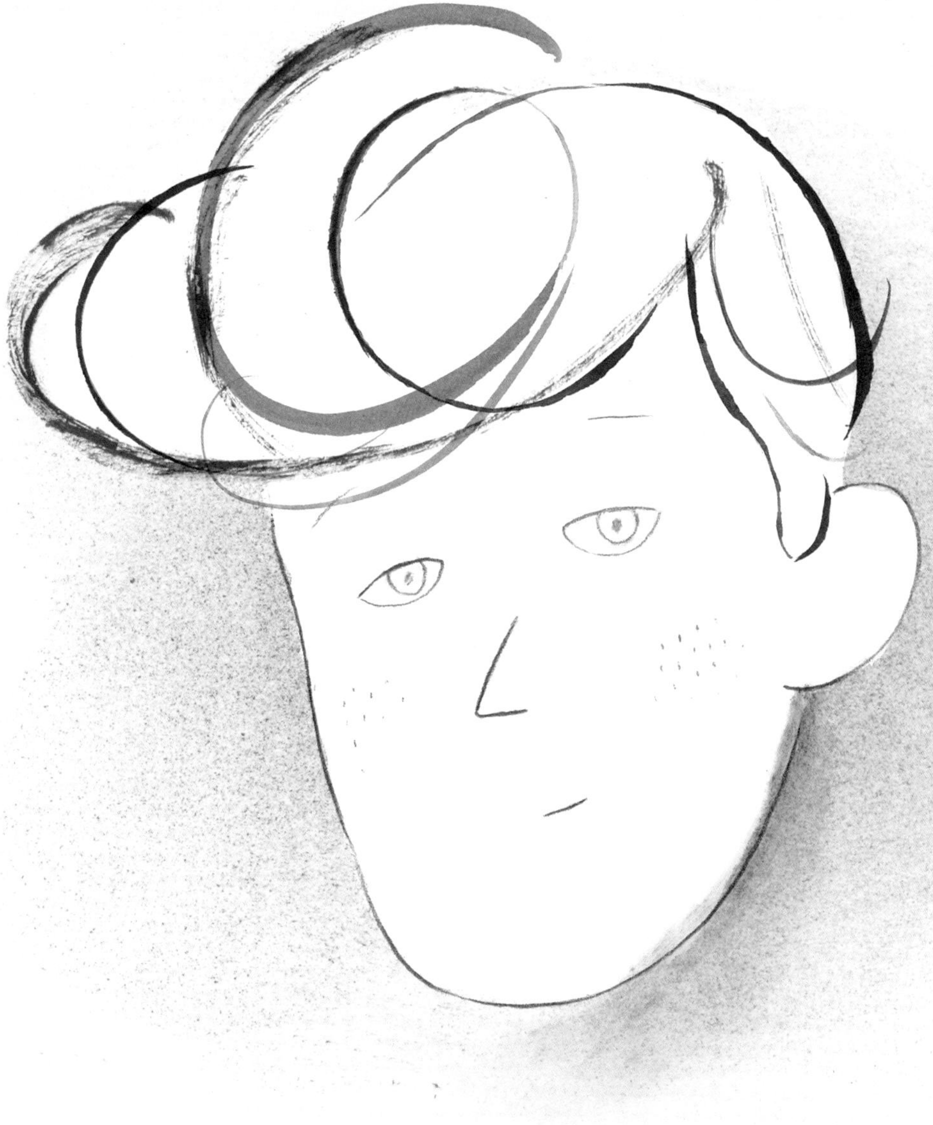

Truffle's brother's name is Louis. Now that he's in high school, he's into robotics, basketball and sarcasm.

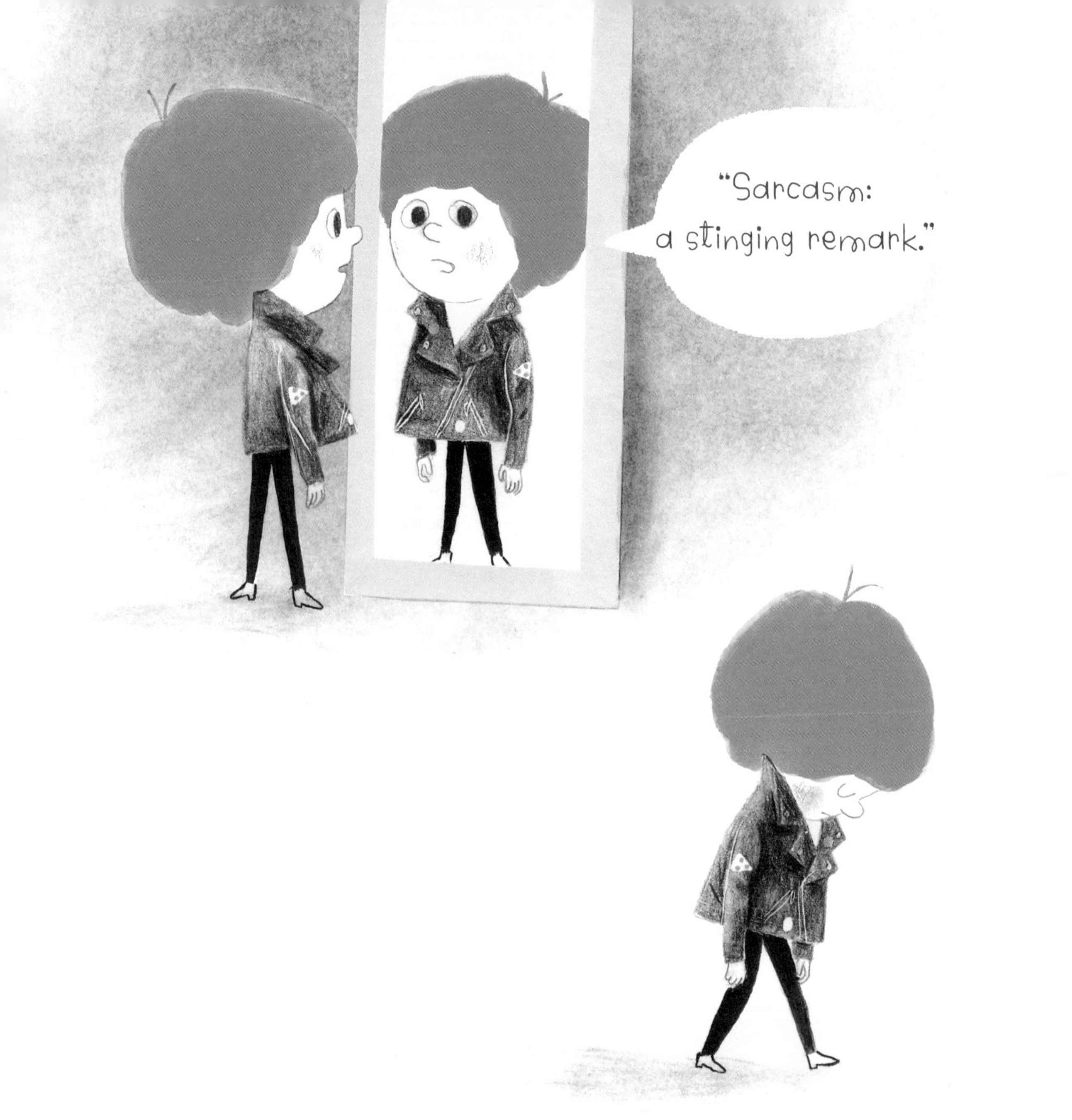
"Sarcasm: a stinging remark."

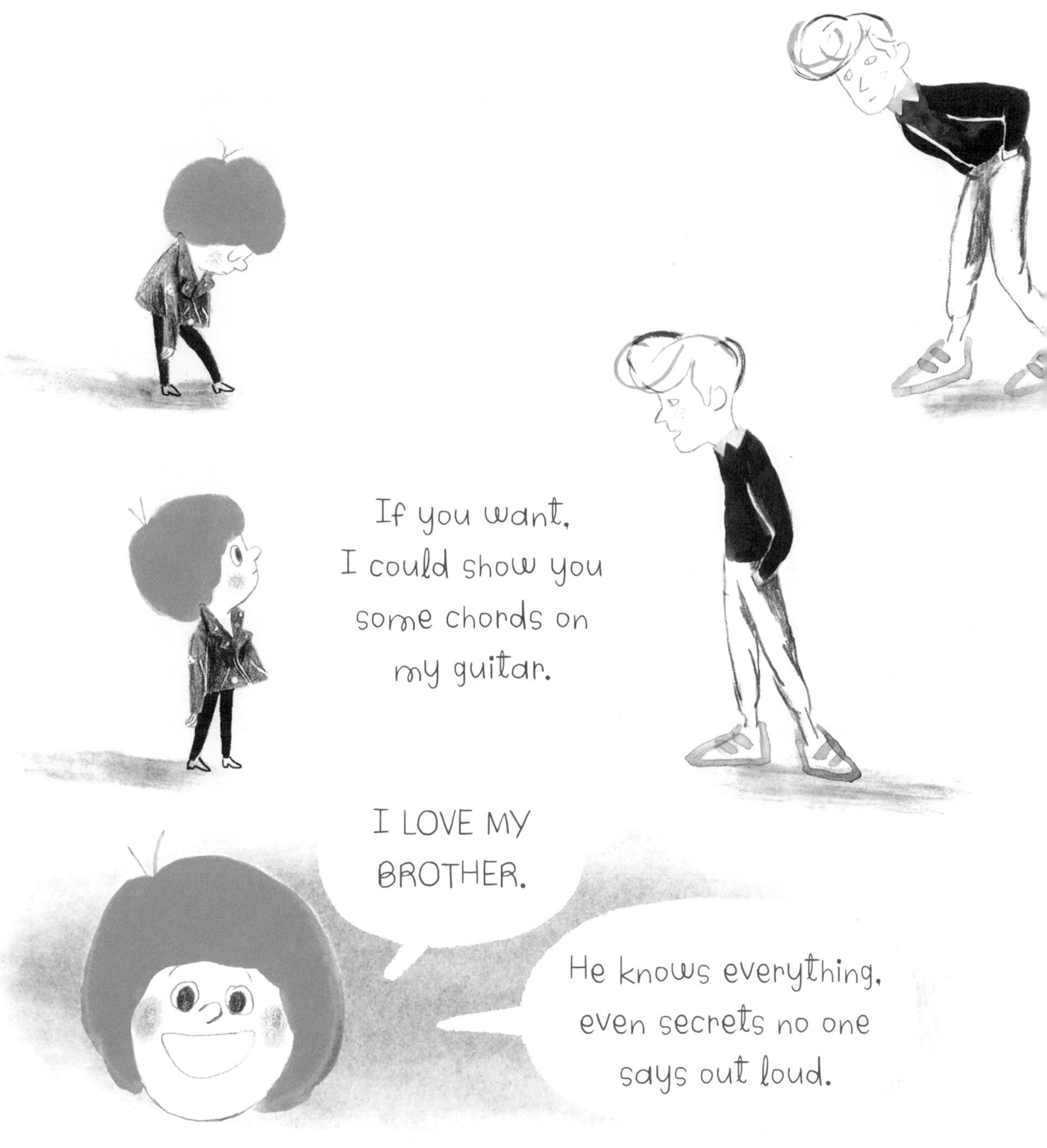
If you want, I could show you some chords on my guitar.
I LOVE MY BROTHER.
He knows everything, even secrets no one says out loud.

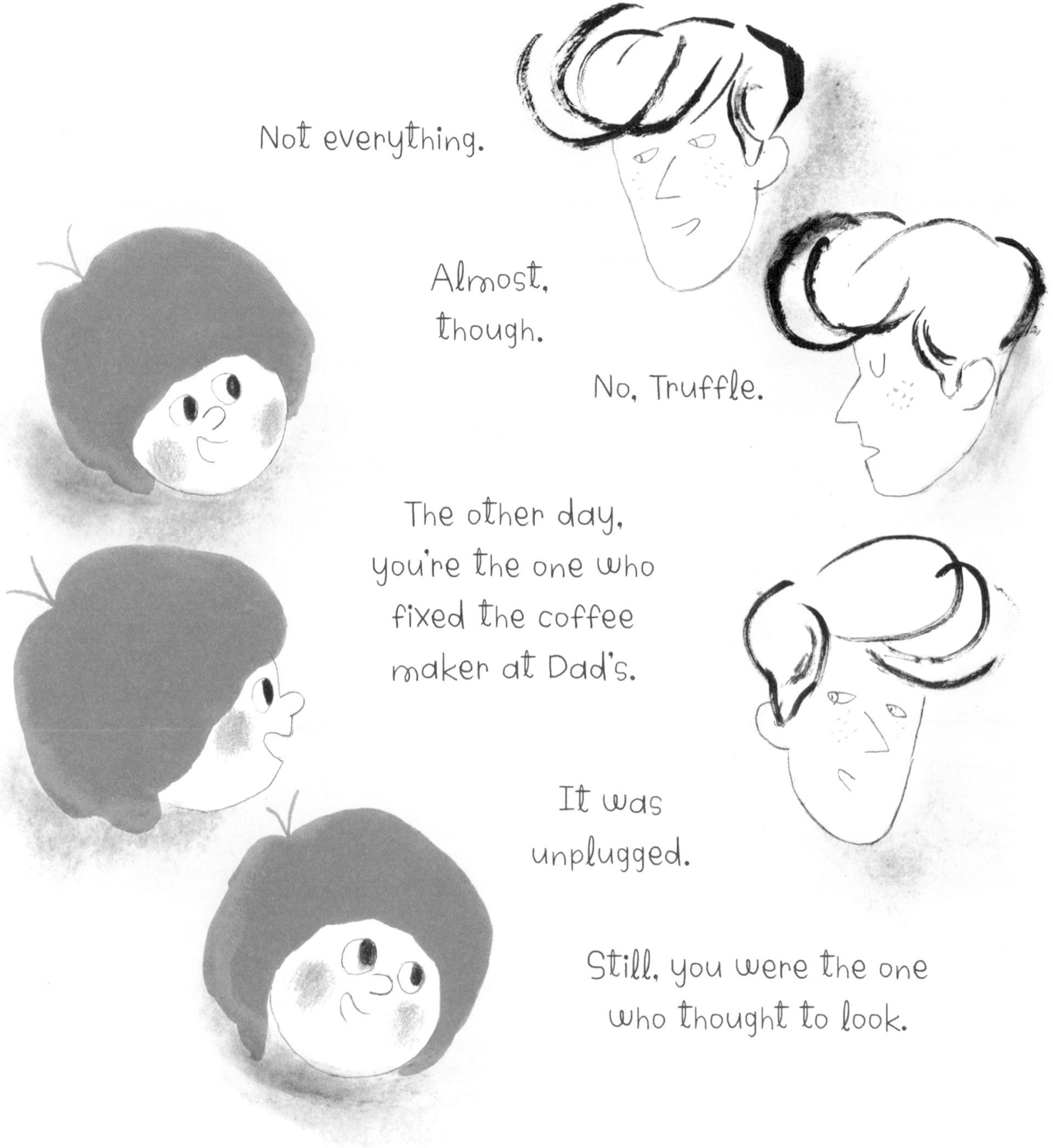
Not everything.
Almost, though.
No, Truffle.
The other day, you're the one who fixed the coffee maker at Dad's.
It was unplugged.
Still, you were the one who thought to look.

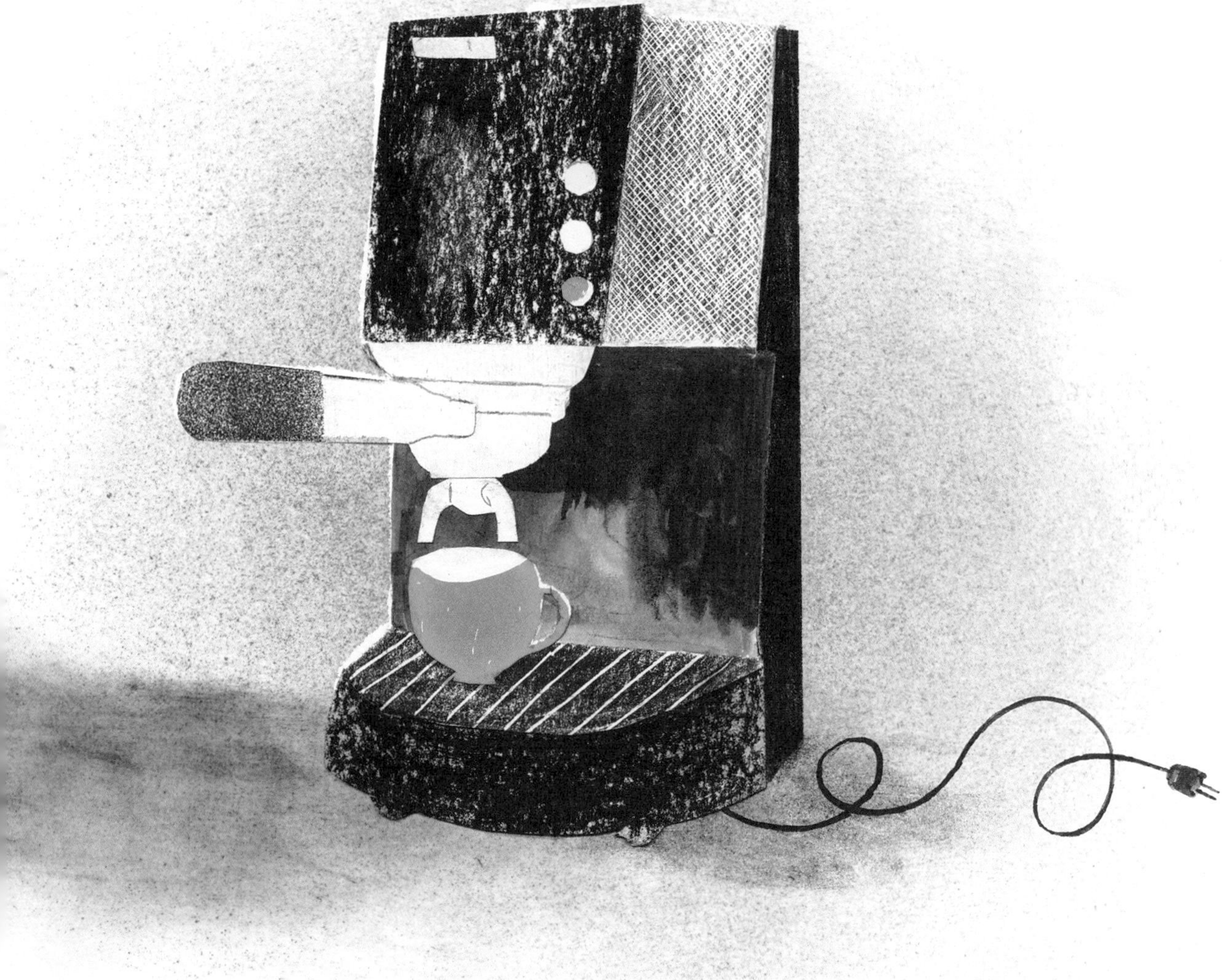

Truffle and his dad have a lot in common, like forgetting to think of certain things from time to time.

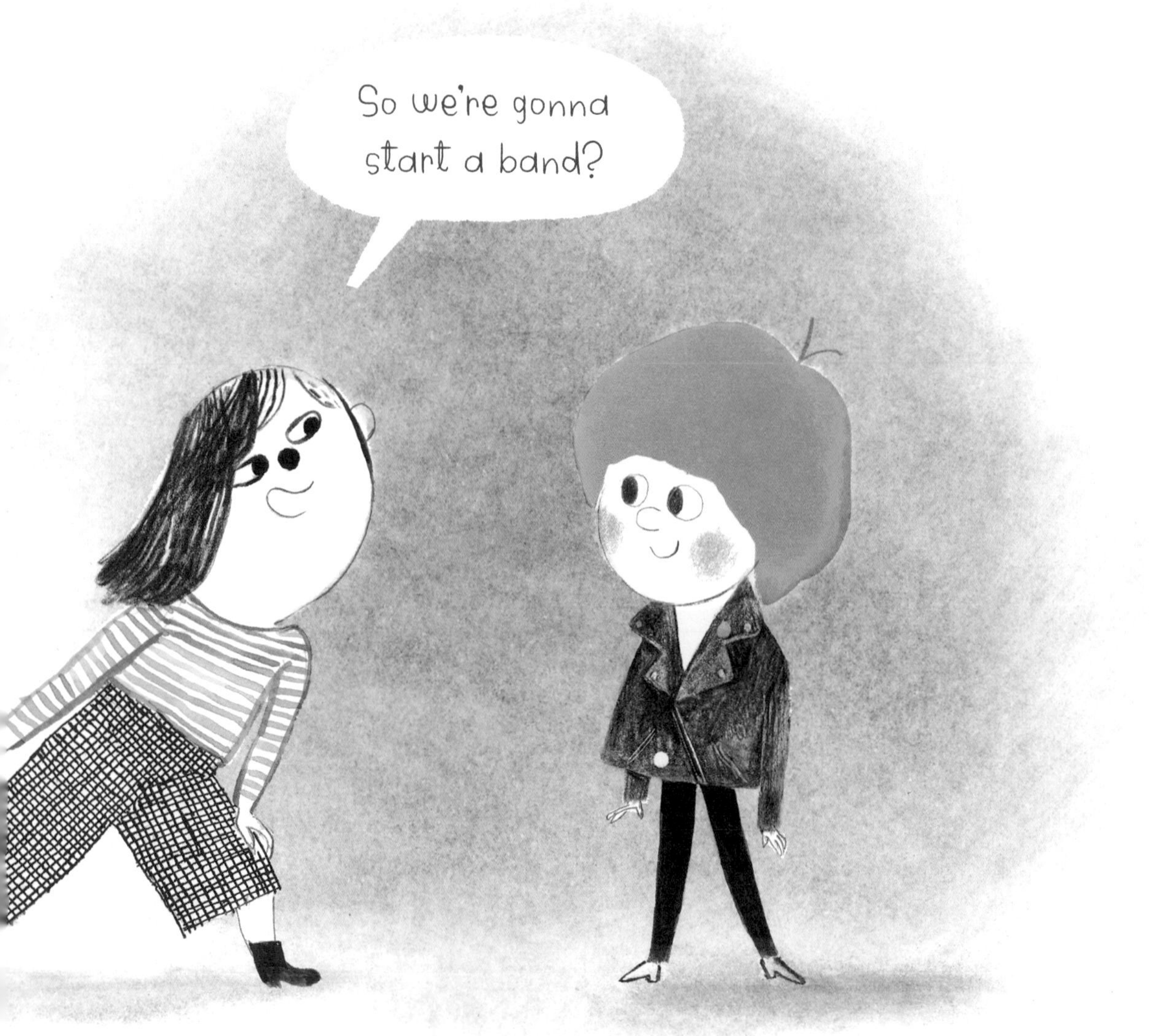
So we're gonna start a band?

Flo is Truffle's best friend.
They've known each other
since the day they were born.

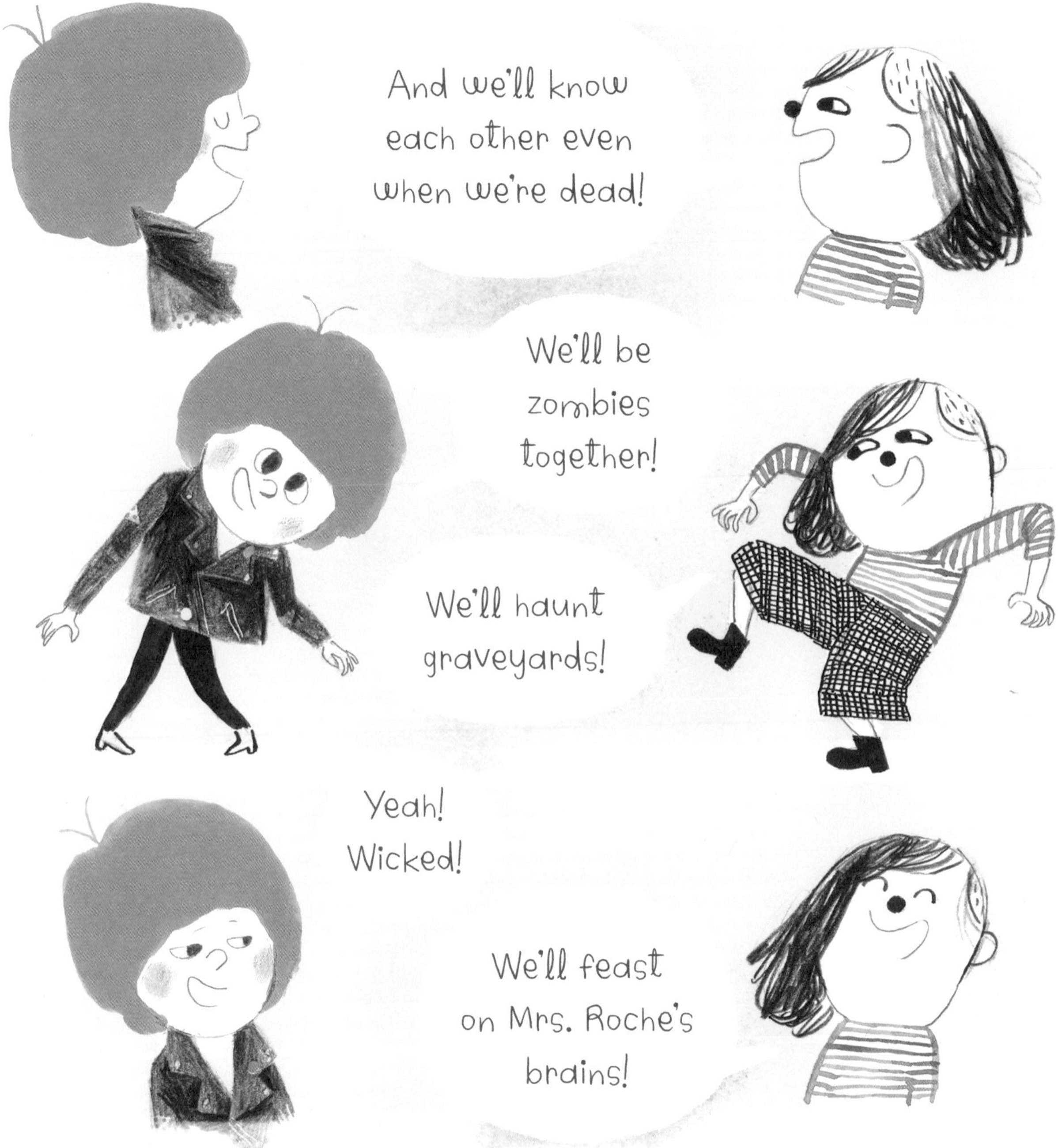
And we'll know each other even when we're dead!
We'll be zombies together!
We'll haunt graveyards!
Yeah! Wicked!
We'll feast on Mrs. Roche's brains!

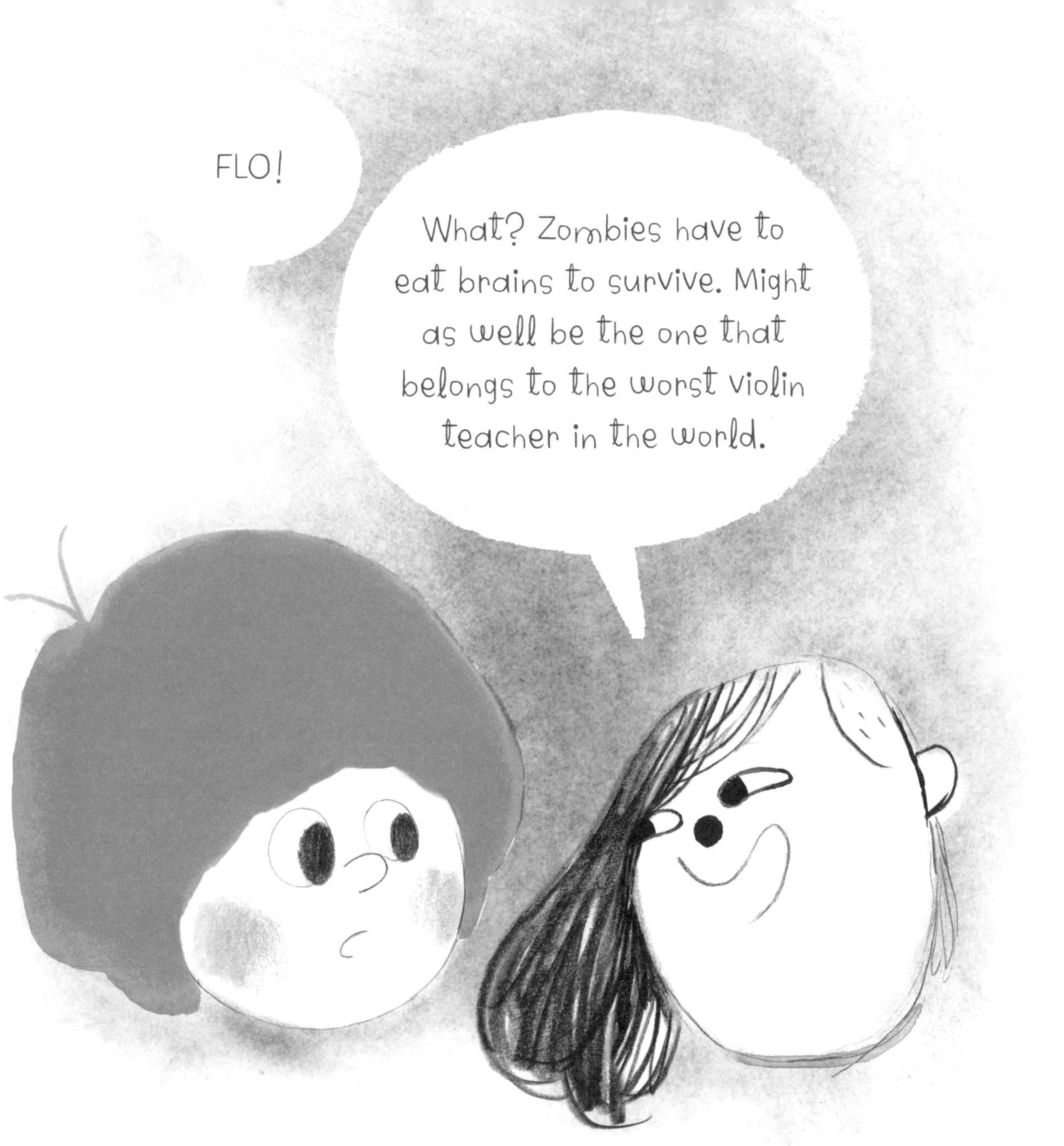
FLO!
What? Zombies have to eat brains to survive. Might as well be the one that belongs to the worst violin teacher in the world.

Flo's a real rebel.

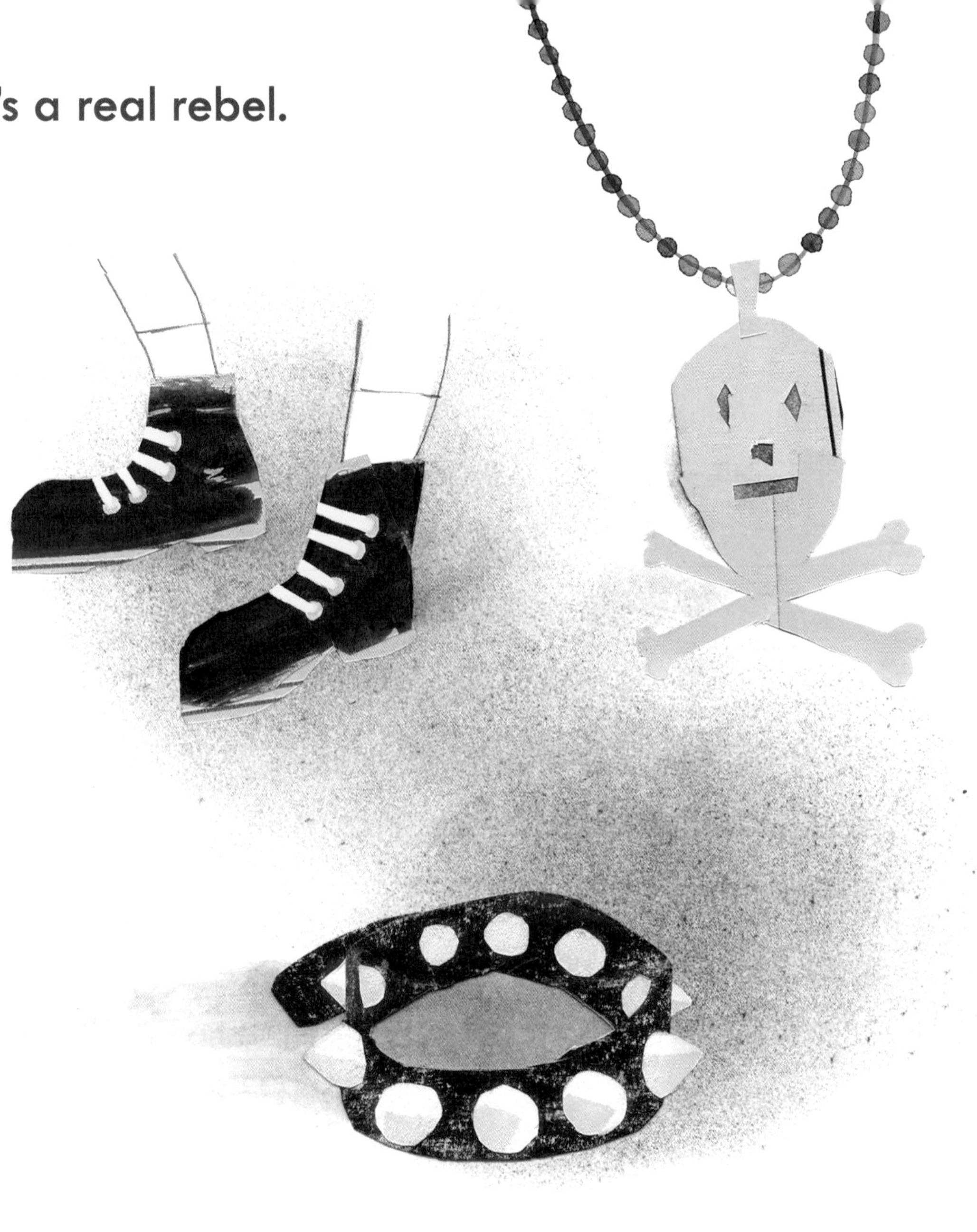

Truffle thinks she'd be great on drums.

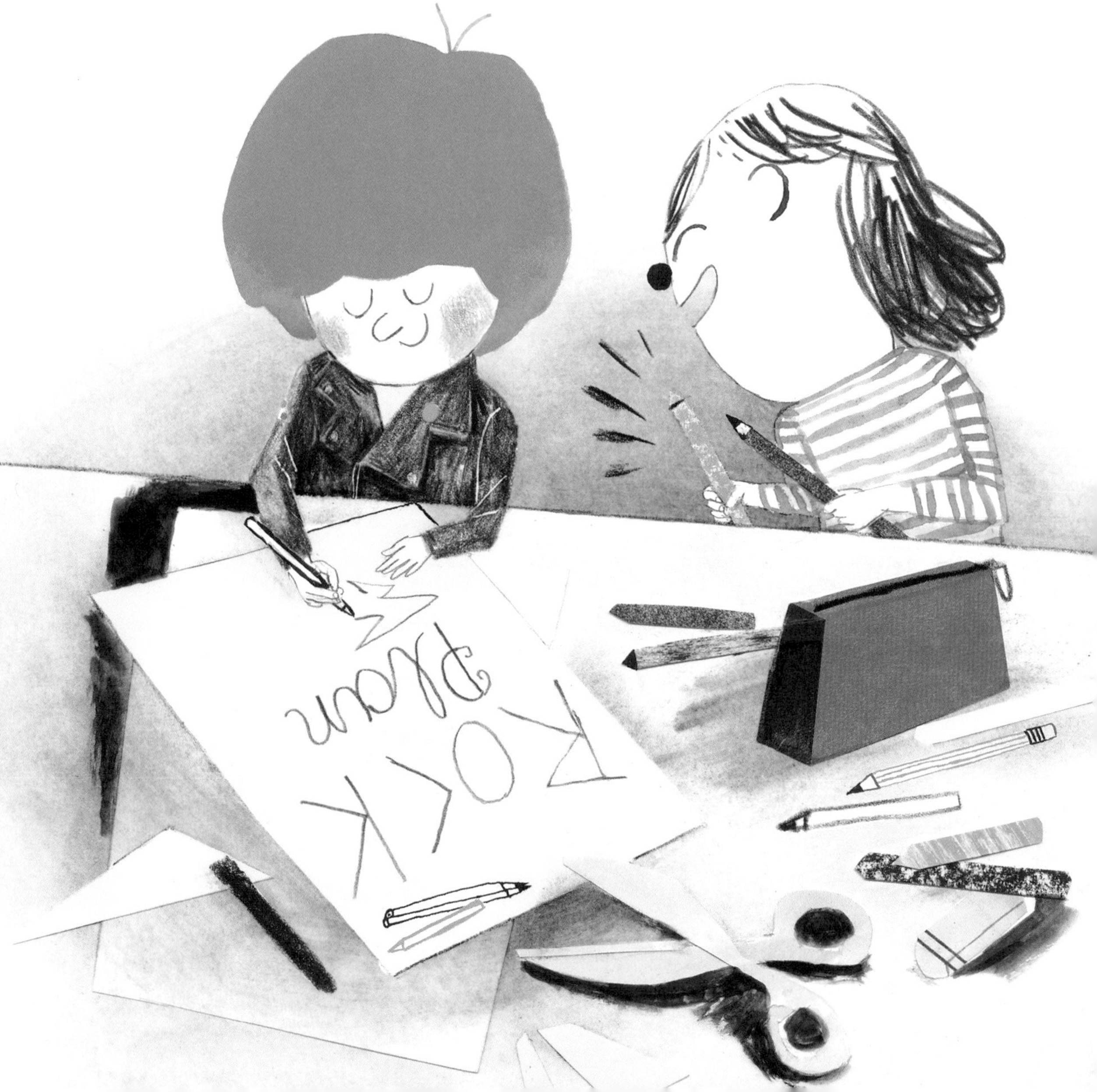
ROCK

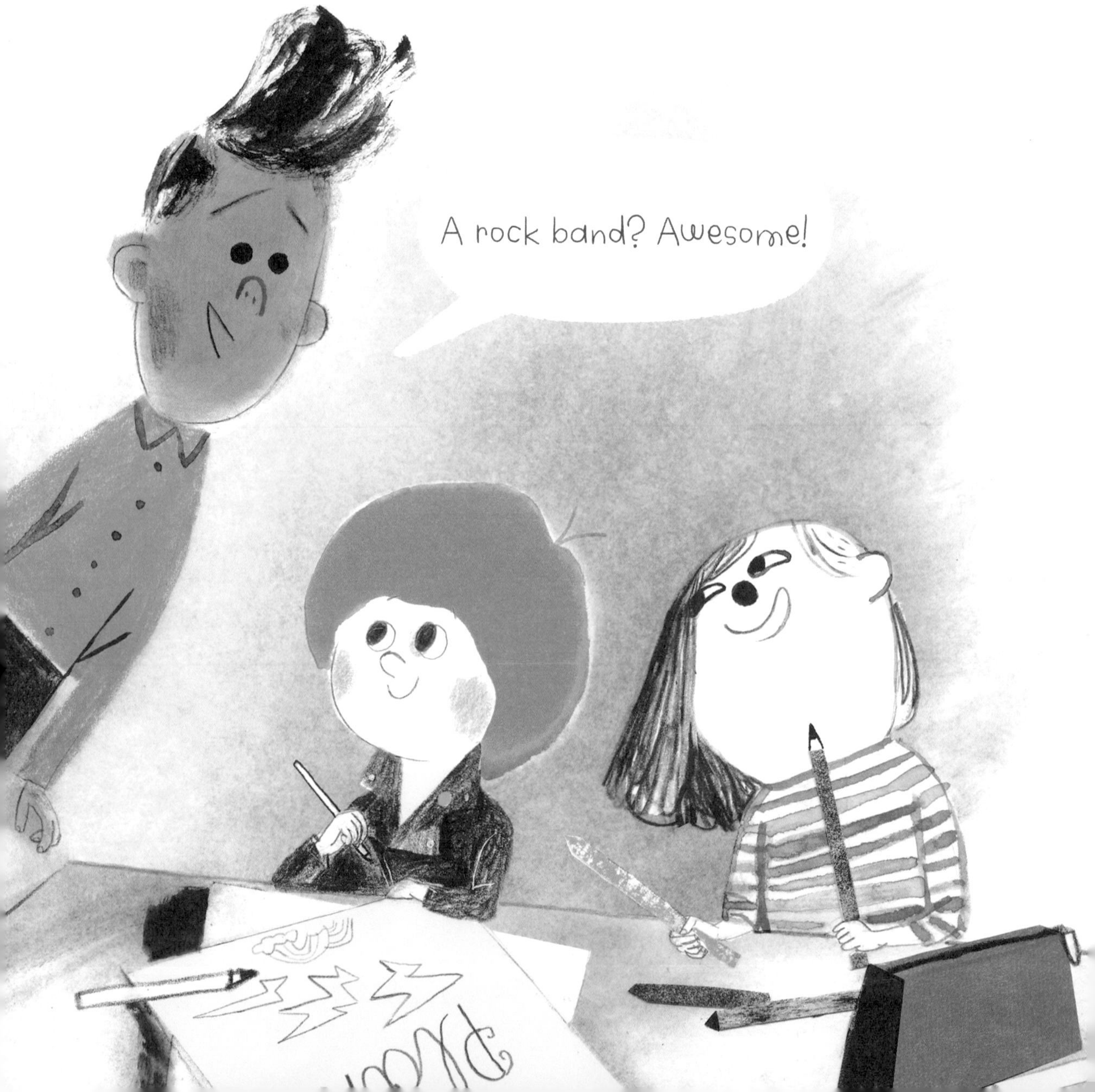
A rock band? Awesome!

Riad is Truffle's other best friend.

He's probably the nicest person in the universe.

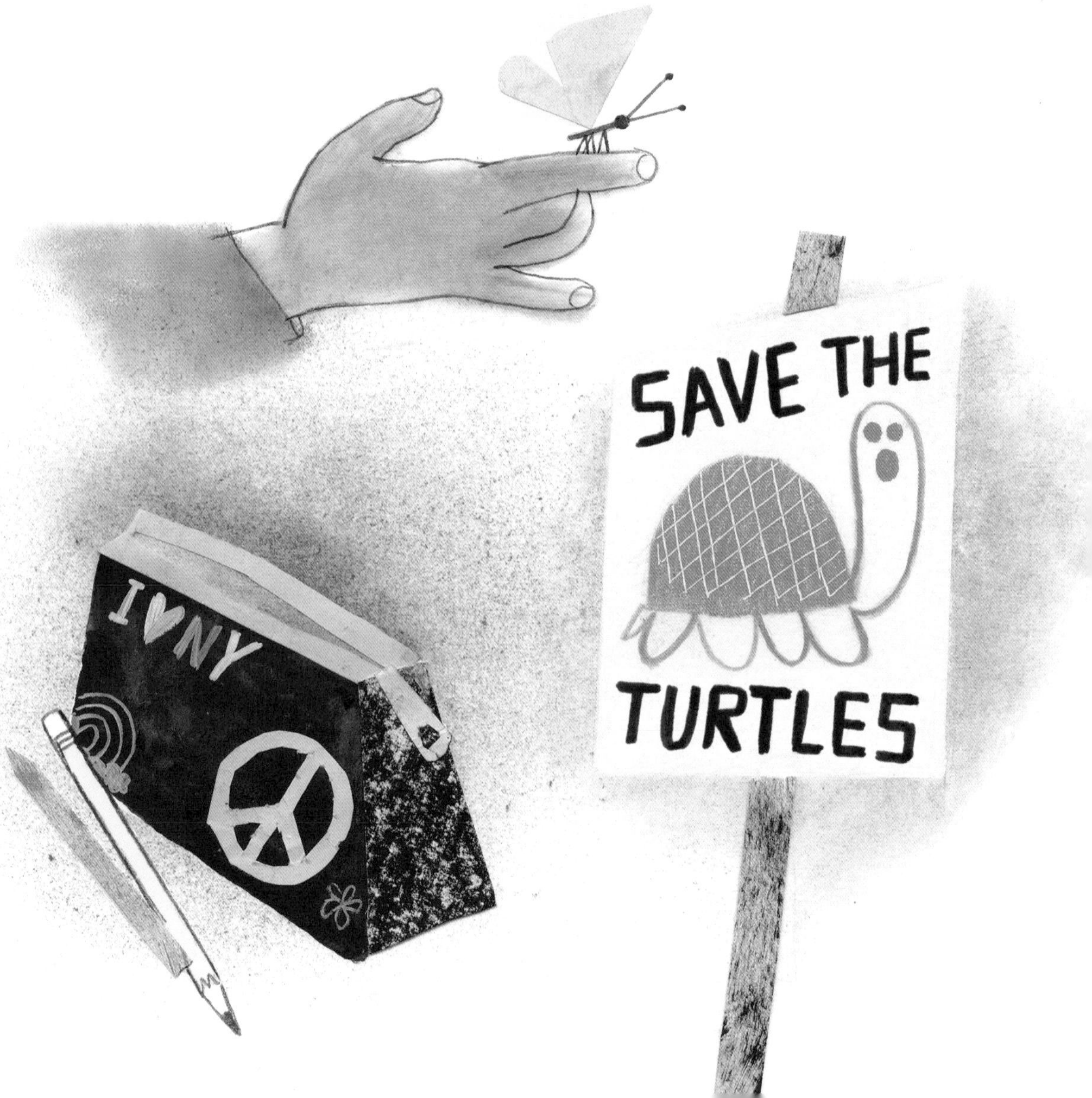
I ♥ NY
SAVE THE TURTLES

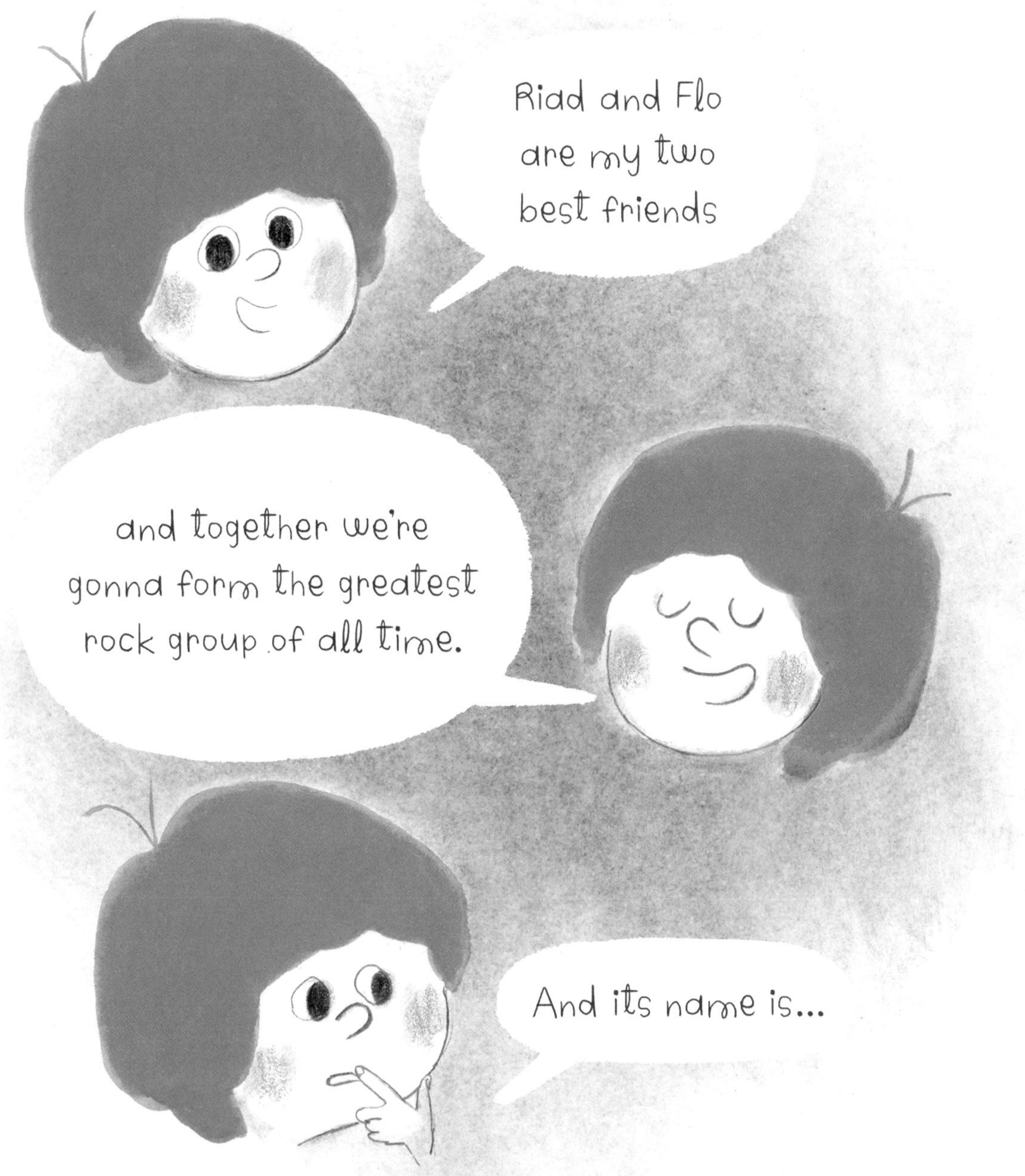
Riad and Flo are my two best friends
and together we're gonna form the greatest rock group of all time.
And its name is...

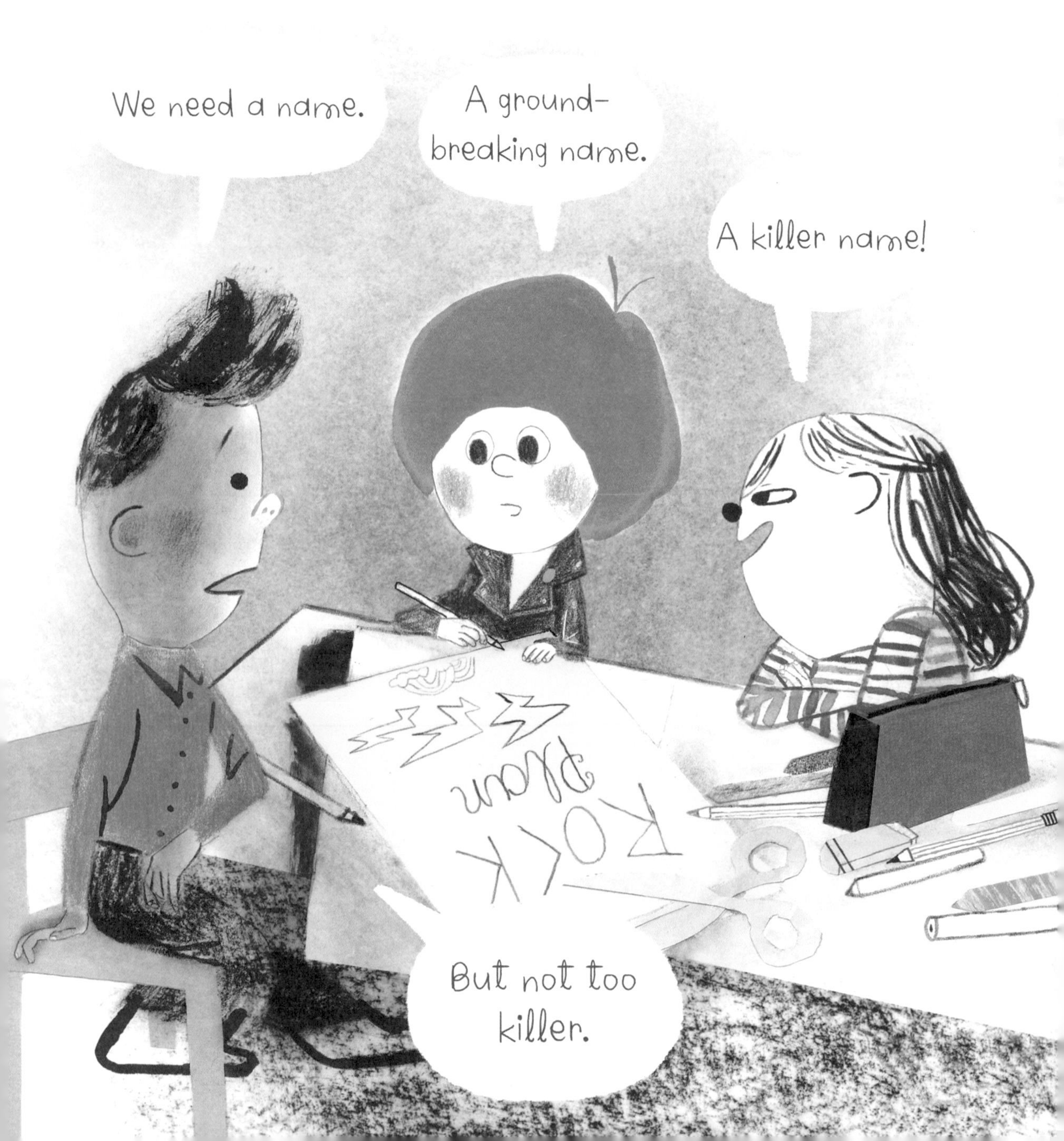
We need a name.
A ground-breaking name.
A killer name!
But not too killer.

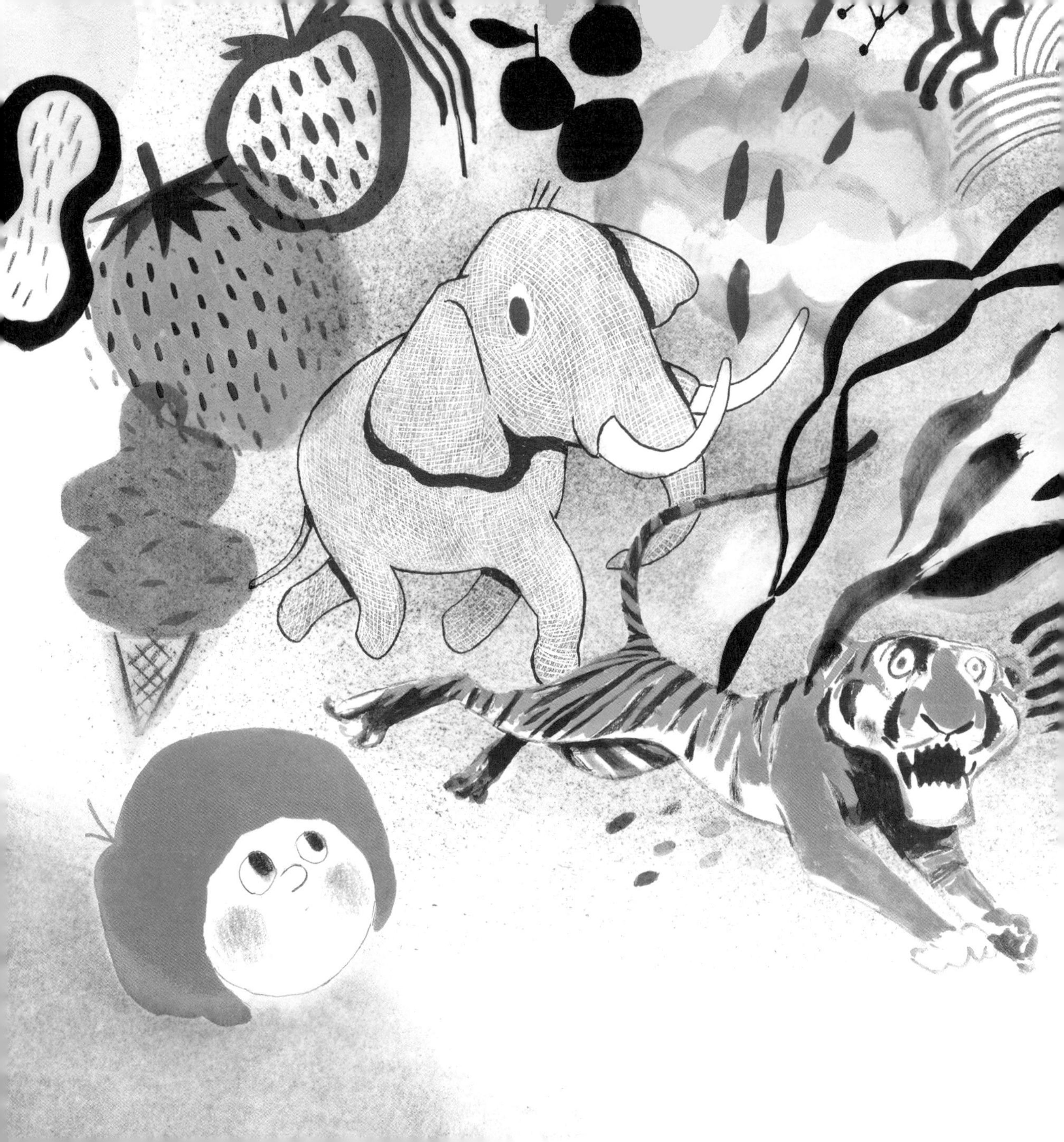

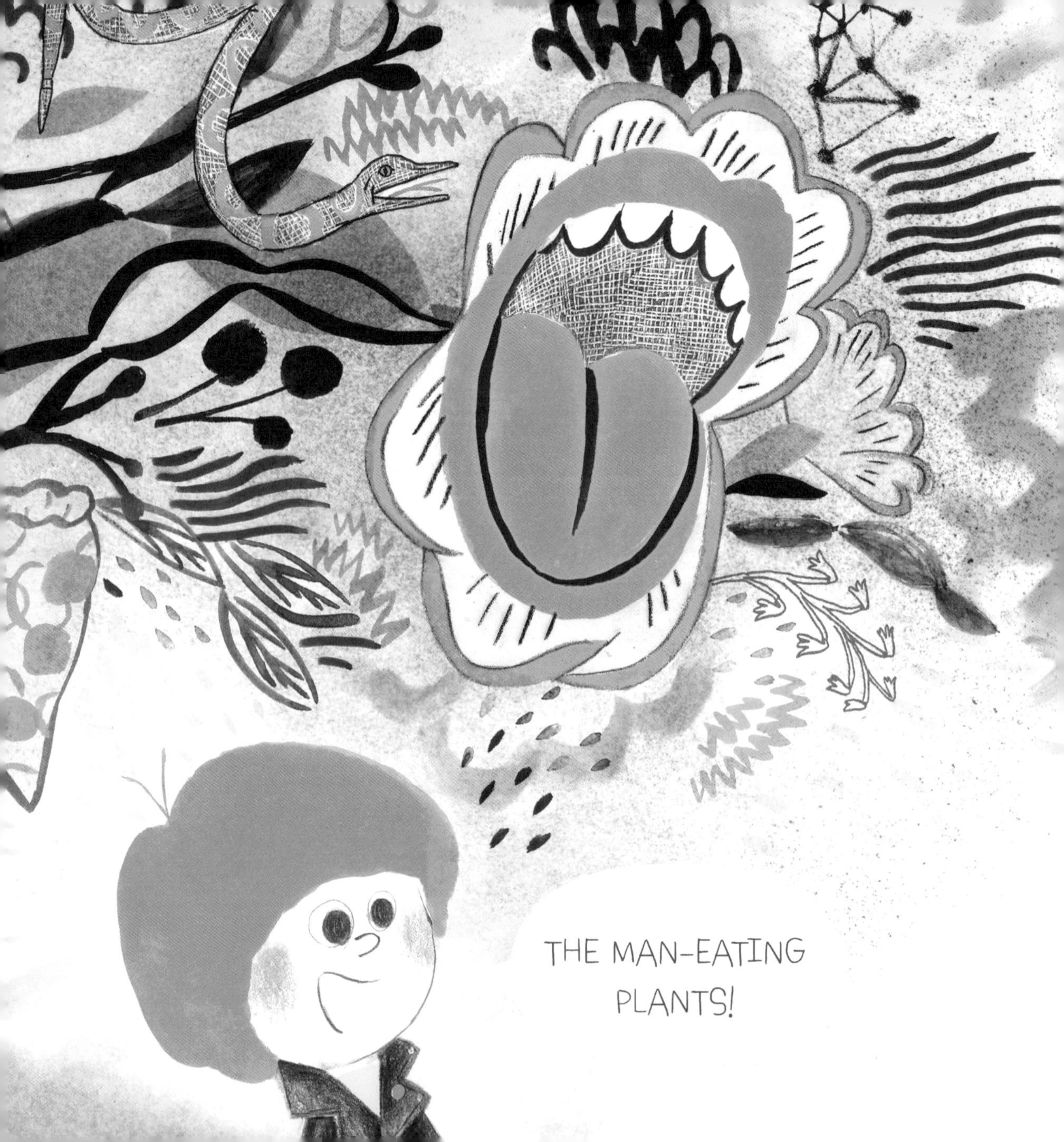

THE MAN-EATING PLANTS!

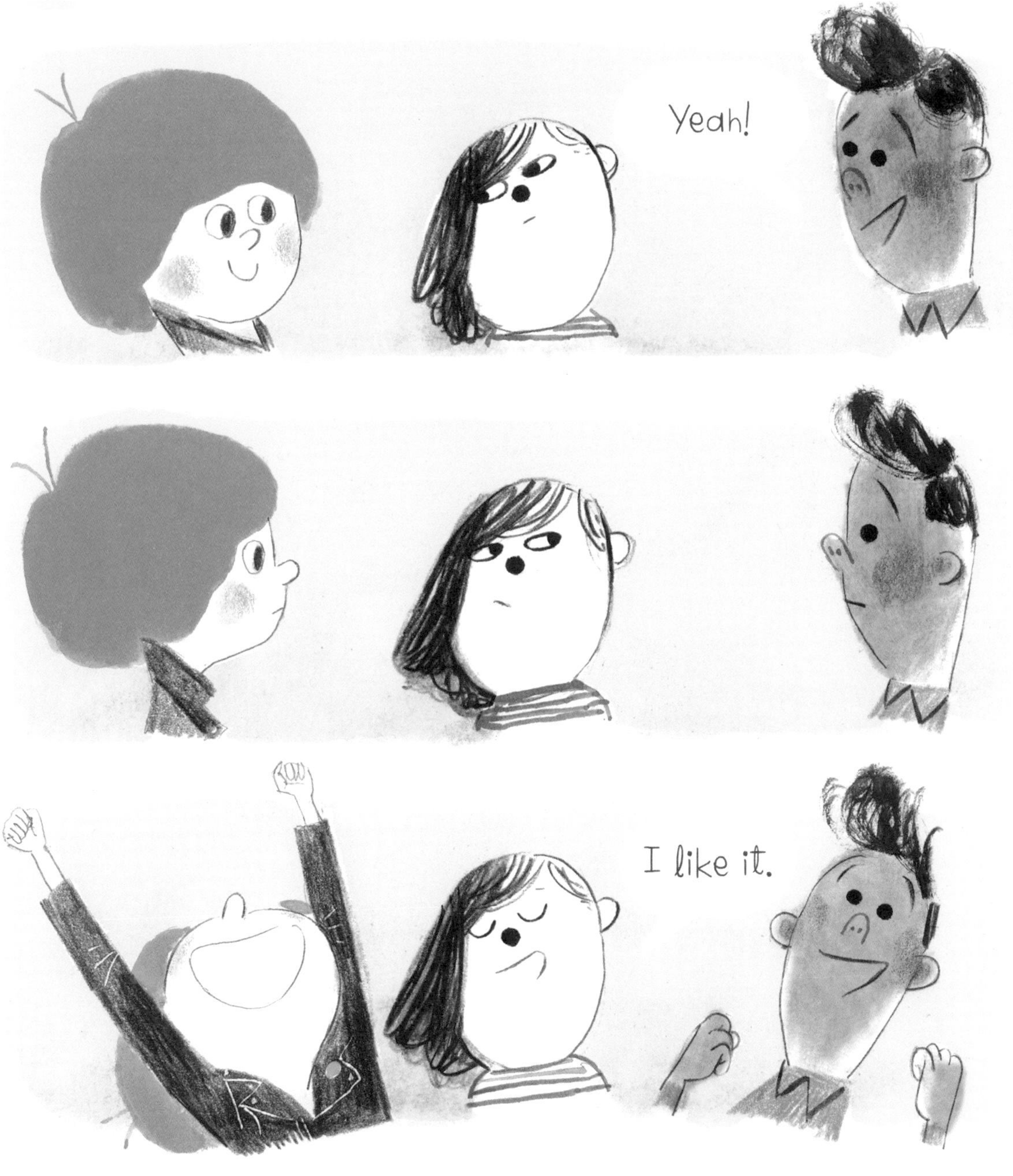
Yeah!
I like it.

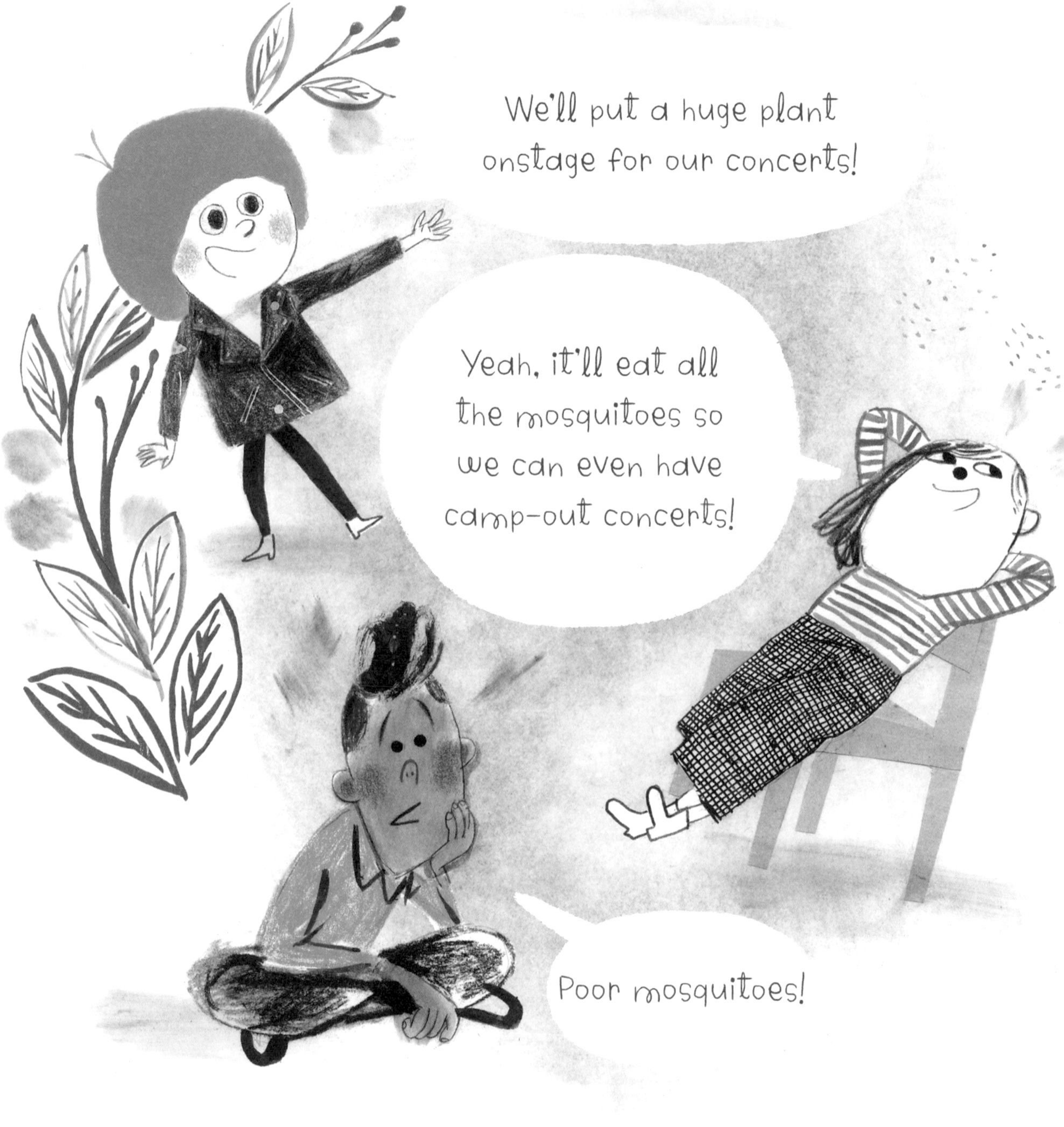
We'll put a huge plant onstage for our concerts!
Yeah, it'll eat all the mosquitoes so we can even have camp-out concerts!
Poor mosquitoes!

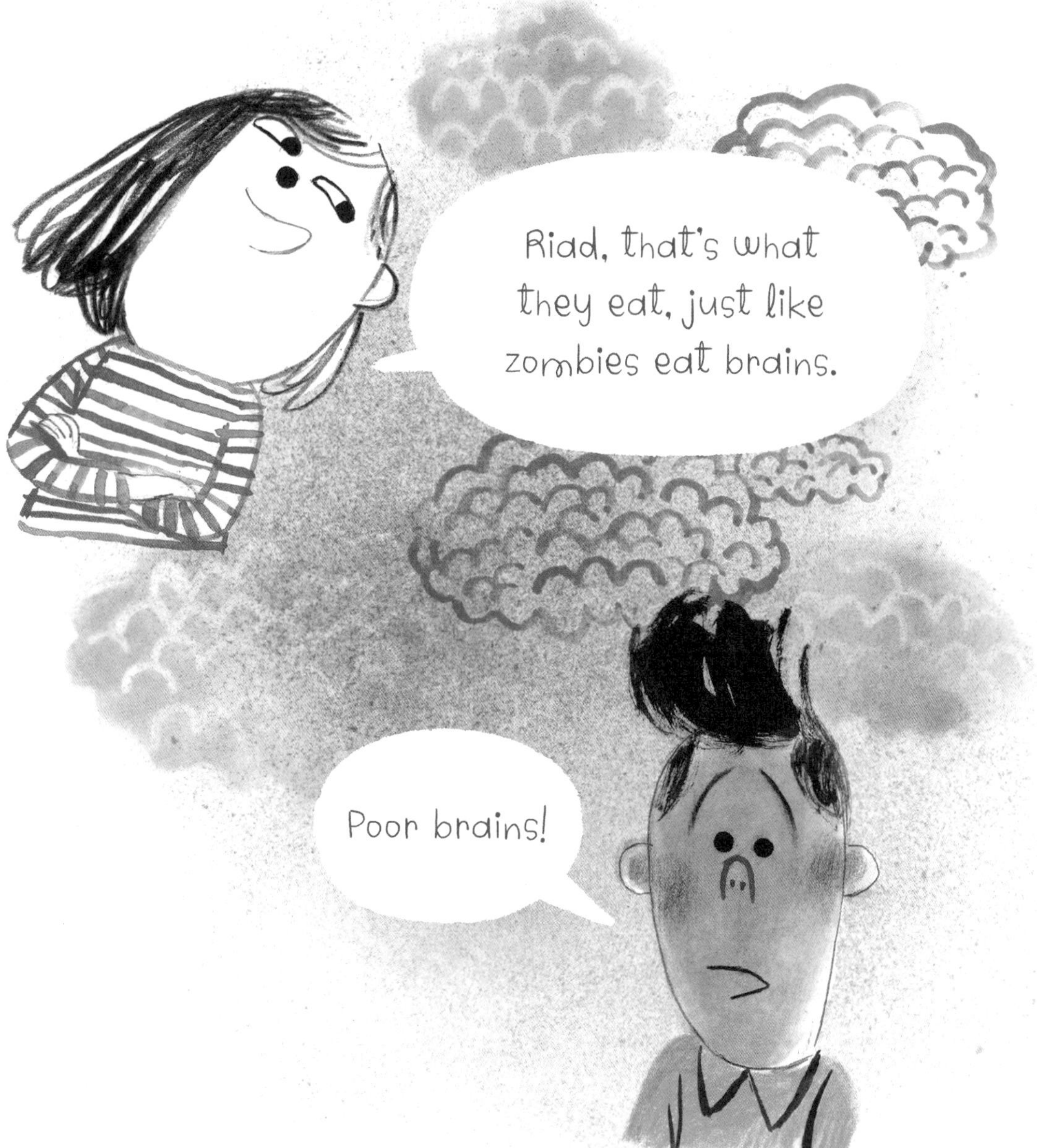
Riad, that's what they eat, just like zombies eat brains.
Poor brains!

Truffle can already picture himself.

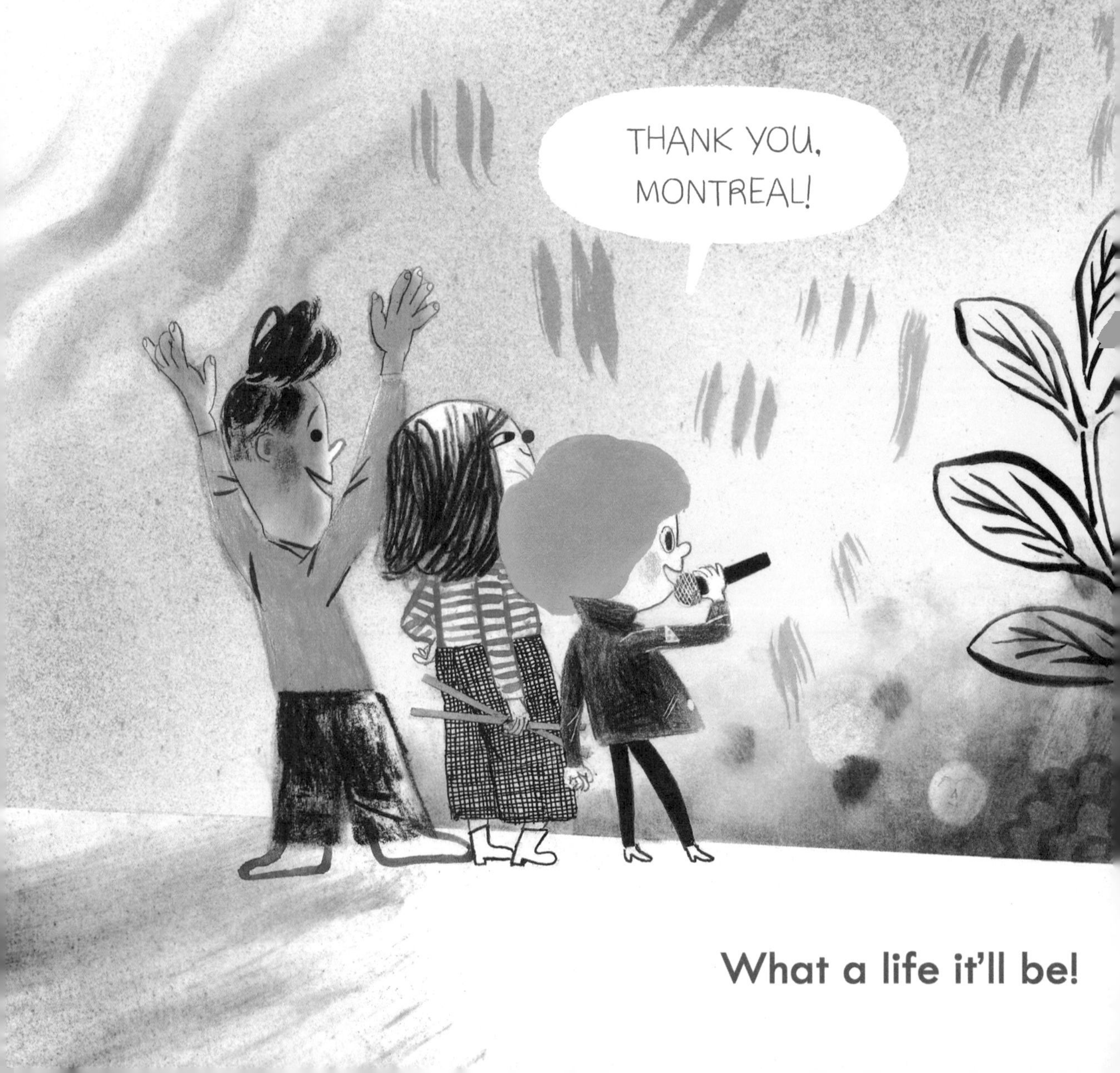
THANK YOU, MONTREAL!

What a life it'll be!

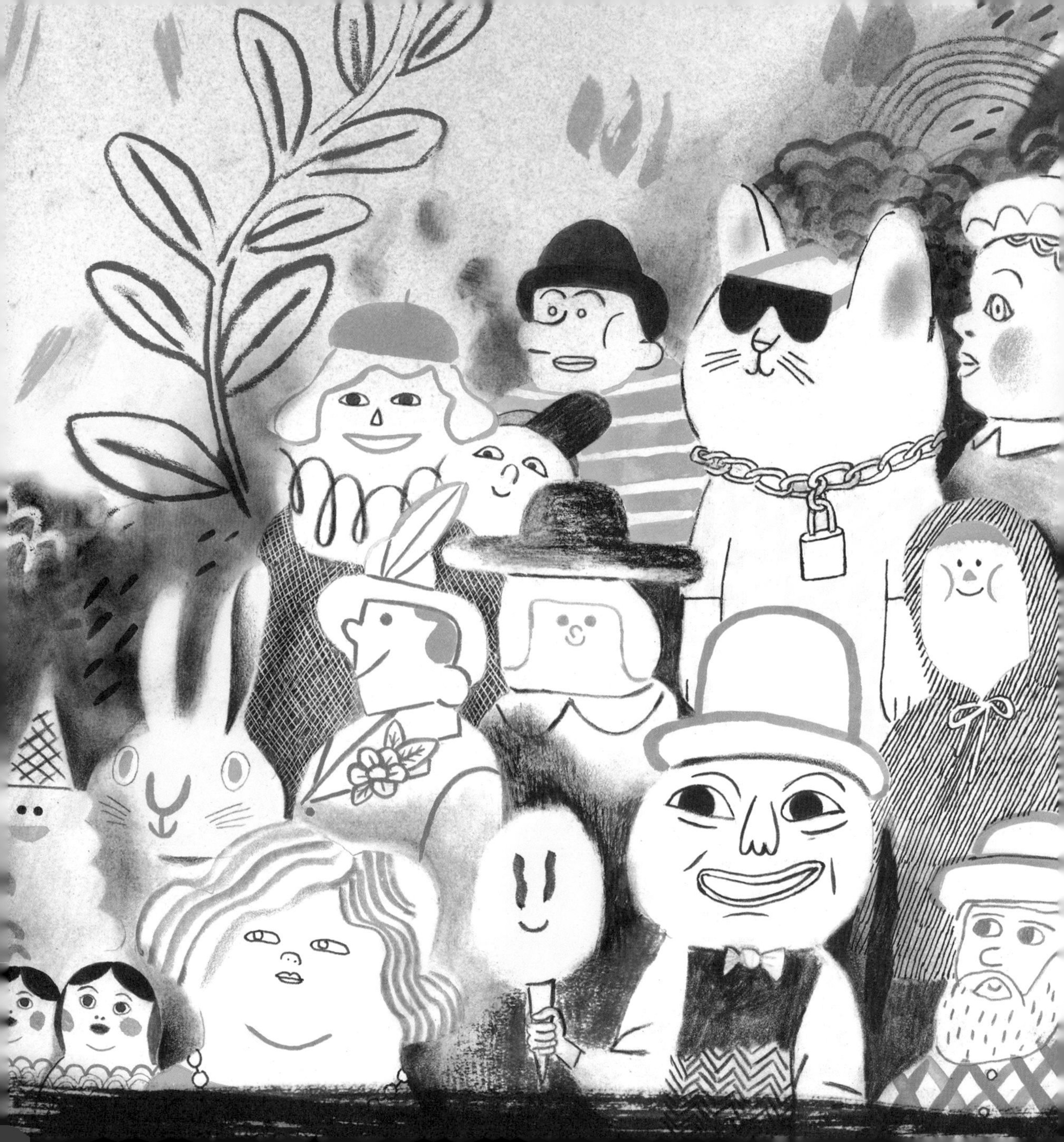

Of course, one of these days, they'll have to start making music, but…

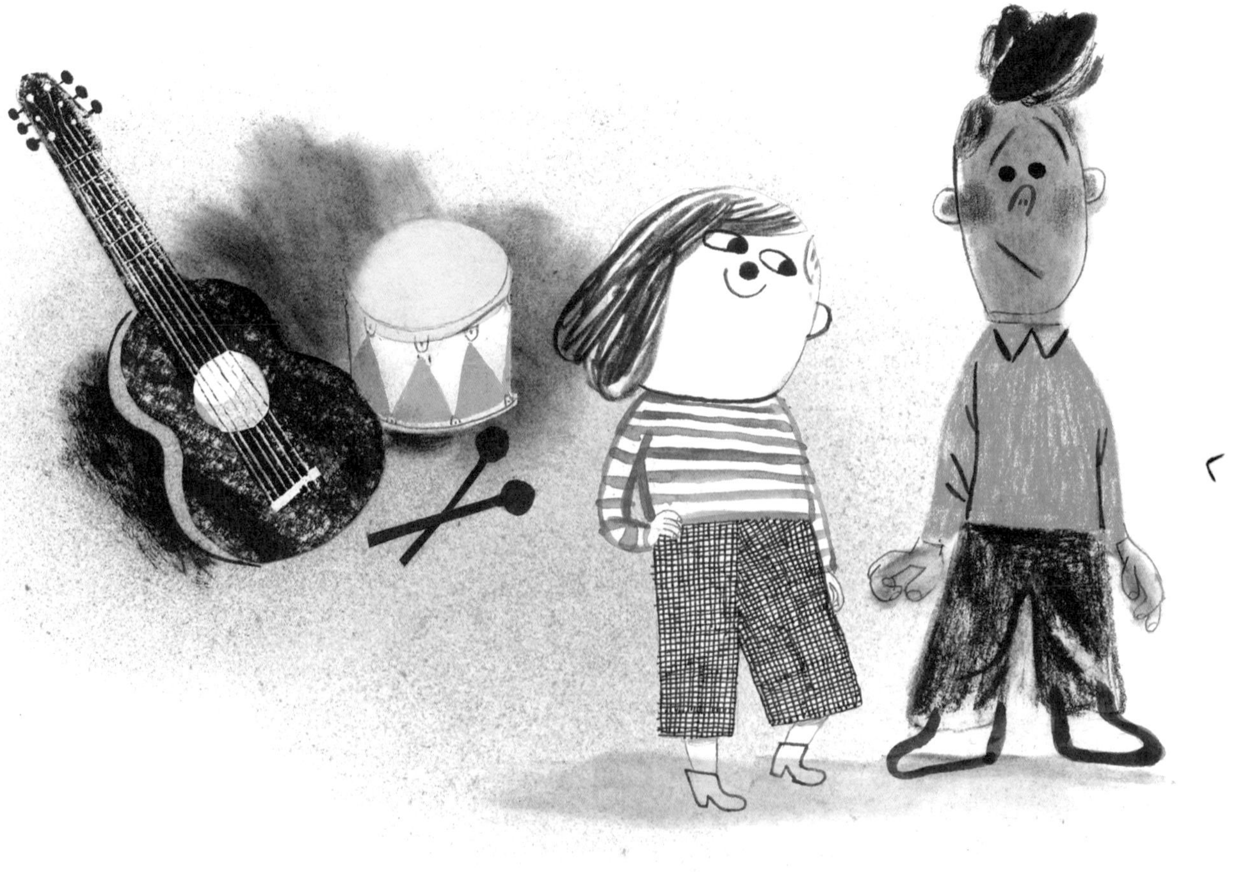

That's a minor detail.

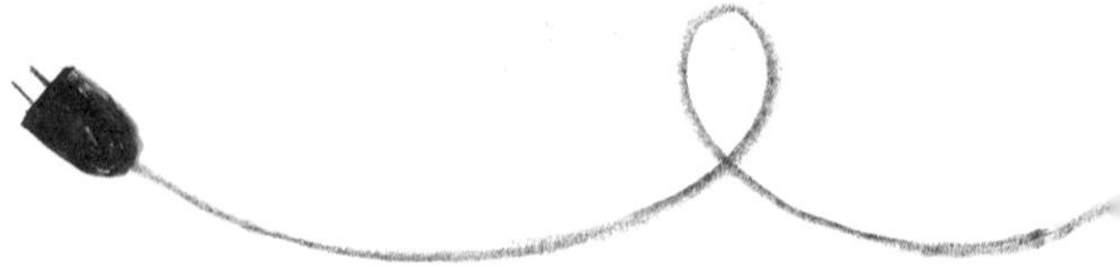

For now...

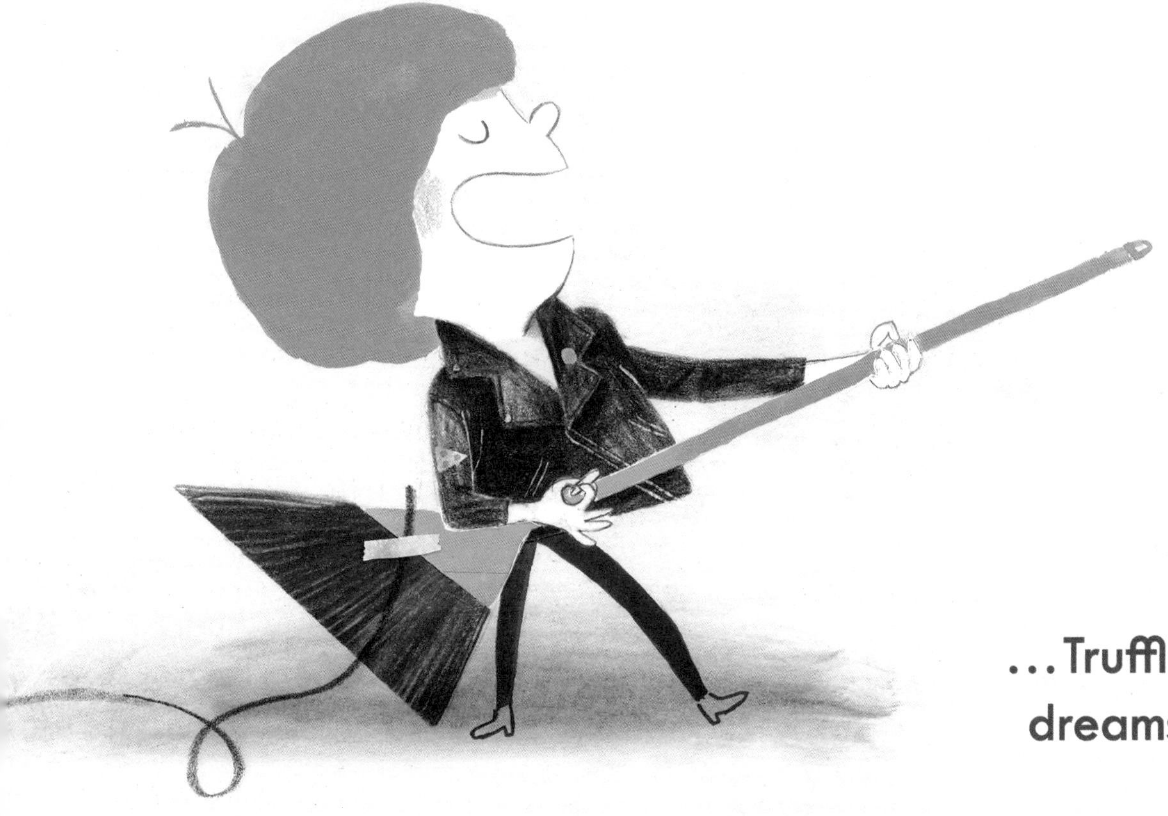

...Truffle
dreams.

TRUFFLE LOVES NINA

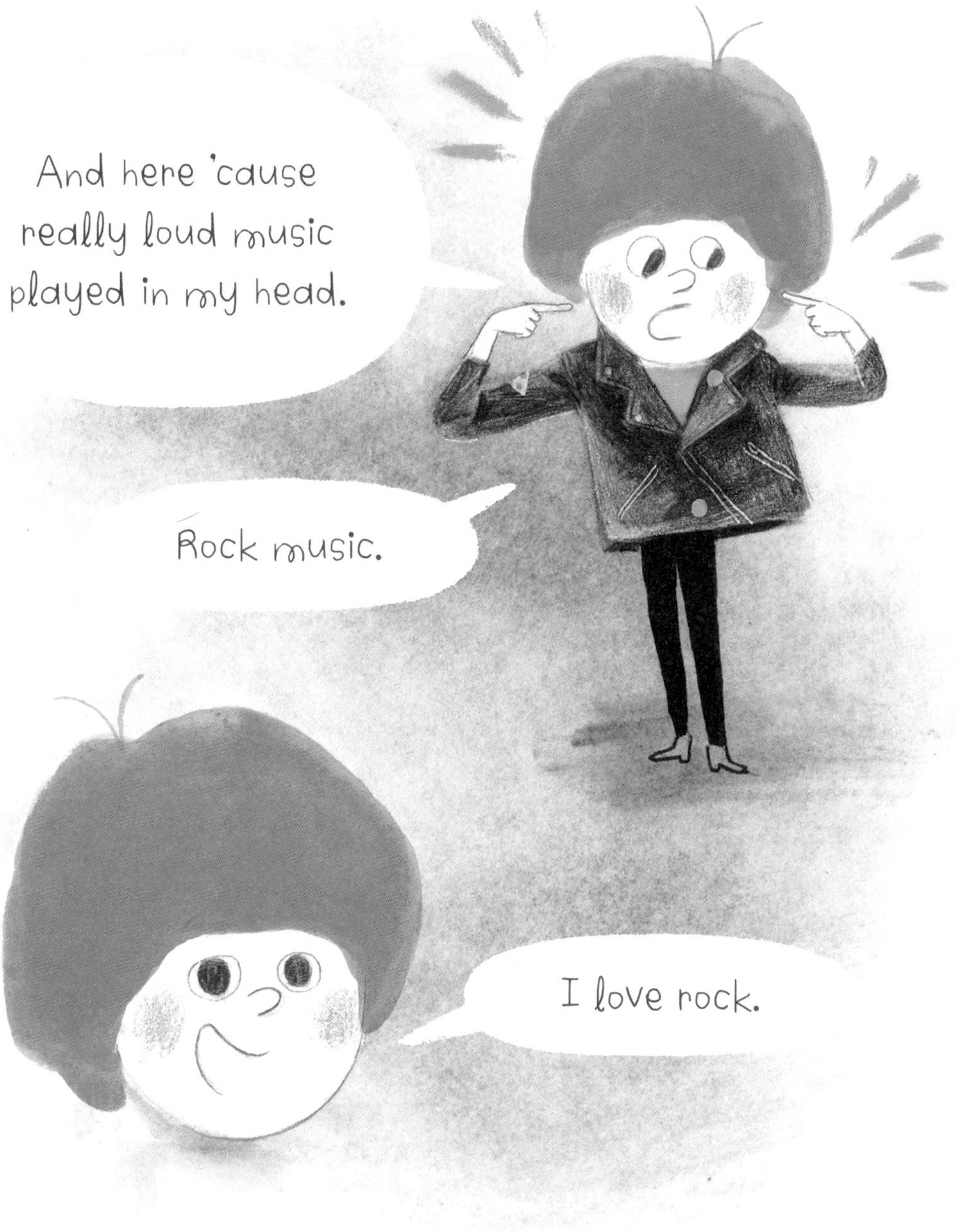
And here 'cause really loud music played in my head.
Rock music.
I love rock.

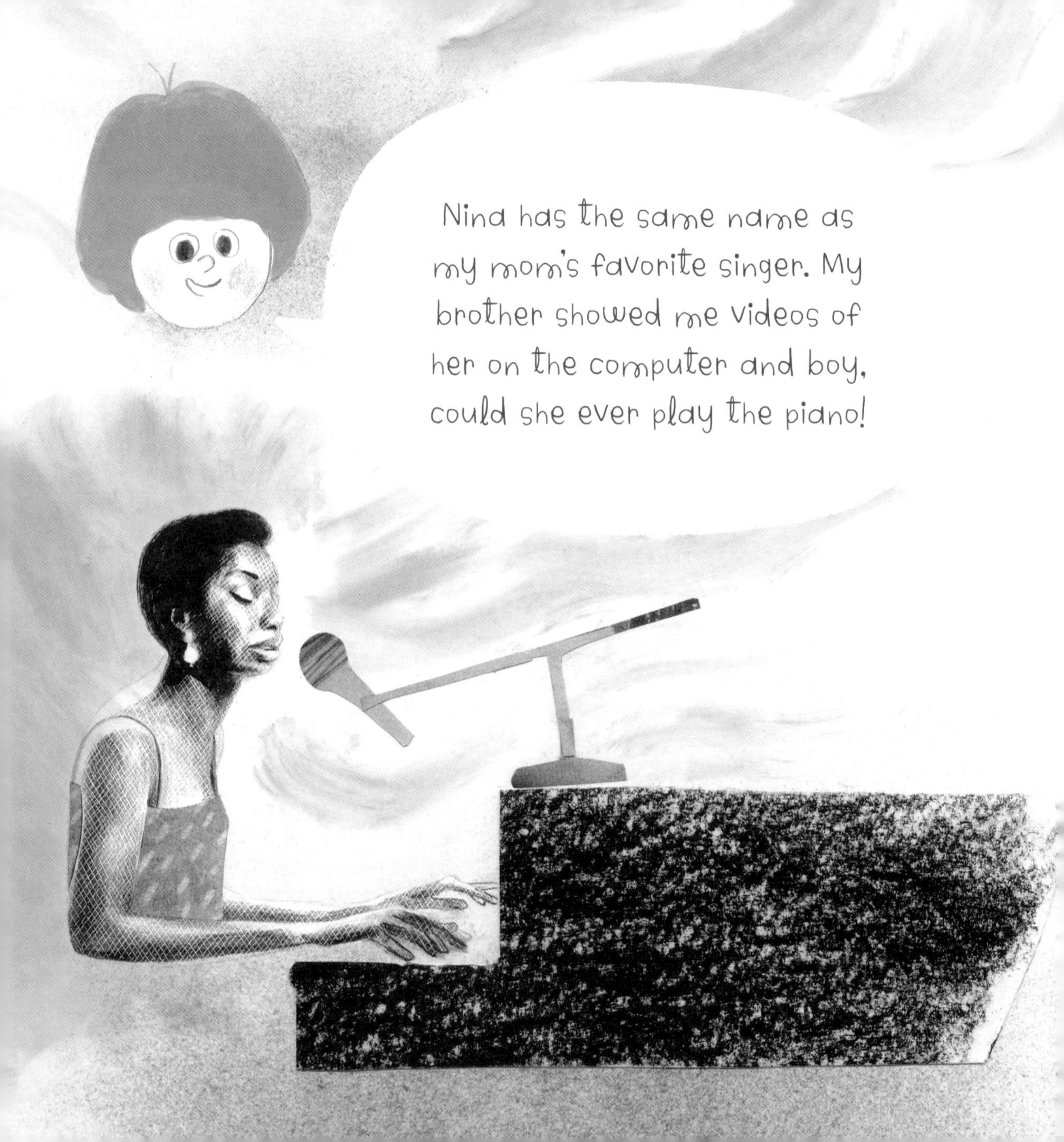
Nina has the same name as my mom's favorite singer. My brother showed me videos of her on the computer and boy, could she ever play the piano!

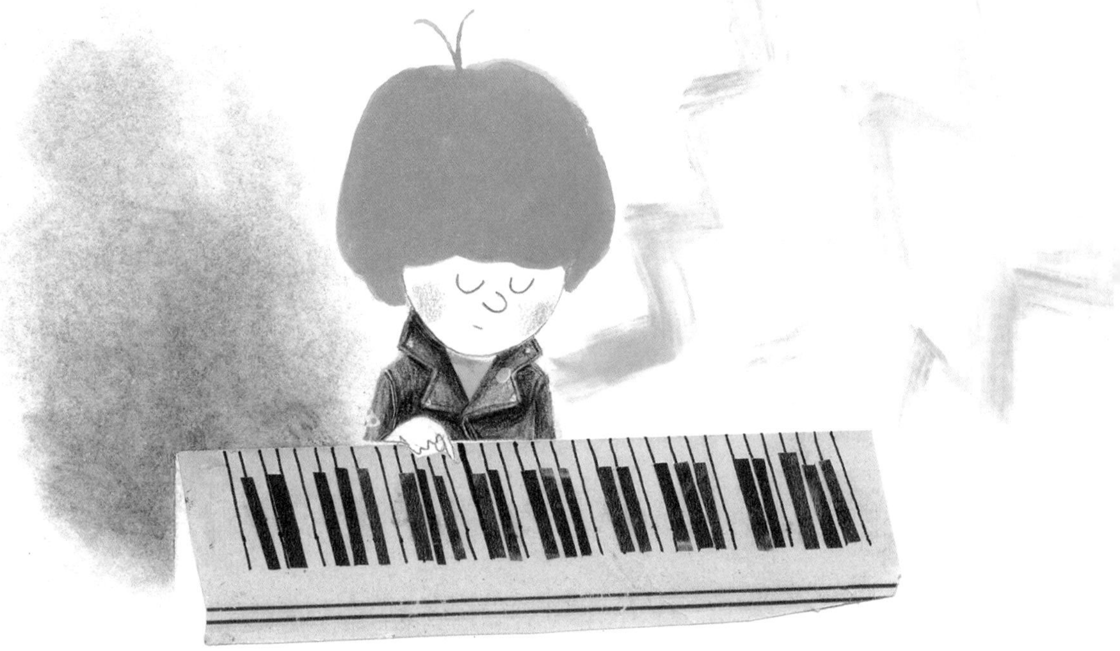

Truffle knows how to play the piano,
but with only one finger.

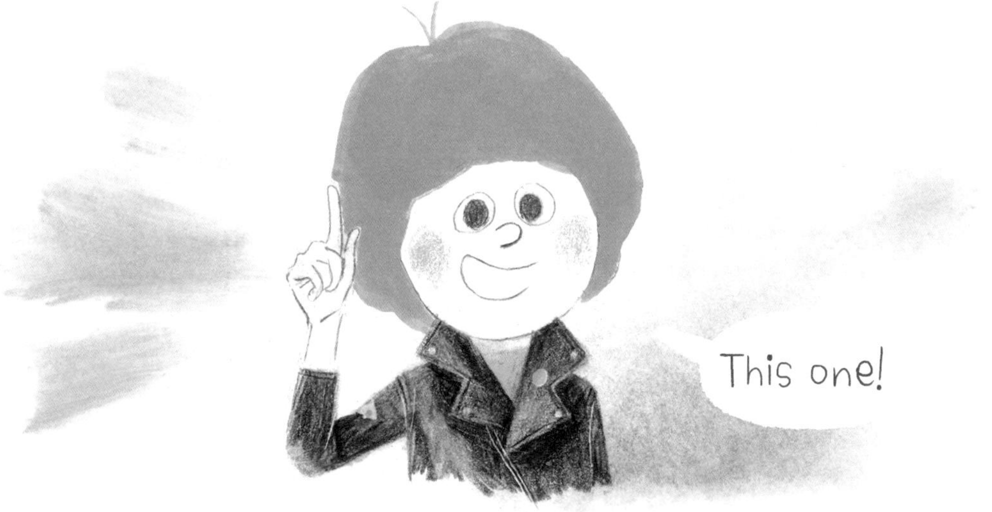
This one!

Ever since he asked Nina to be his girlfriend, Truffle has felt shy around her and doesn't know what to say.

Usually, Truffle always has something to say.

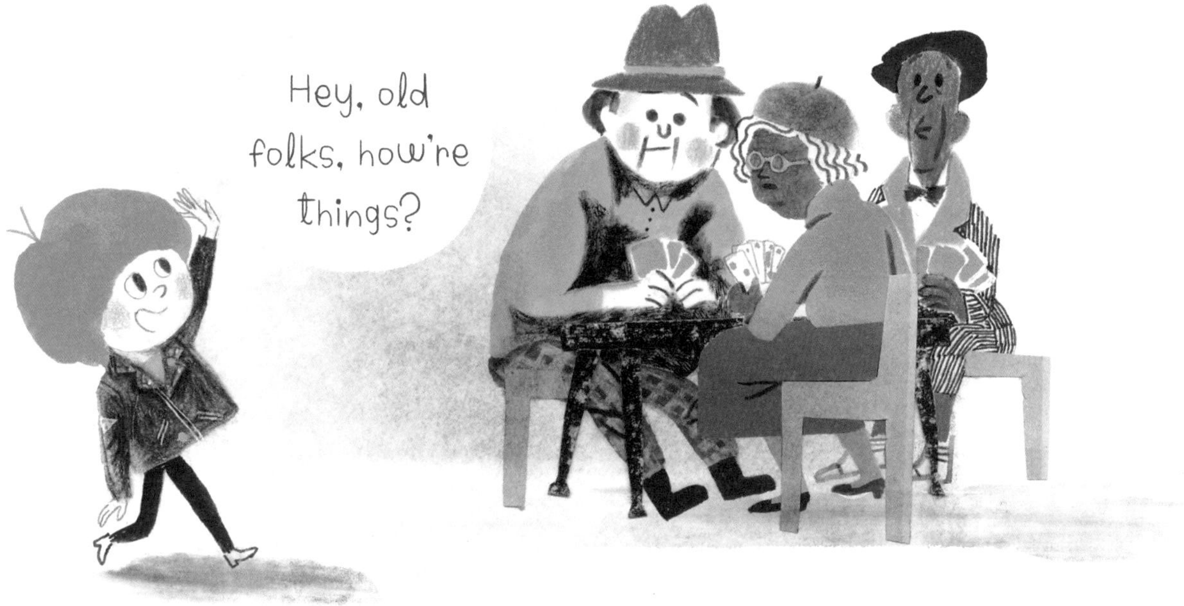
Hey, old folks, how're things?

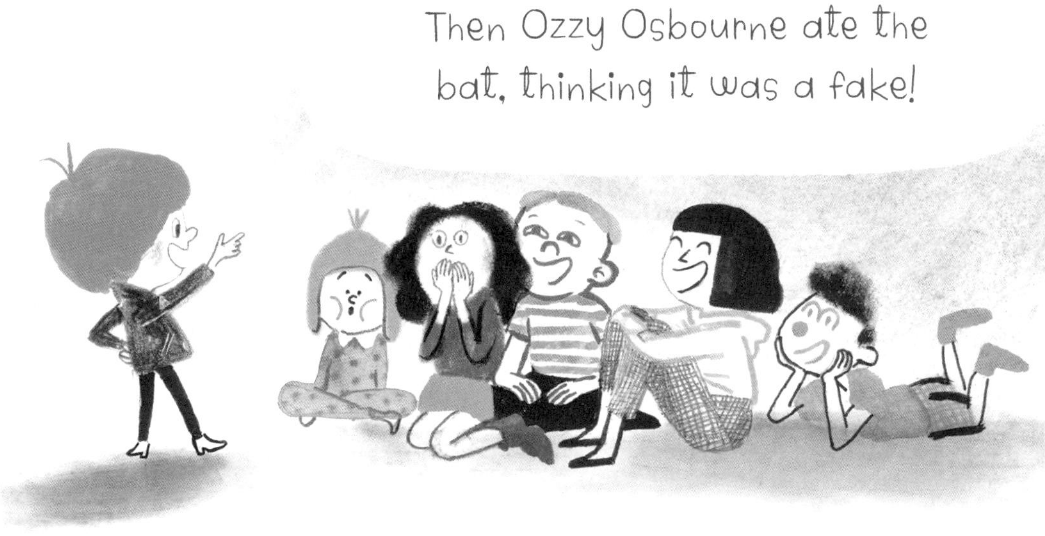
Then Ozzy Osbourne ate the bat, thinking it was a fake!

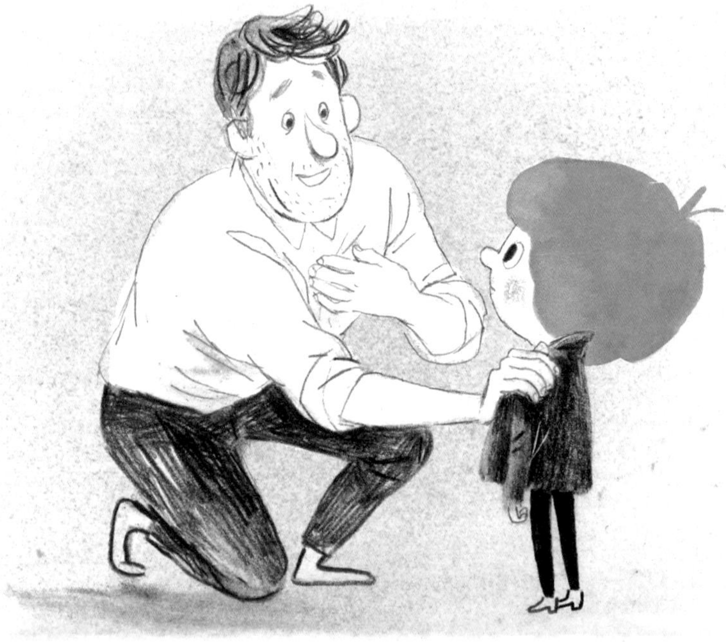

His dad suggested he let his heart do the talking.

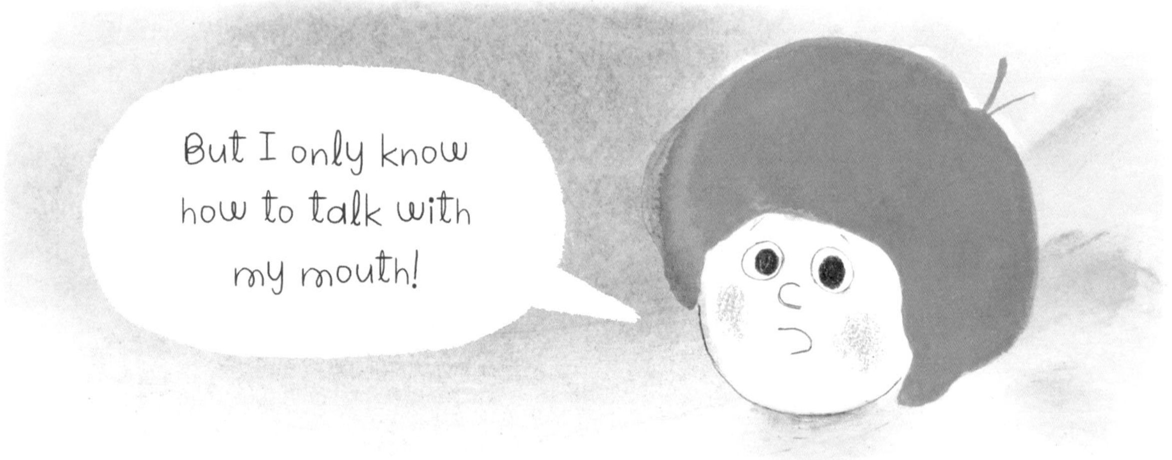
But I only know how to talk with my mouth!

Truffle asked his brother how he could get his heart to talk seeing that Louis knows pretty well everything.

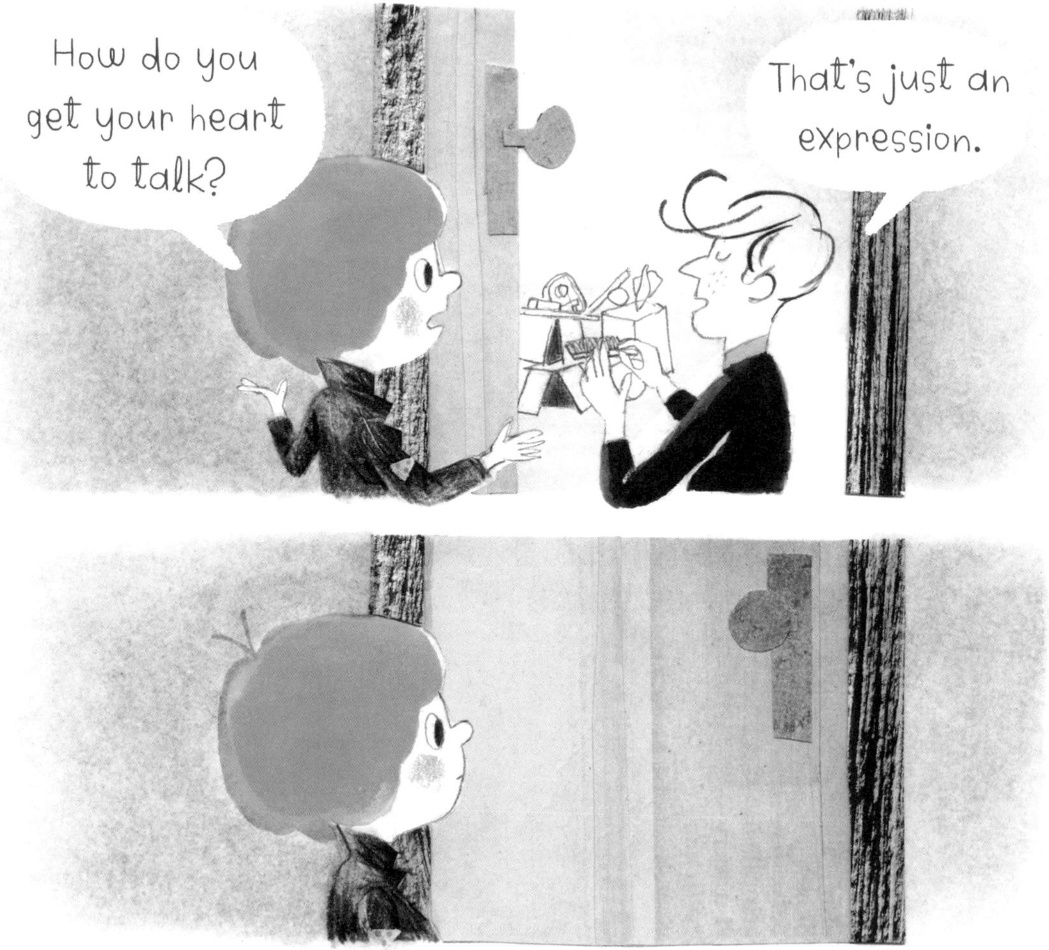
How do you get your heart to talk?
That's just an expression.

Then Louis shut the door in his face because, in high school, they get lots of homework.

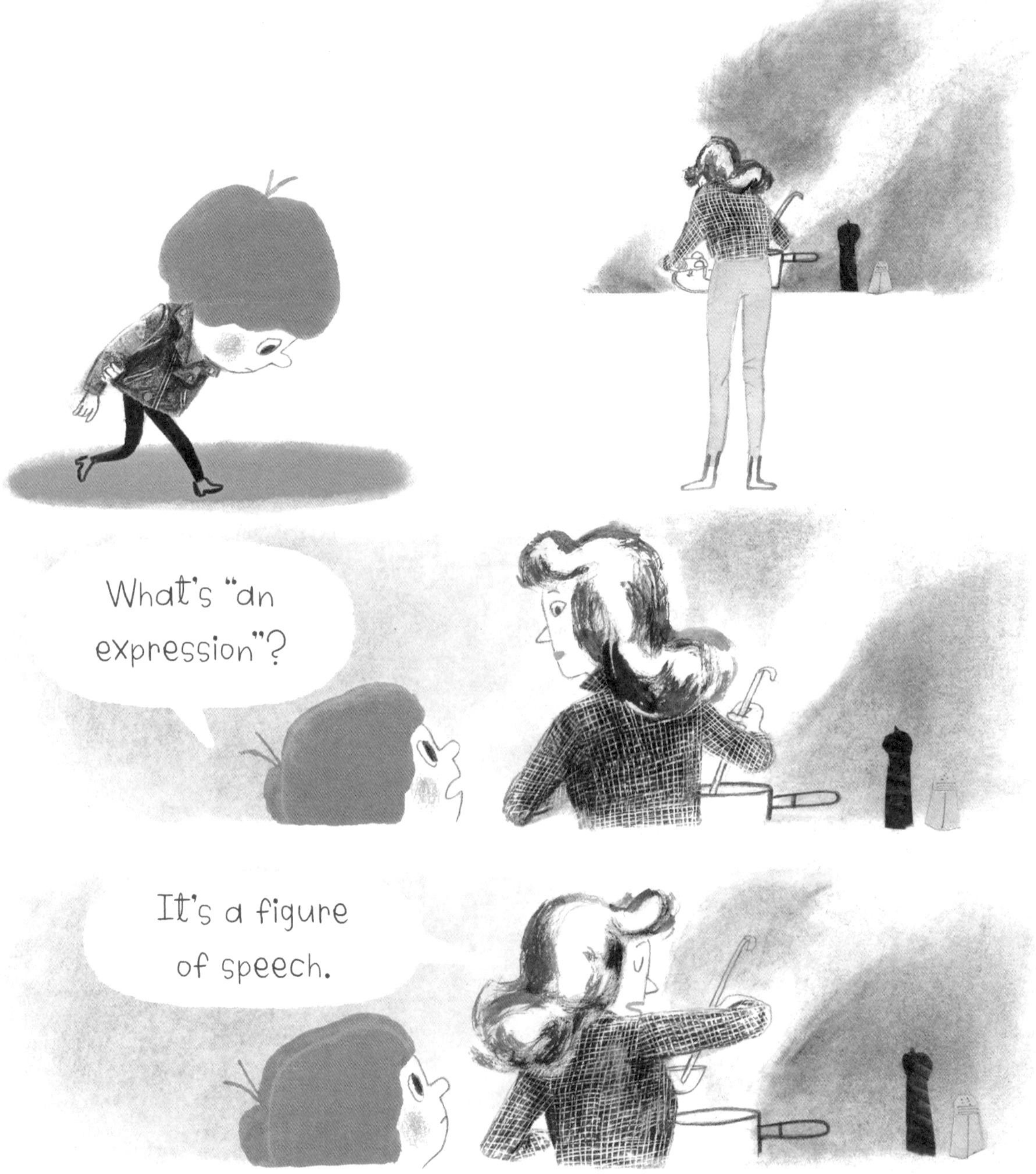
What's "an expression"?
It's a figure of speech.

His dad told him to let his heart do the talking, which is an expression, which is a figure of speech.

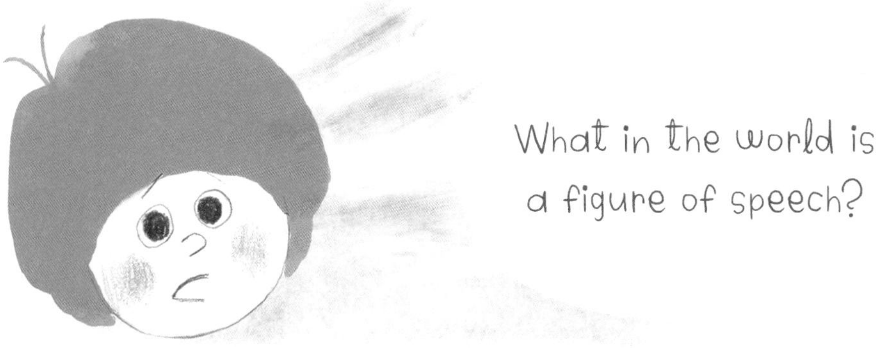
What in the world is a figure of speech?

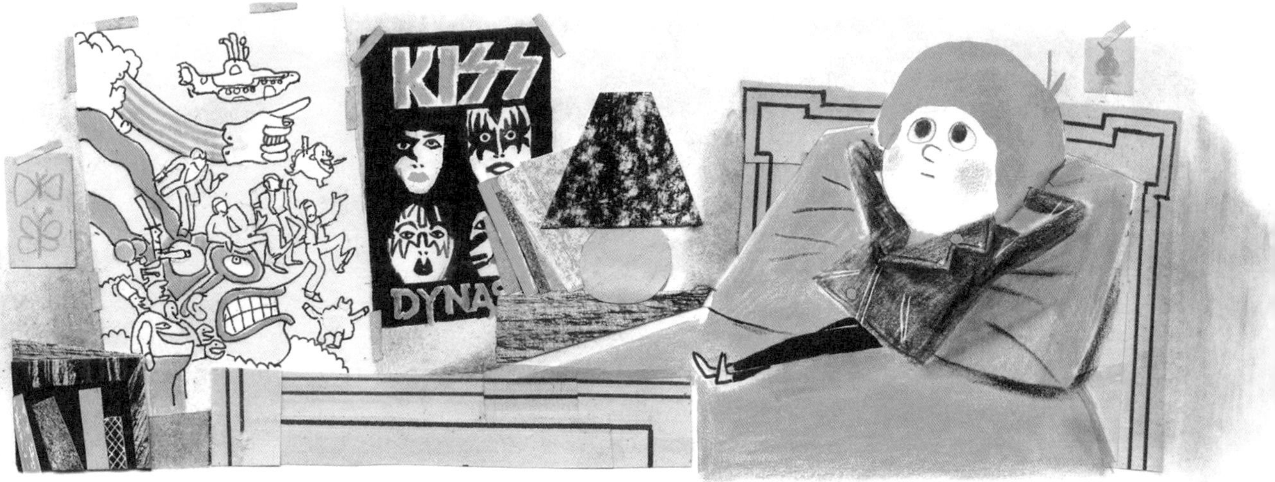
KISS
DYNA

Flo says you can find almost any answer you want in a book, as long as it isn't a math book. Truffle likes rock music better, but books are okay, too.

So, on library day, he asked the man behind the counter if he had a book on figures of speech.

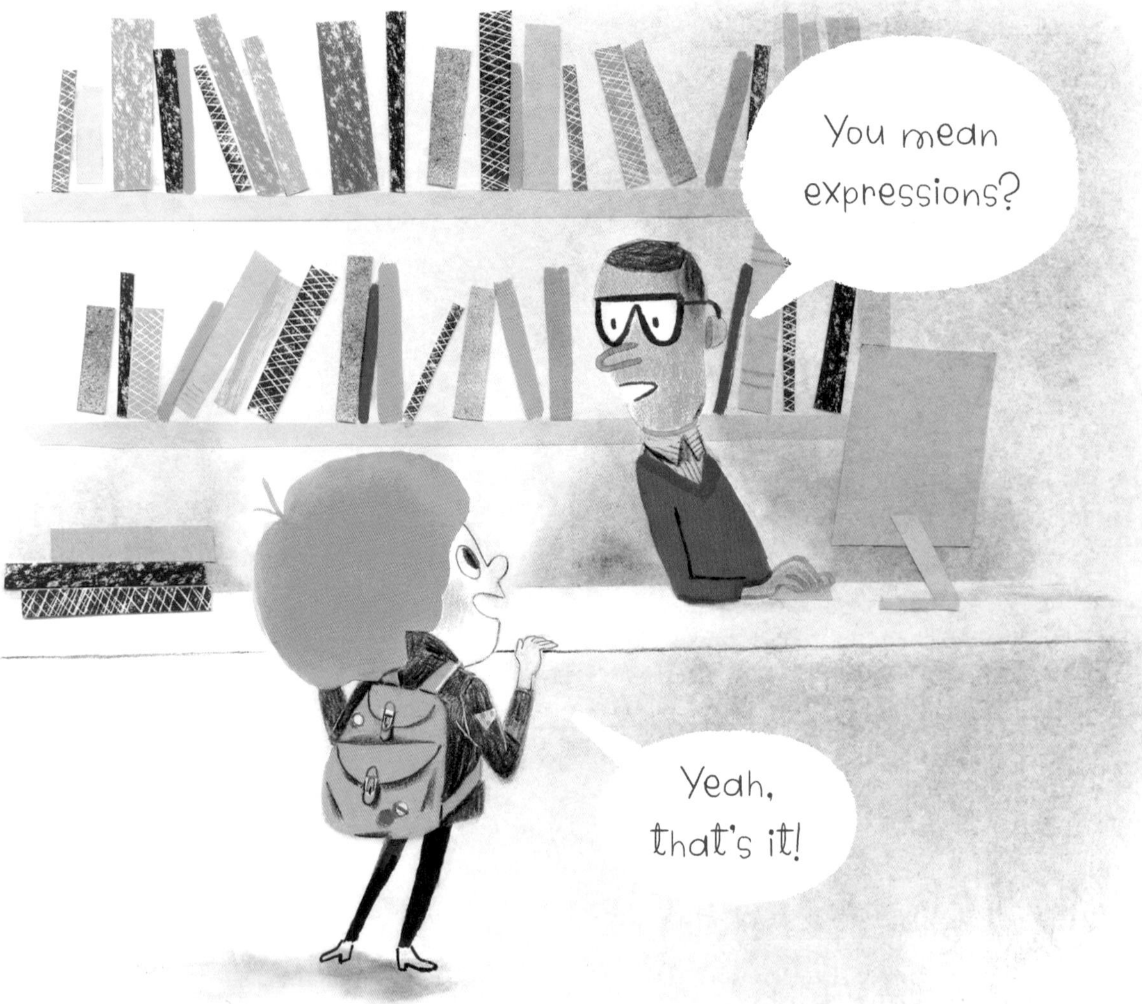
You mean expressions?
Yeah, that's it!

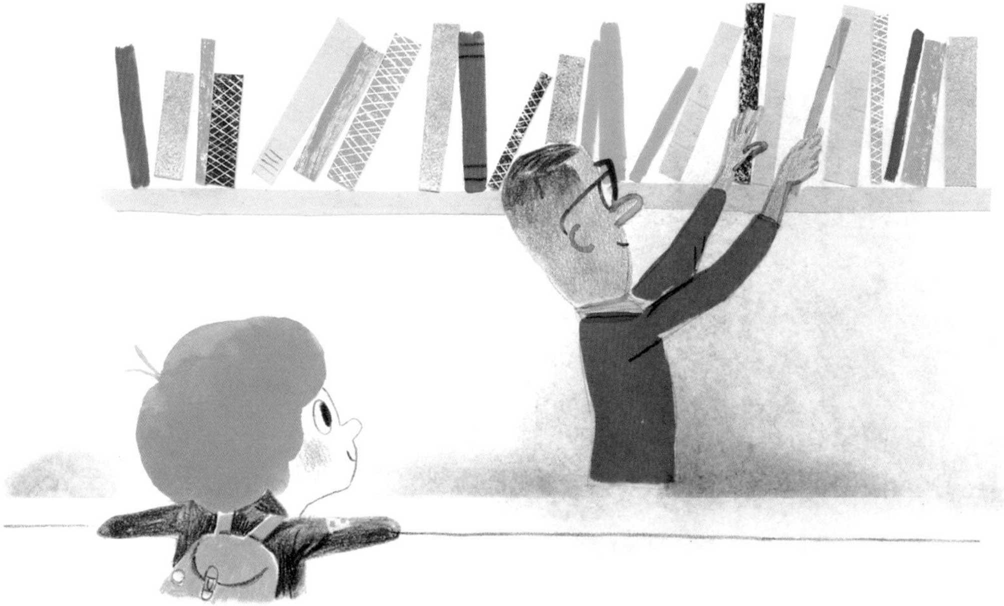

That counter man is smart.

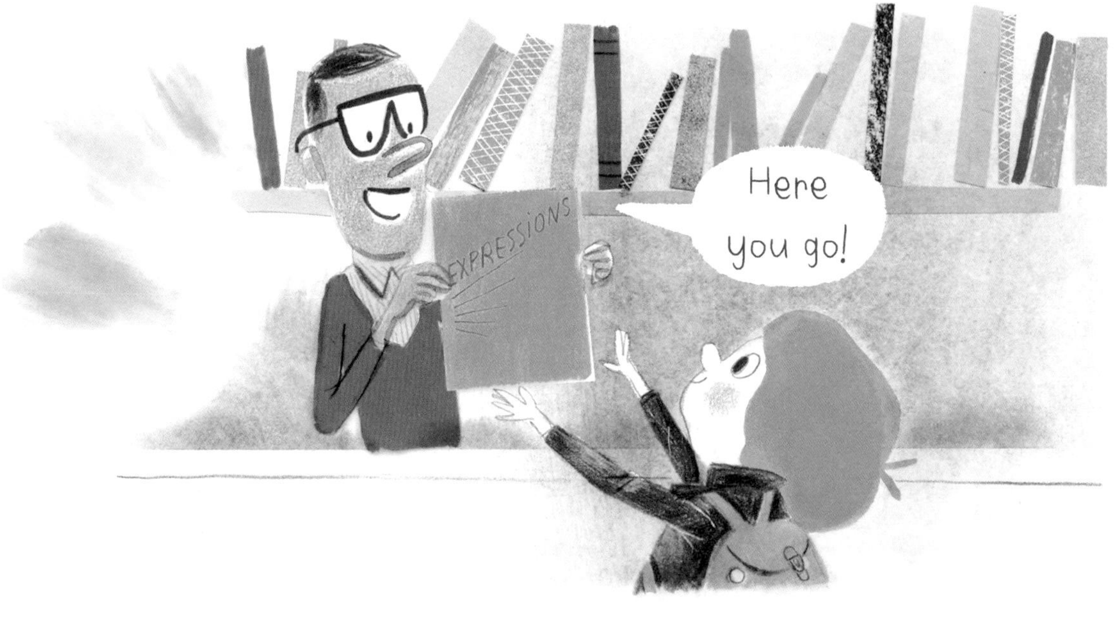
EXPRESSIONS
Here you go!

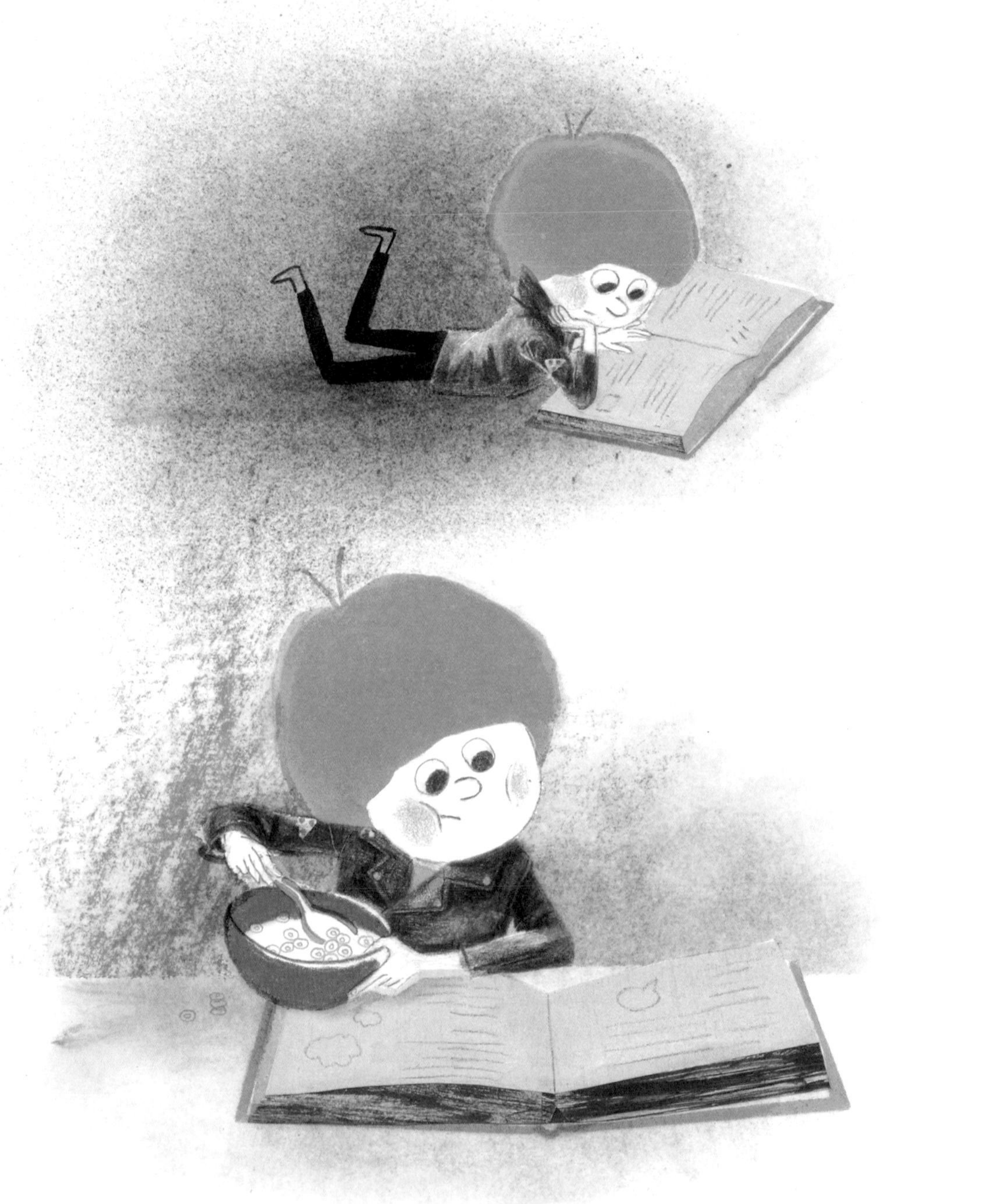

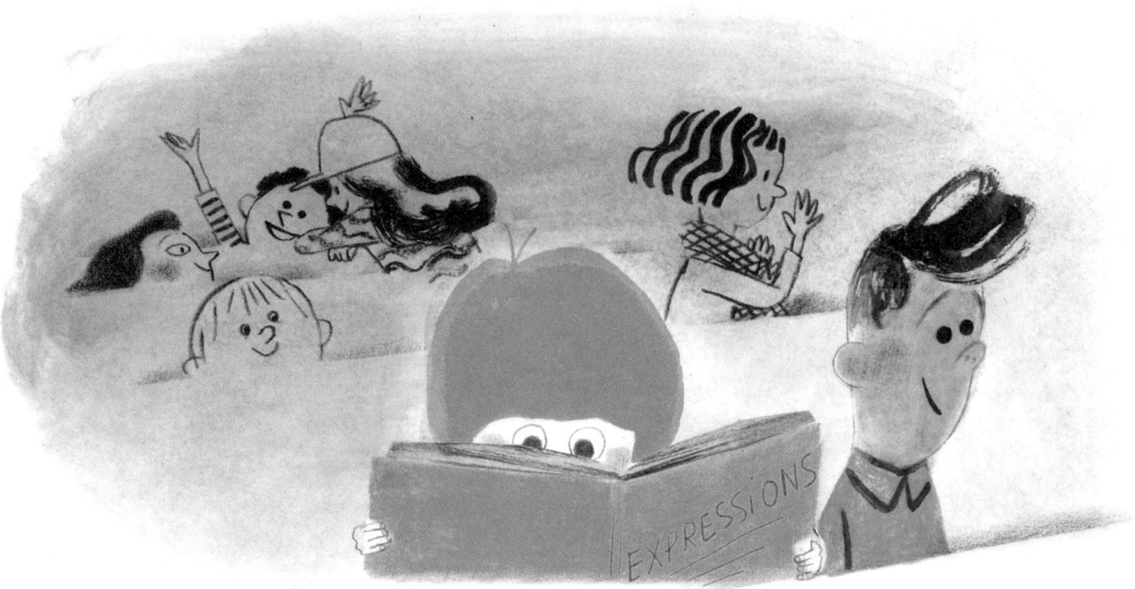
EXPRESSIONS

"A Rolling Stone gathers no moss."

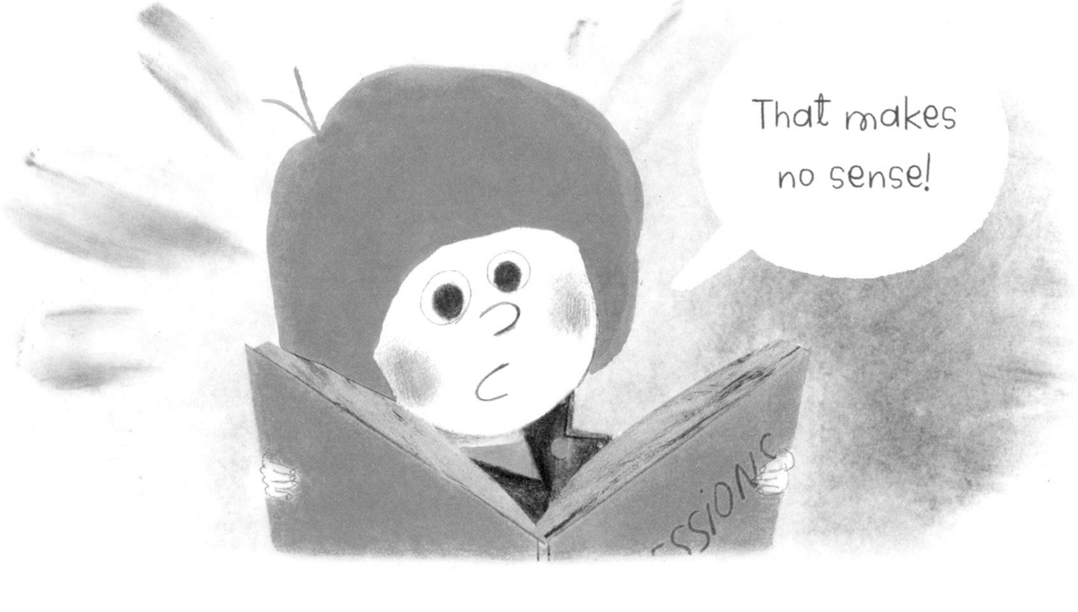
That makes no sense!

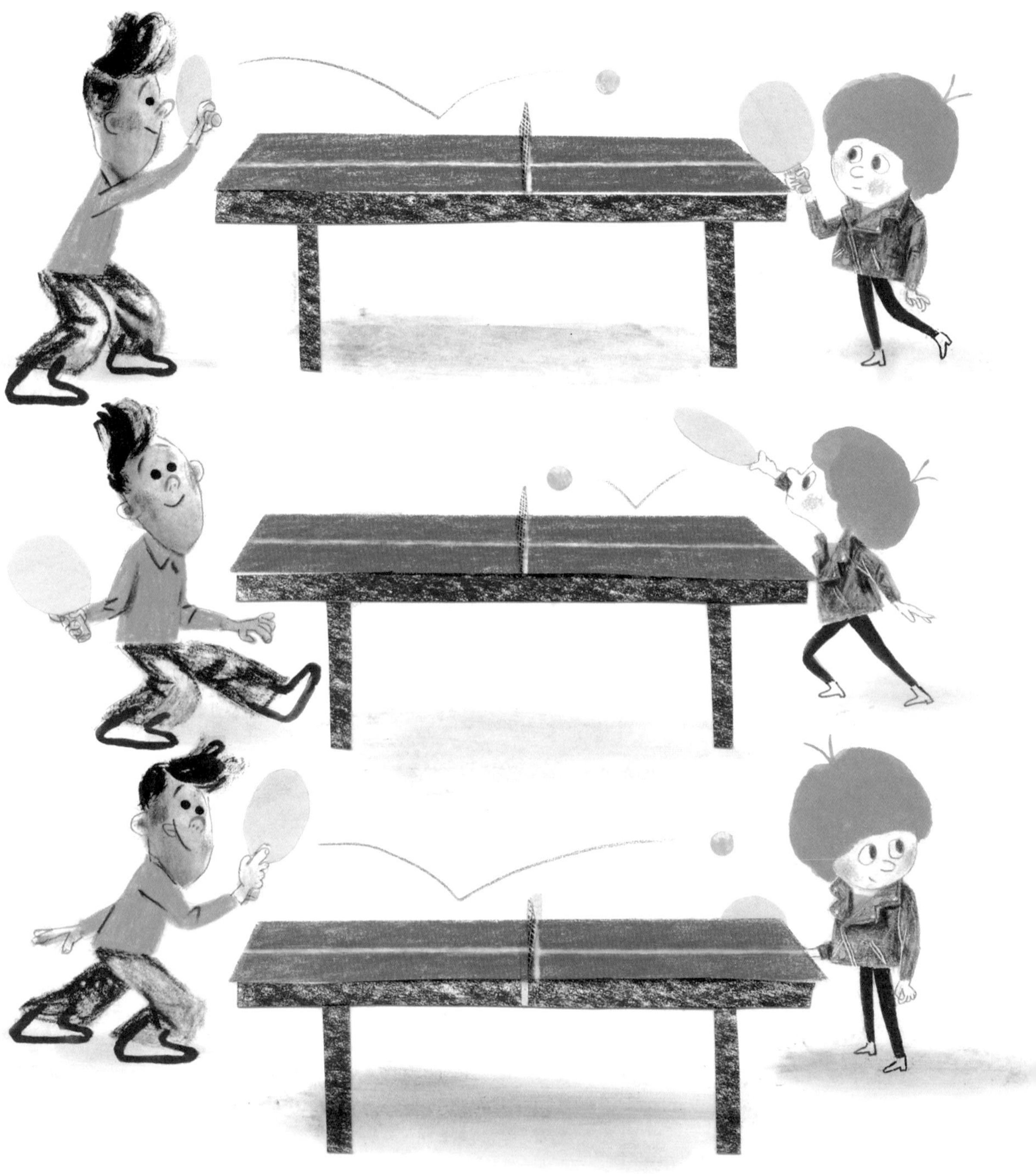

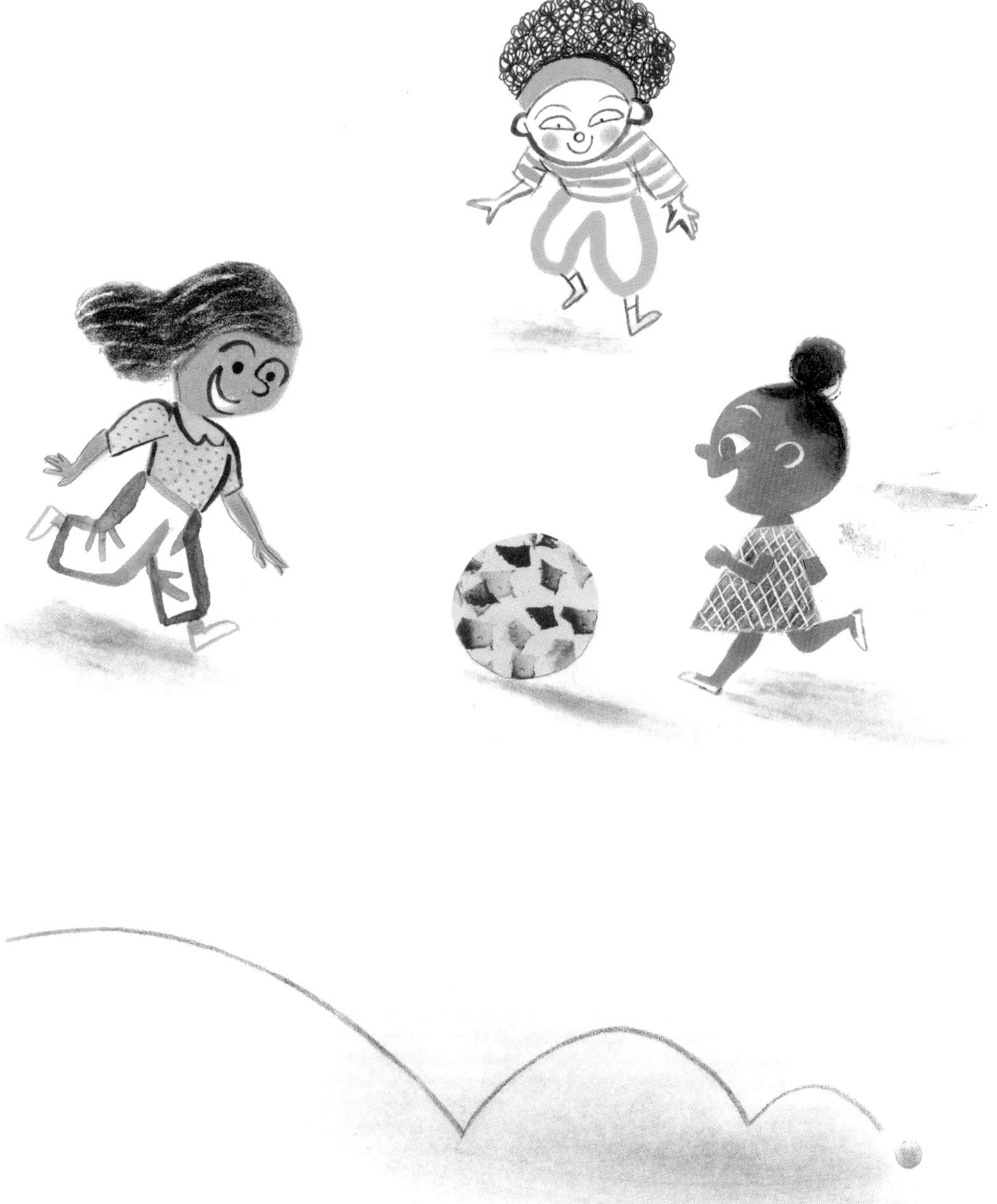

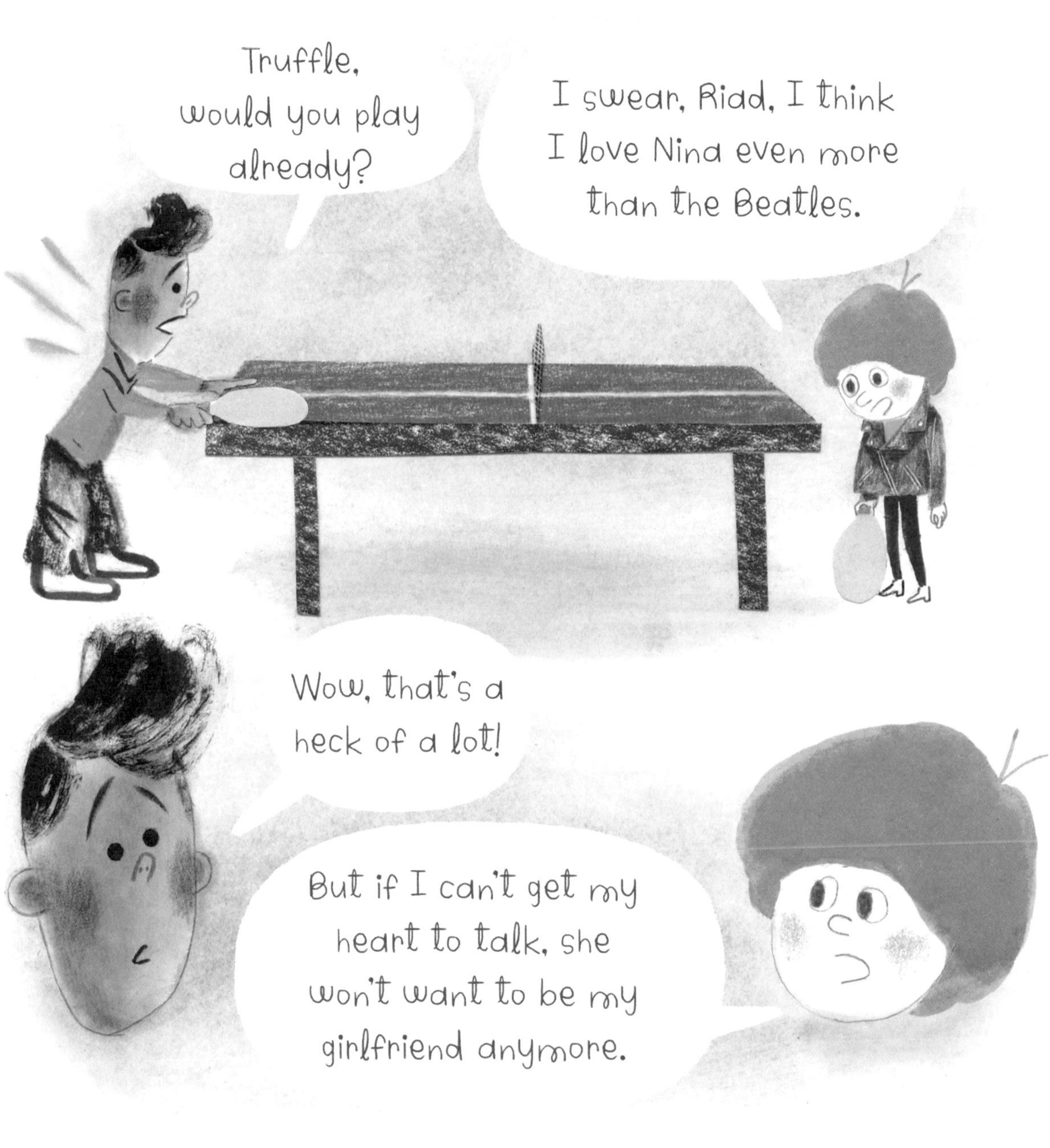

Truffle, would you play already?
I swear, Riad, I think I love Nina even more than the Beatles.
Wow, that's a heck of a lot!
But if I can't get my heart to talk, she won't want to be my girlfriend anymore.

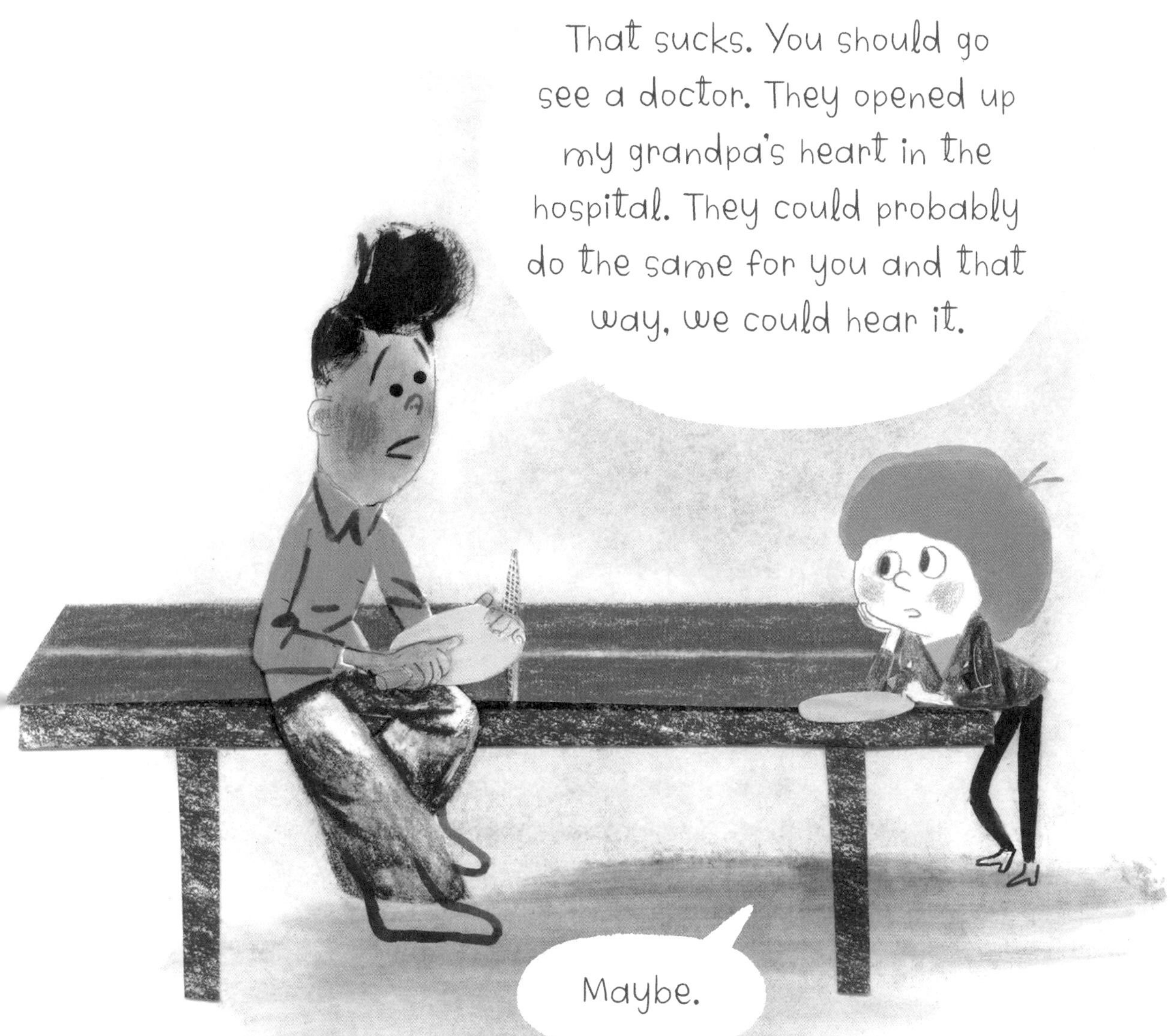
That sucks. You should go see a doctor. They opened up my grandpa's heart in the hospital. They could probably do the same for you and that way, we could hear it.
Maybe.

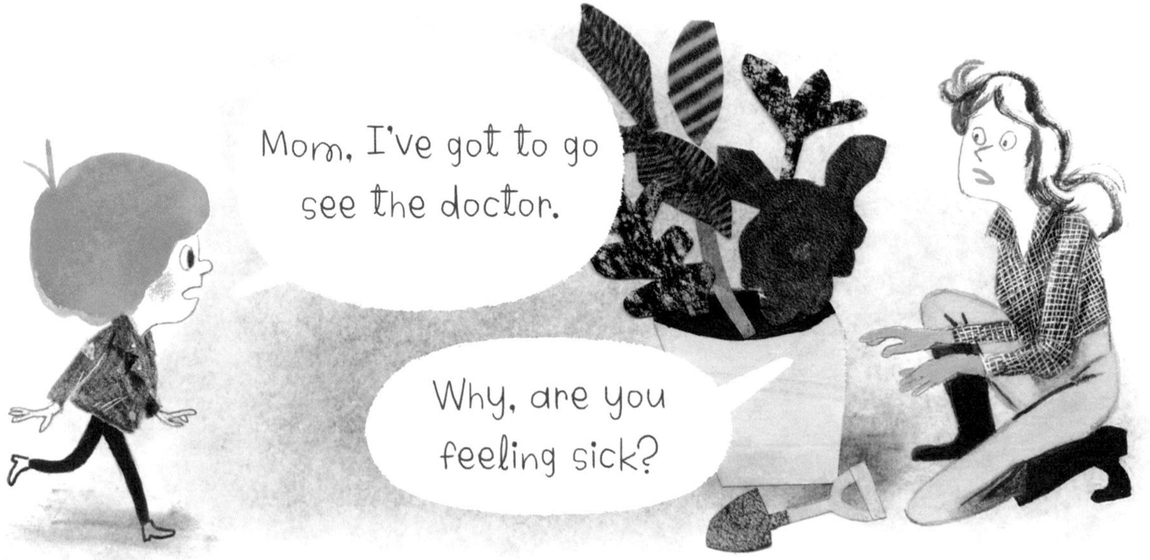
Mom, I've got to go see the doctor.
Why, are you feeling sick?

Truffle's mother always worries whenever the word "doctor" is mentioned.

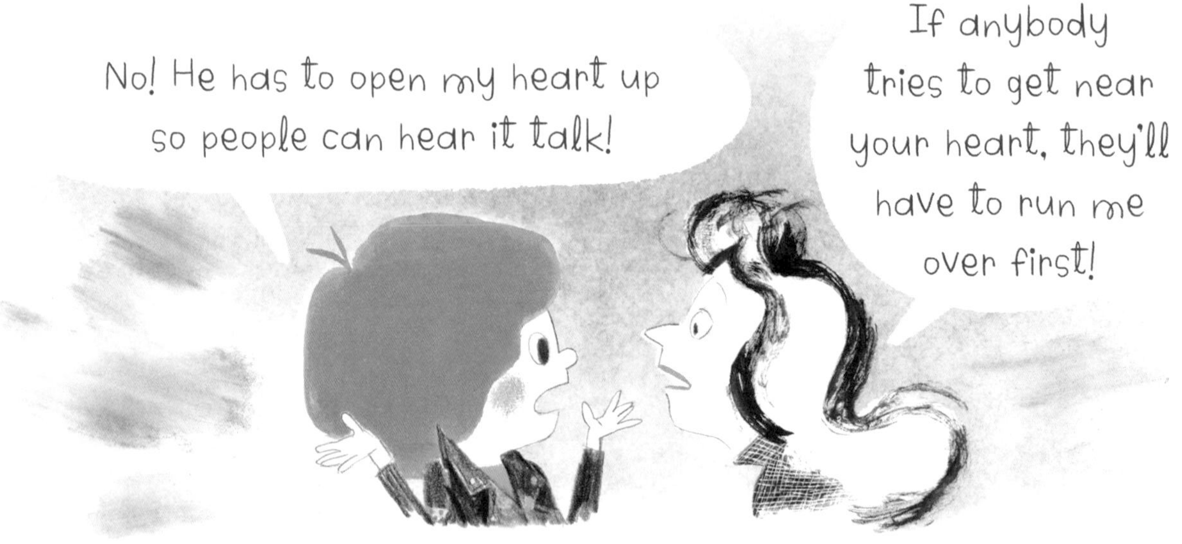
No! He has to open my heart up so people can hear it talk!
If anybody tries to get near your heart, they'll have to run me over first!

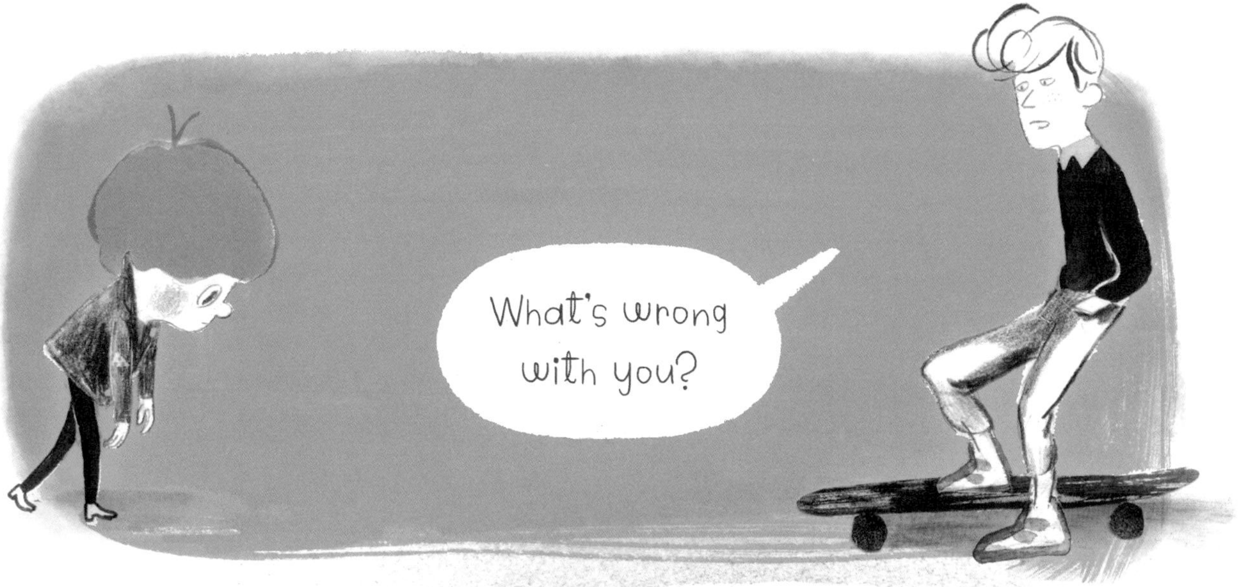
What's wrong with you?

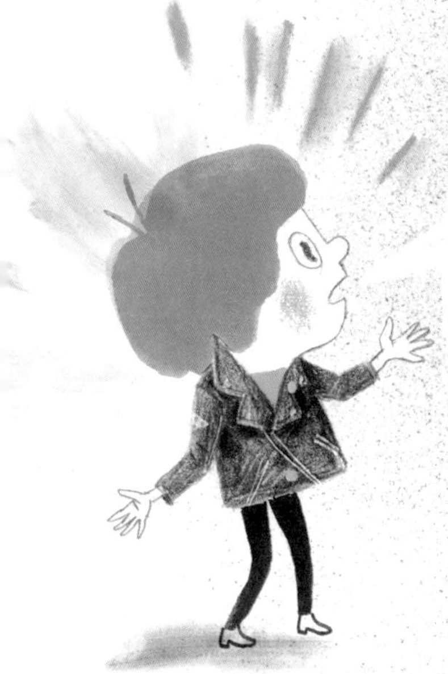

I want Nina and me to stay together, but I don't know what to say to her, and Dad told me to let my heart do the talking, which is an expression, which is a figure of speech, and Riad's grandpa had the doctors open up his heart, but Mom says she'd rather they run her over with a car and I don't want her to get smashed to a pulp!

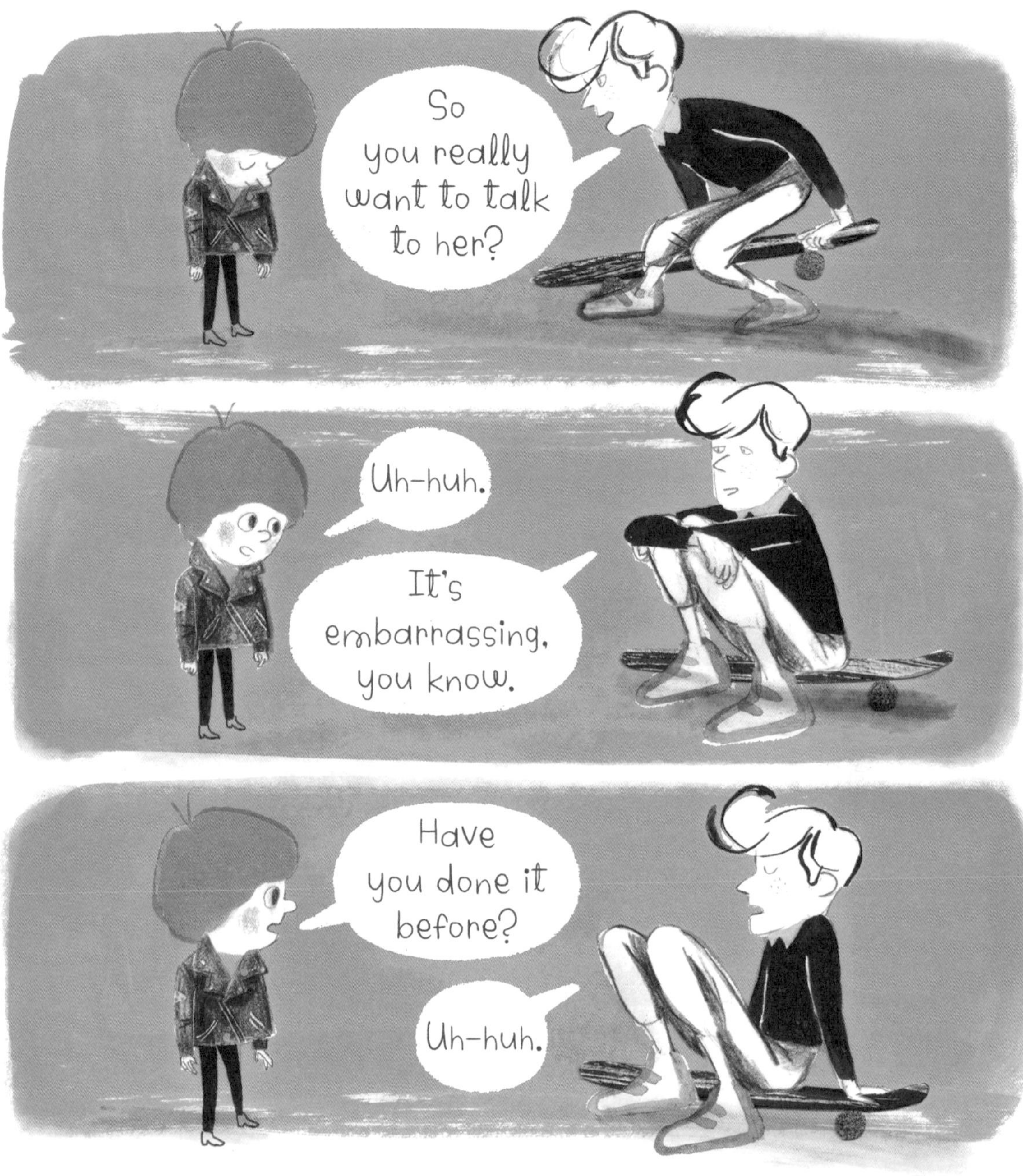
So you really want to talk to her?
Uh-huh.
It's embarrassing, you know.
Have you done it before?
Uh-huh.

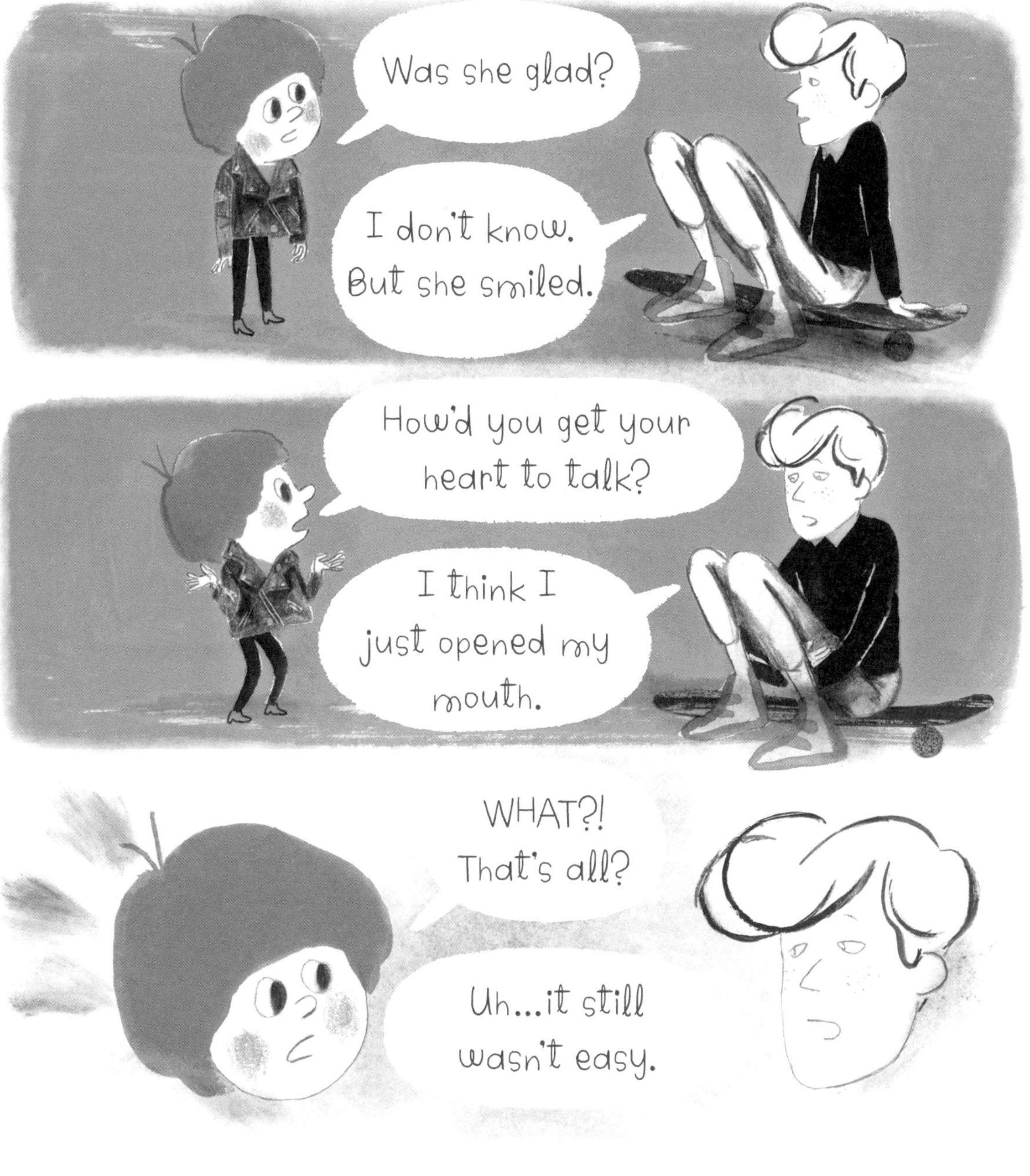
Was she glad?
I don't know. But she smiled.
How'd you get your heart to talk?
I think I just opened my mouth.
WHAT?! That's all?
Uh...it still wasn't easy.

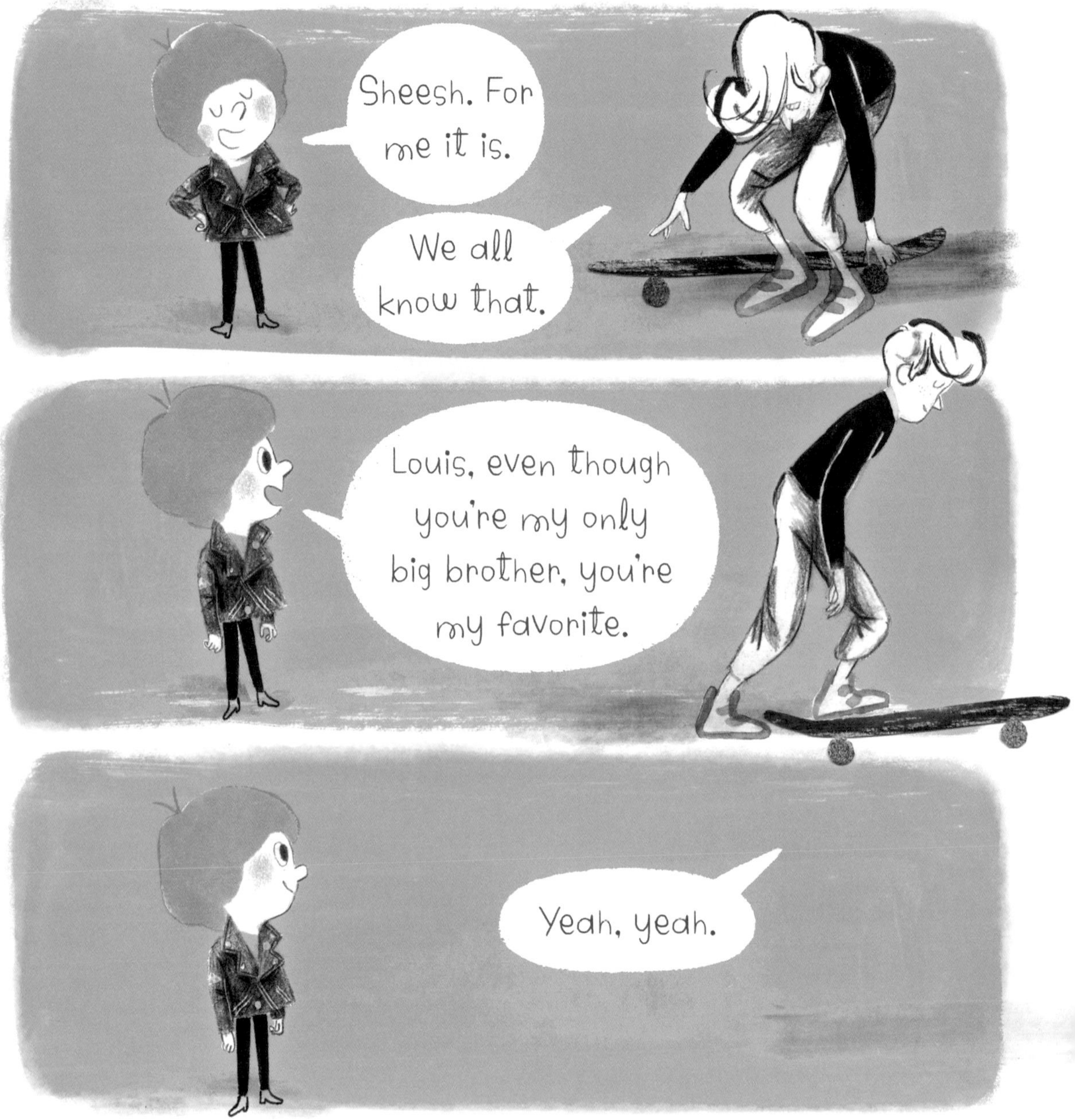
Sheesh. For me it is.
We all know that.
Louis, even though you're my only big brother, you're my favorite.
Yeah, yeah.

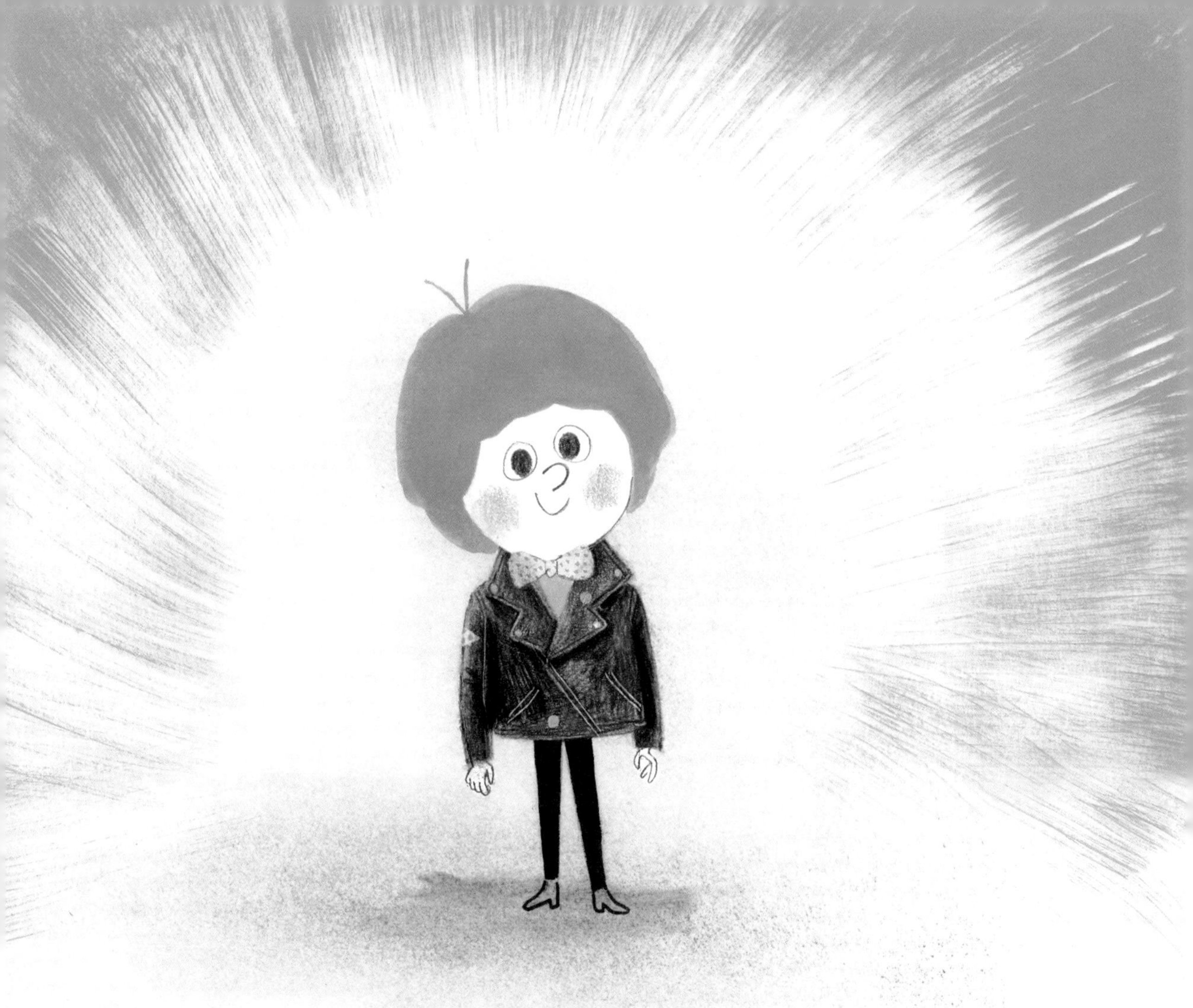

The next day, Truffle put on his lucky suspenders, Flo's bow tie and his biker jacket with a pizza button on it. He wanted to look his best to talk to Nina.

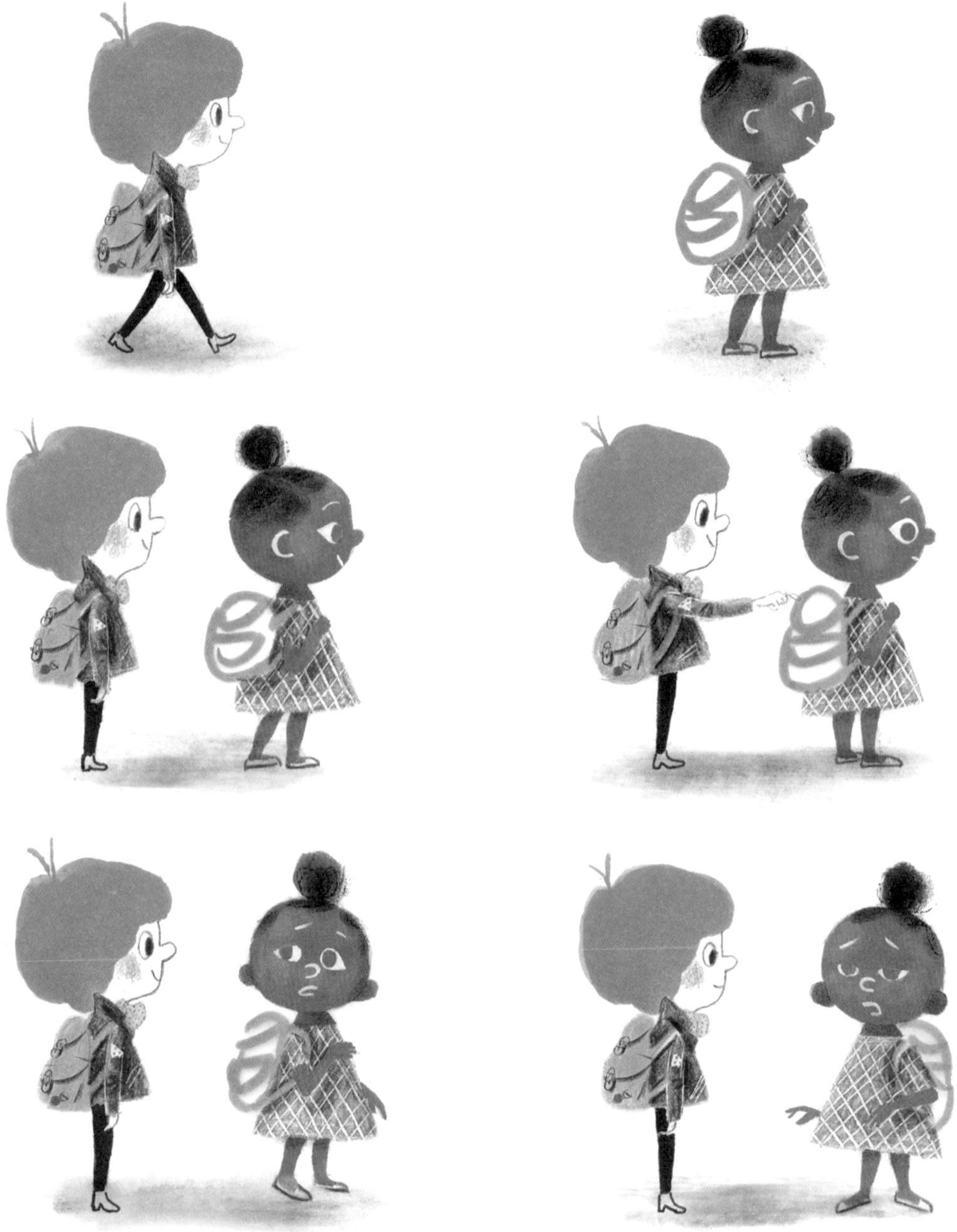

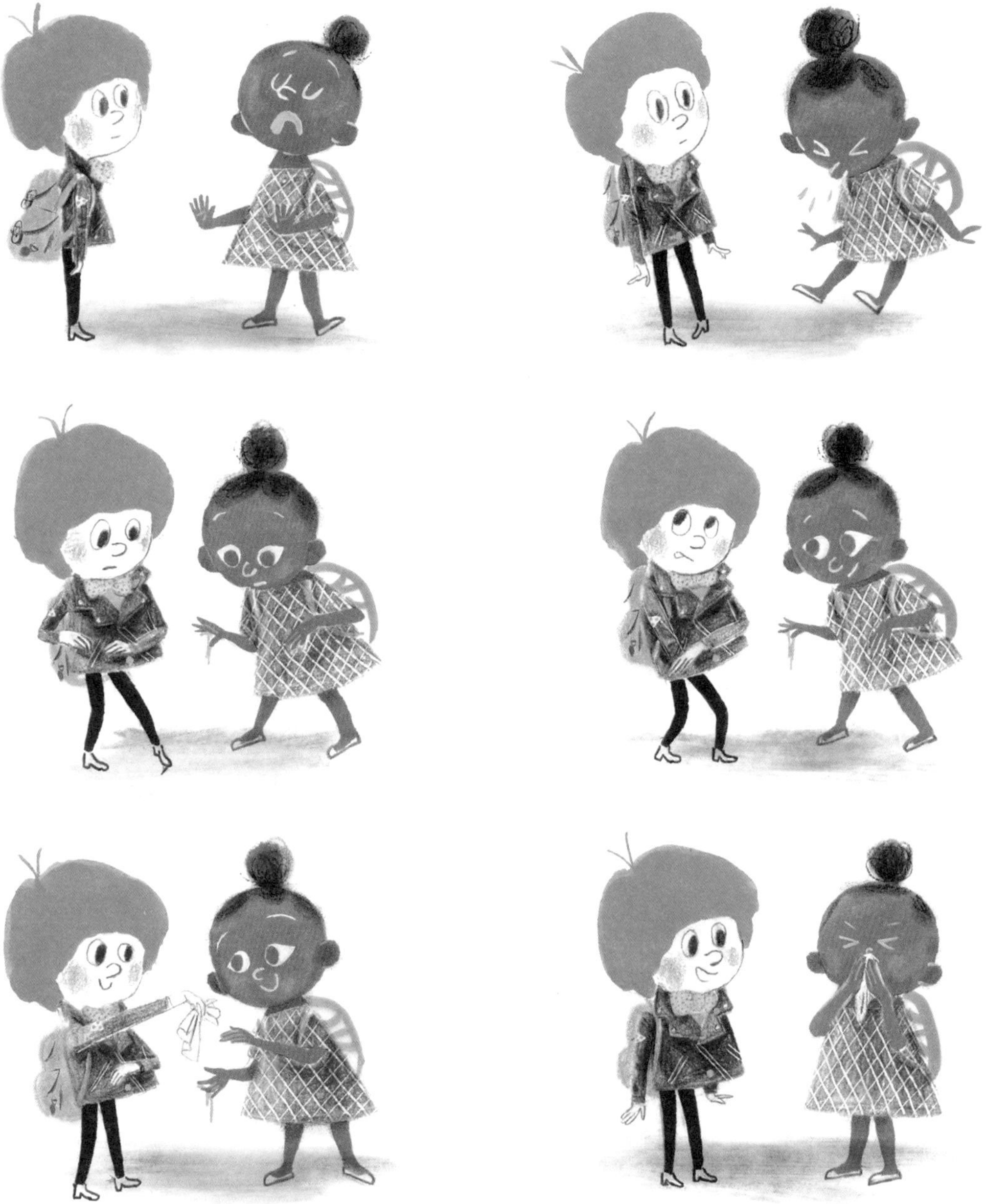

Nina, I want to tell you my heart loves you. It would tell you itself, but I don't want my mom to get run over. So, my mouth is delivering the message. I love you, first because of the way you focus when you write and second because you smell like plants 'cause your dad's a florist.

Okay. Me too, I love you. First because you know Nina Simone who's got the same name as me and second because your pizza button always makes me hungry.

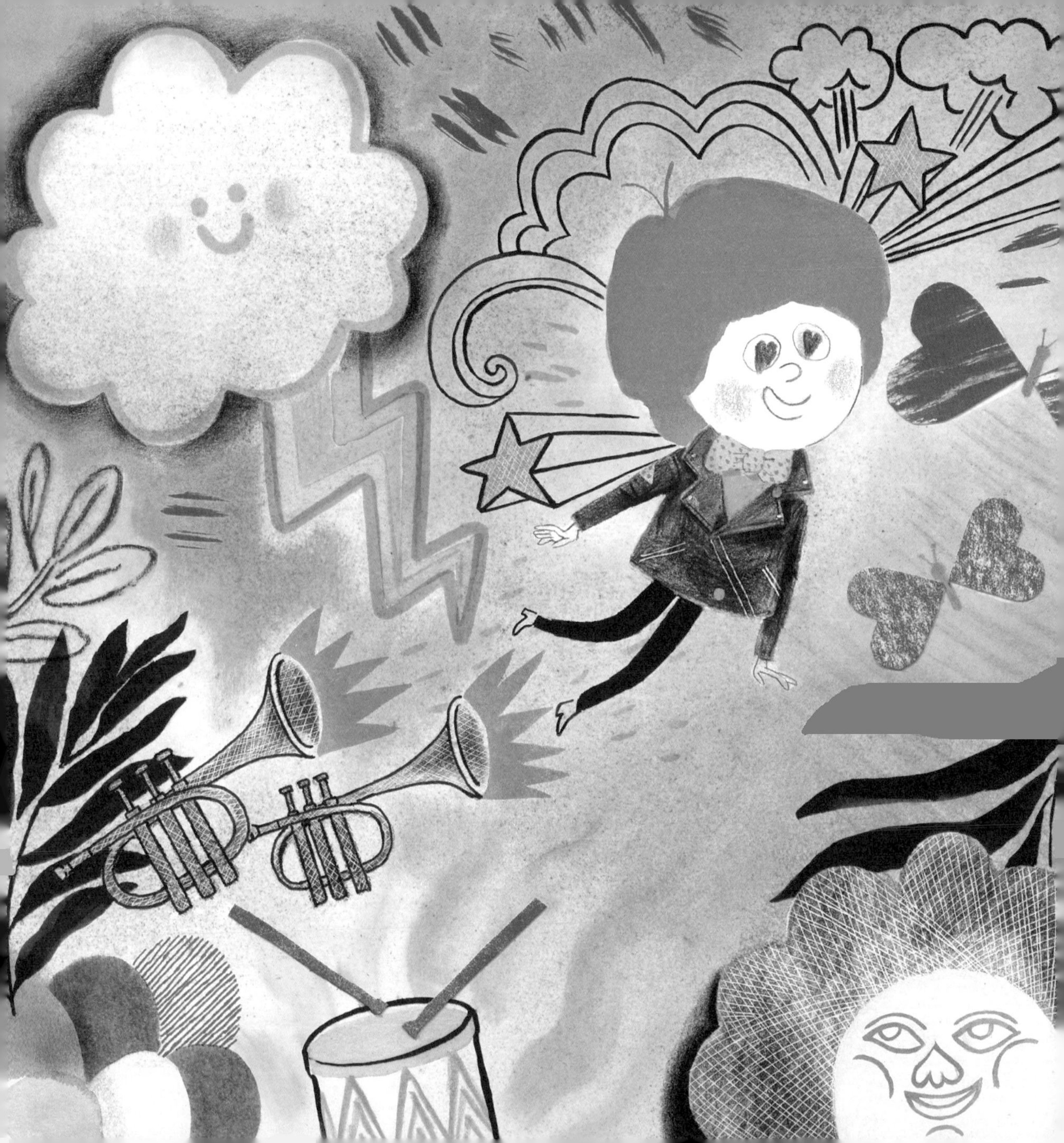

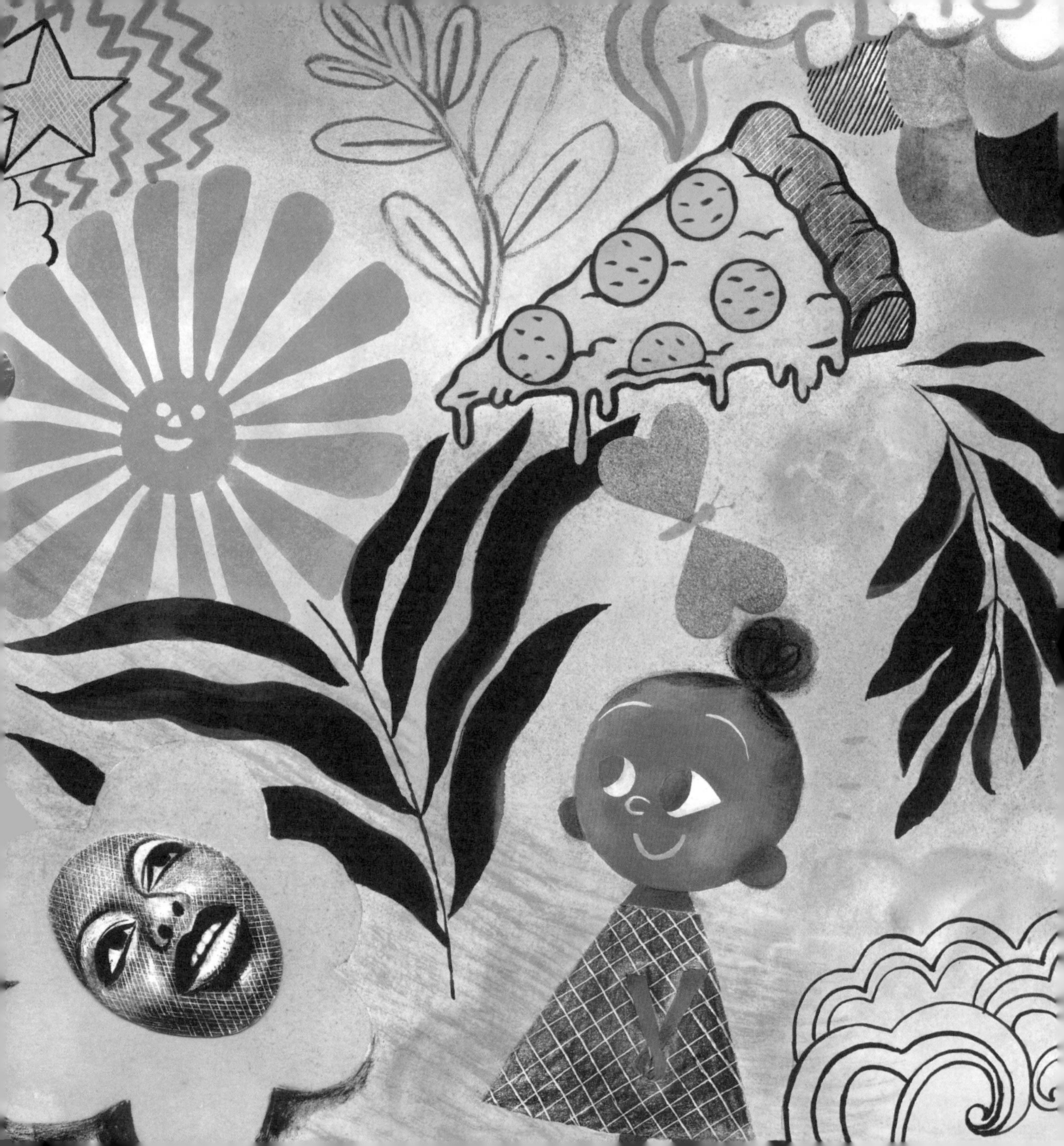

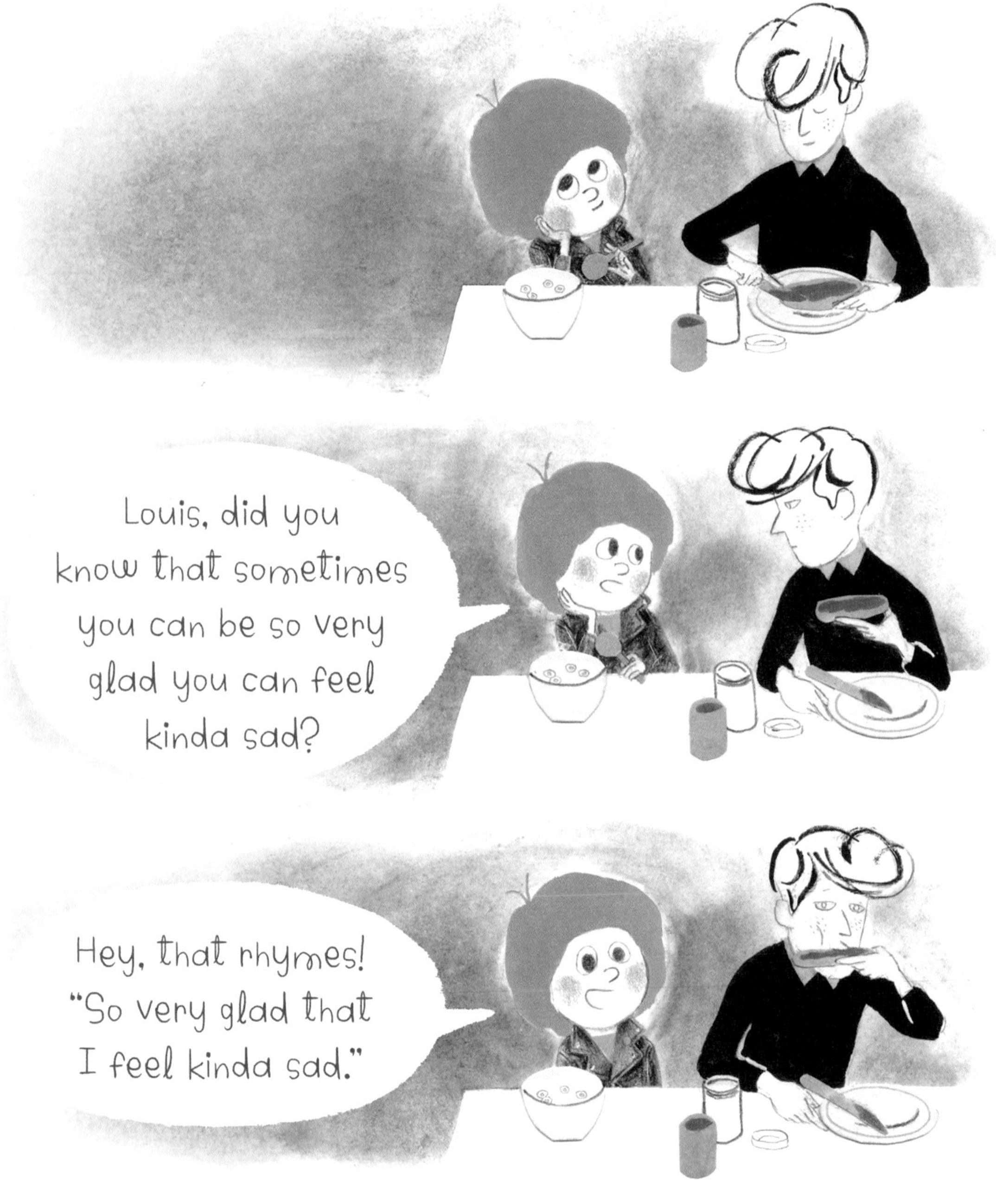
Louis, did you know that sometimes you can be so very glad you can feel kinda sad?
Hey, that rhymes! "So very glad that I feel kinda sad."

So glaaad! Kinda saaaad!

So very

So very

So very glaaaad...

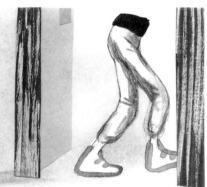

That's how Truffle wrote the first song for his super awesome band, The Man-Eating Plants, who are into retro and garage rock and a little bit of pop even though Flo, Riad and Truffle haven't actually learned how to play an instrument yet.

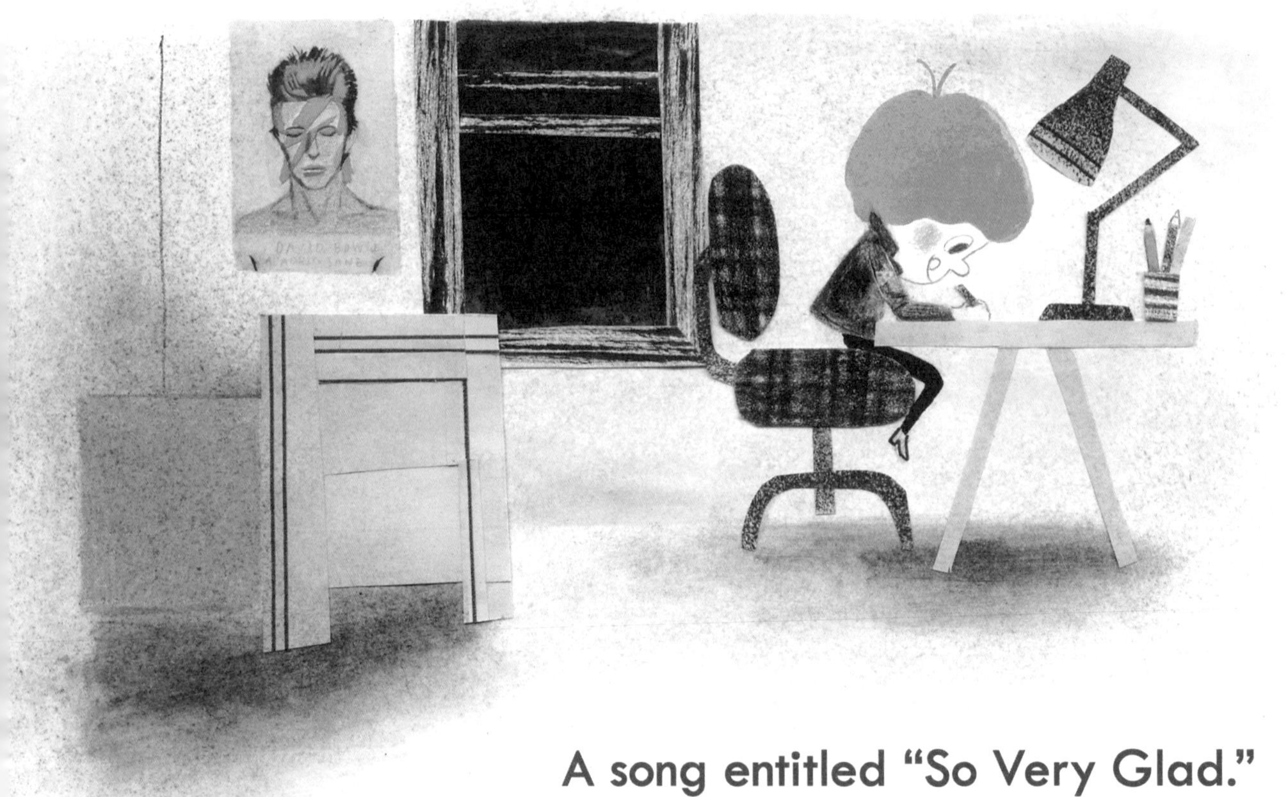

A song entitled "So Very Glad."

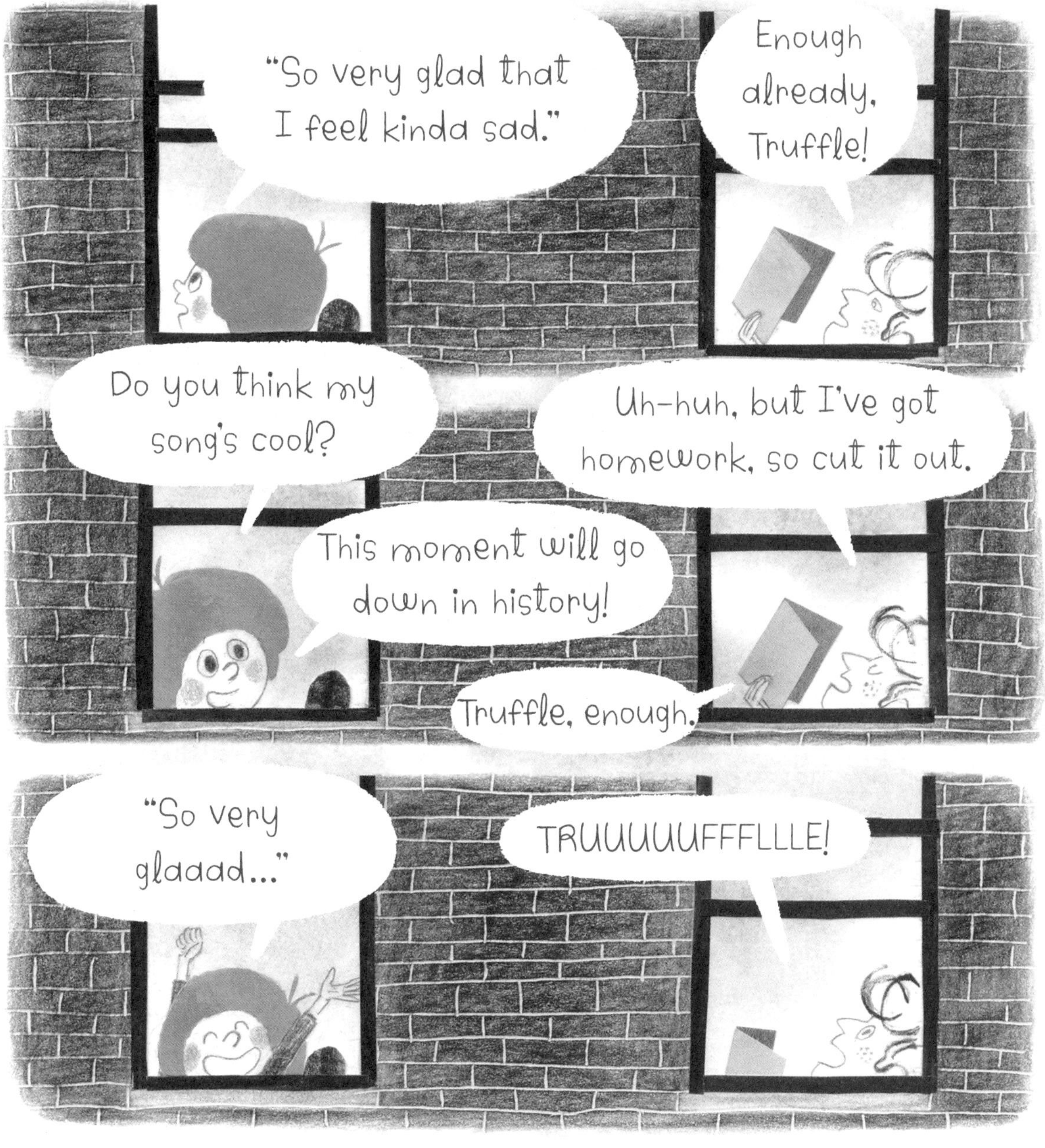
"So very glad that I feel kinda sad."
Enough already, Truffle!
Do you think my song's cool?
Uh-huh, but I've got homework, so cut it out.
This moment will go down in history!
Truffle, enough.
"So very glaaad..."
TRUUUUUFFFLLLE!

TRUFFLE TACKLES EXISTENCE

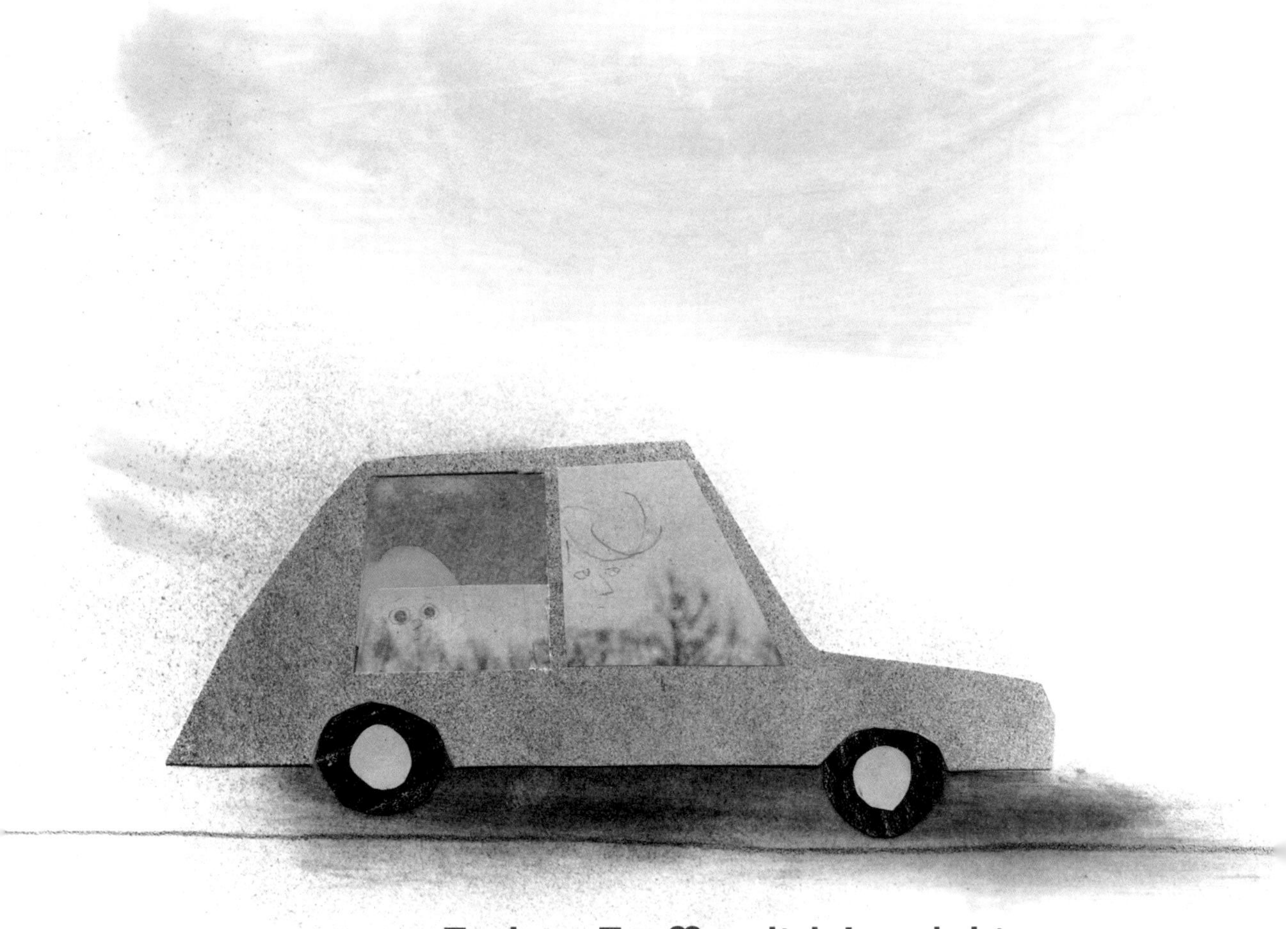

Today, Truffle didn't ask his mom to turn the music on in the car.

Usually, he always asks for a song.

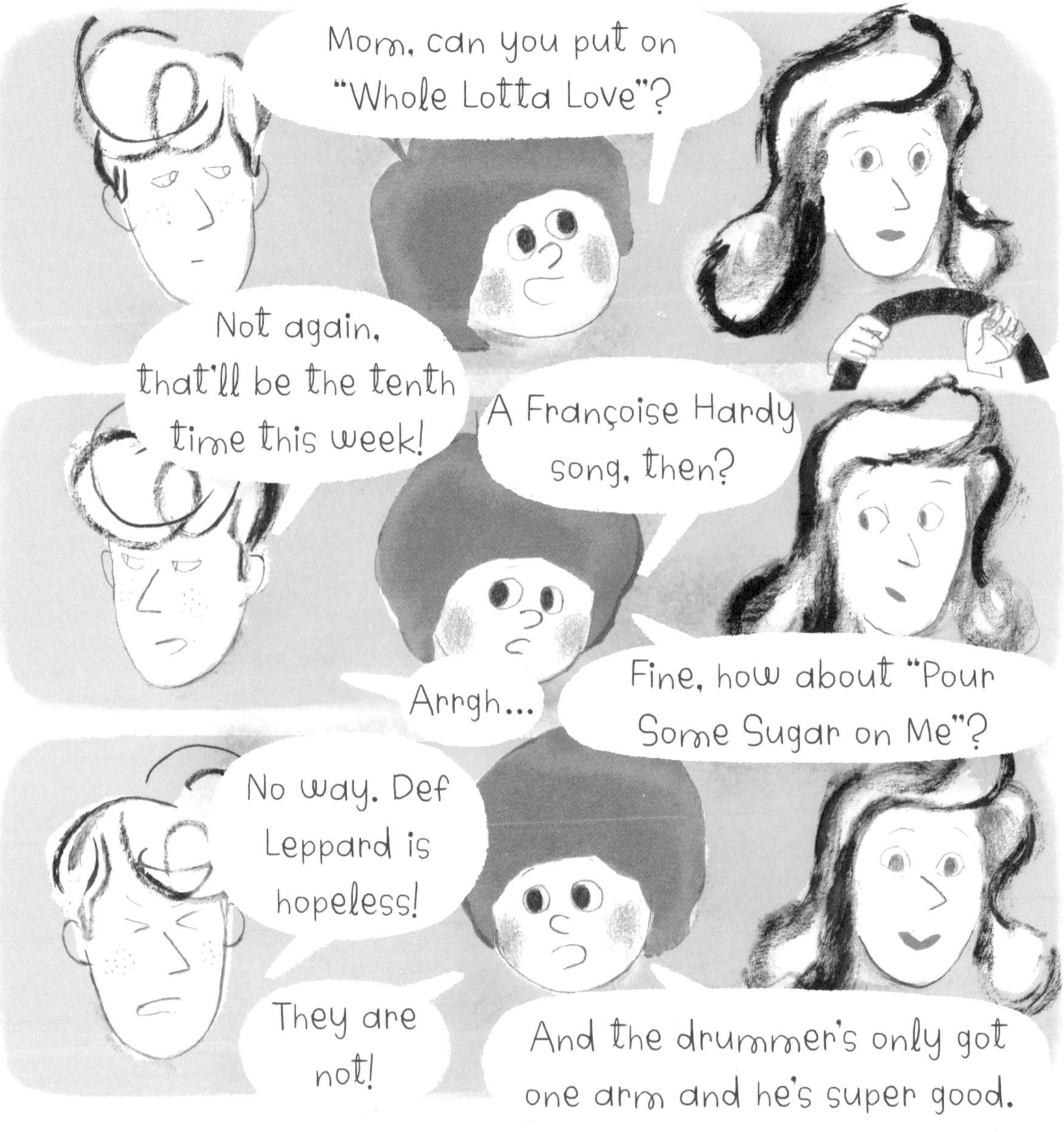
Mom, can you put on "Whole Lotta Love"?
Not again, that'll be the tenth time this week!
A Françoise Hardy song, then?
Arrgh...
Fine, how about "Pour Some Sugar on Me"?
No way. Def Leppard is hopeless!
They are not!
And the drummer's only got one arm and he's super good.

Most days that's the way
it goes. But not today.

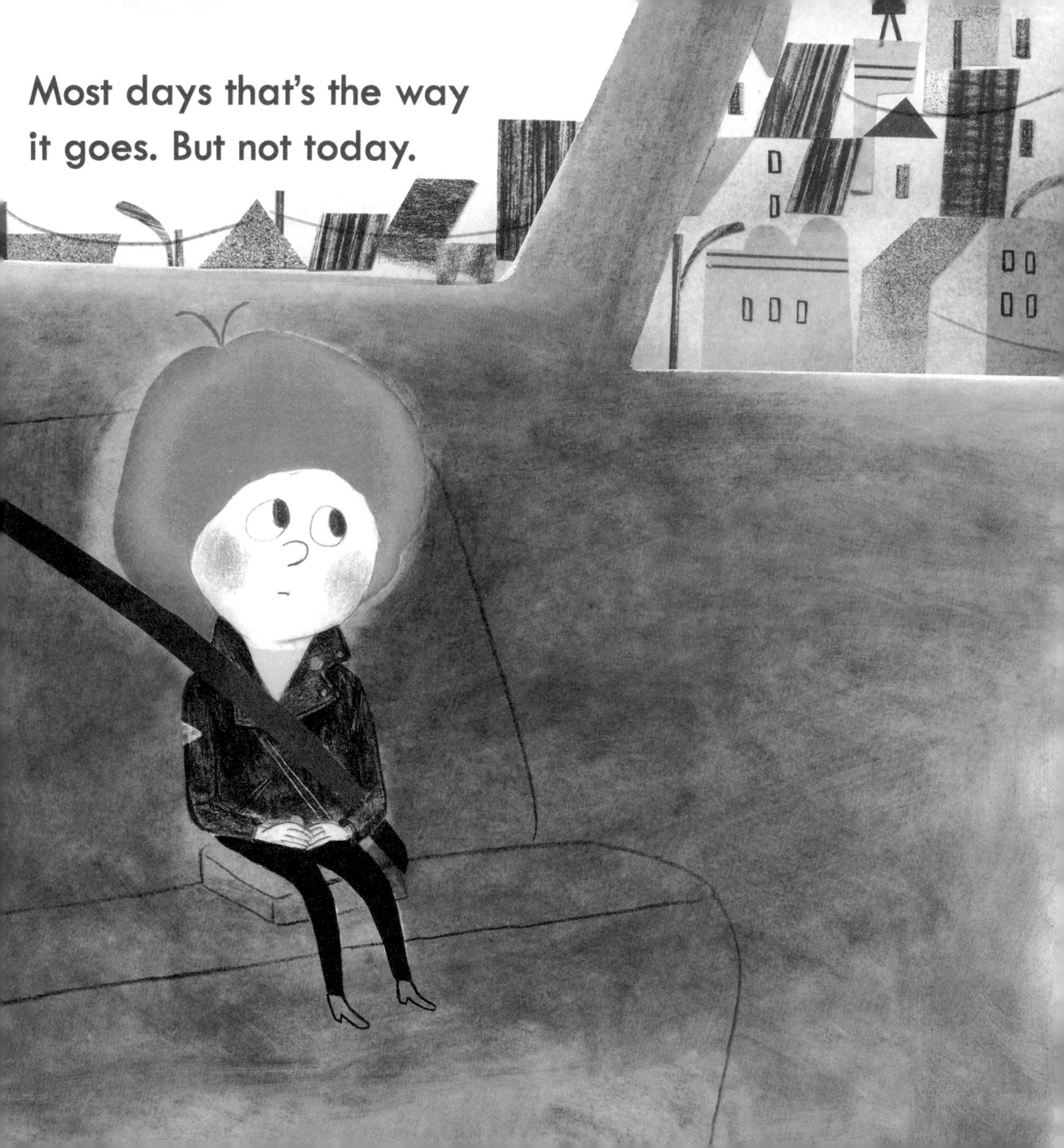

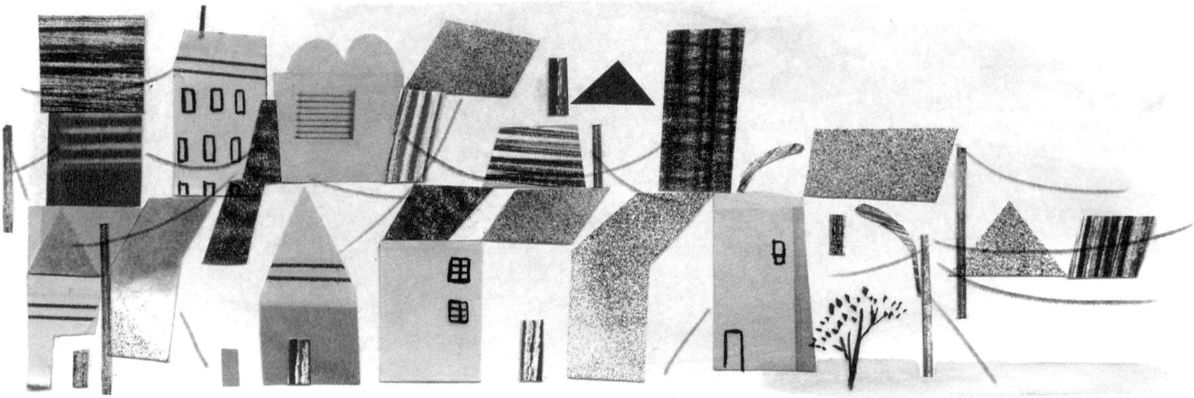
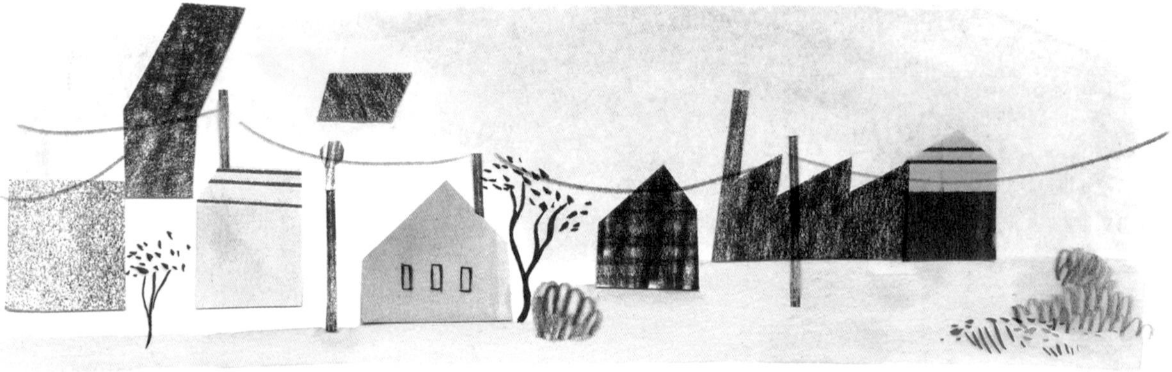
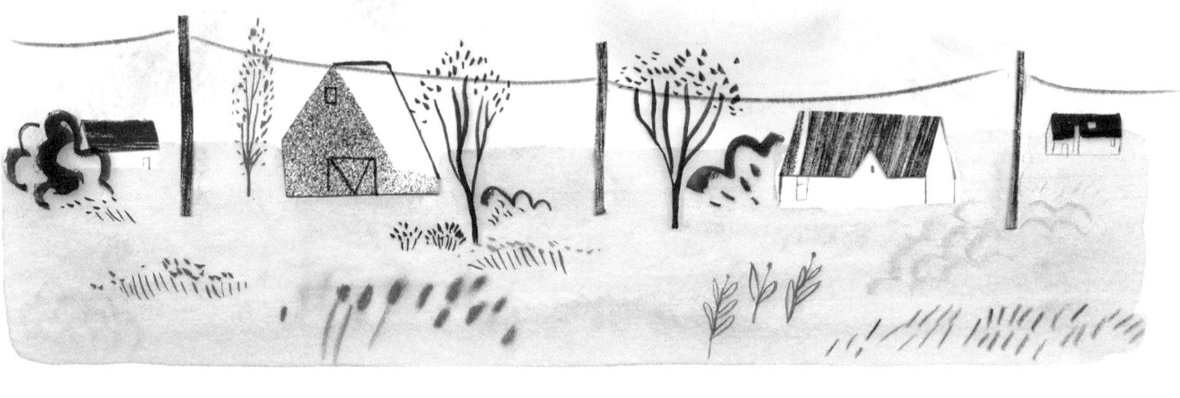

Not that he doesn't feel like listening to music.

I always feel like listening to music!

But today, Truffle thinks it wouldn't be right because of his great-grandma Sybile.

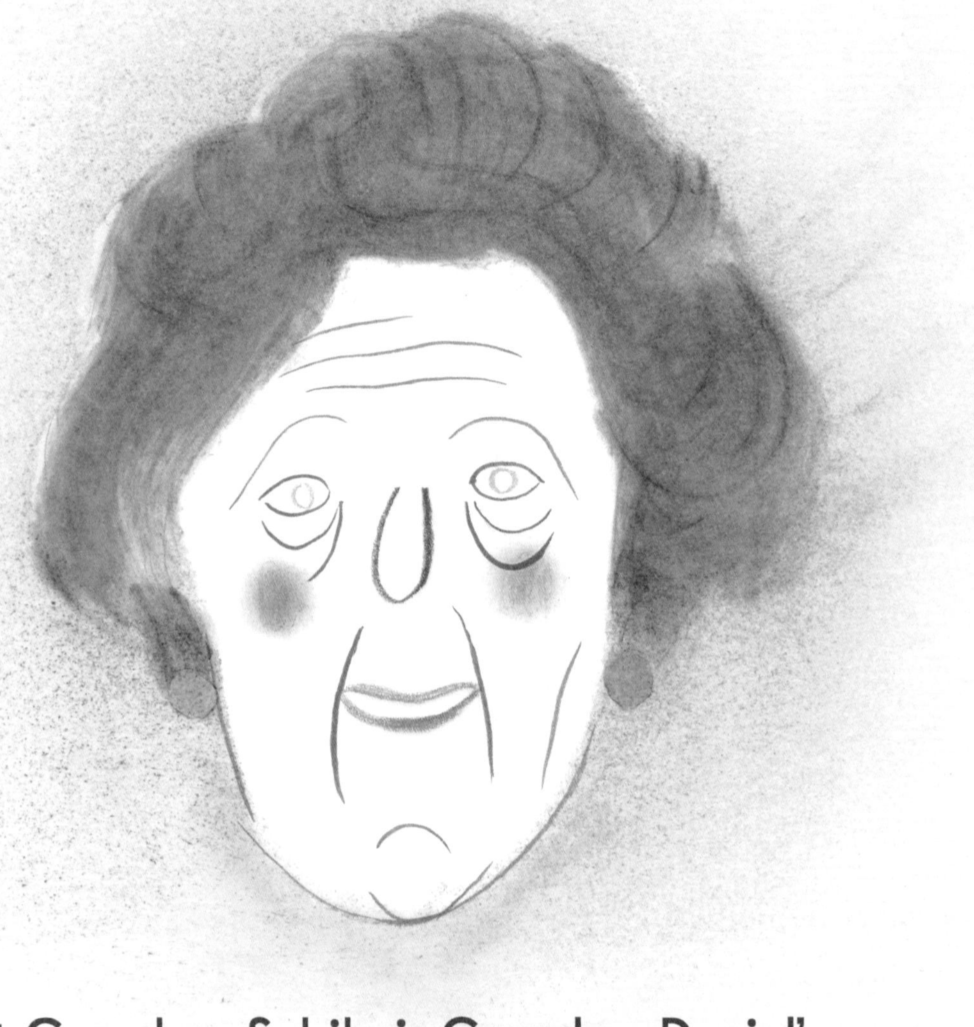

Great-Grandma Sybile is Grandpa Daniel's mom
and Grandpa Daniel is Truffle's dad's dad.

Five days ago, Great-Grandma Sybile died.

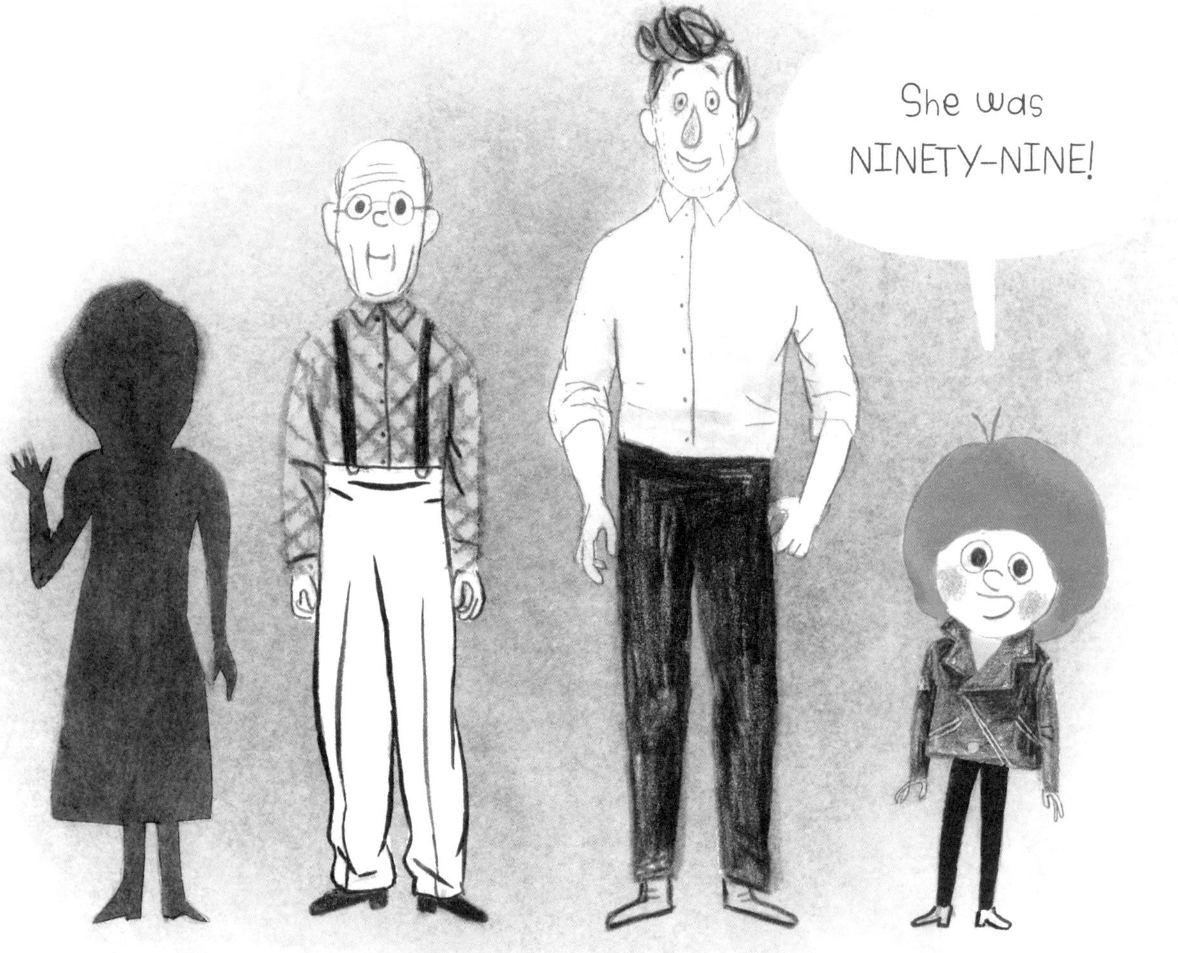
She was
NINETY-NINE!

That's almost a hundred years old.

Truffle didn't see her very often. For one thing, she lived a long way away. Plus she hadn't been doing too well lately.

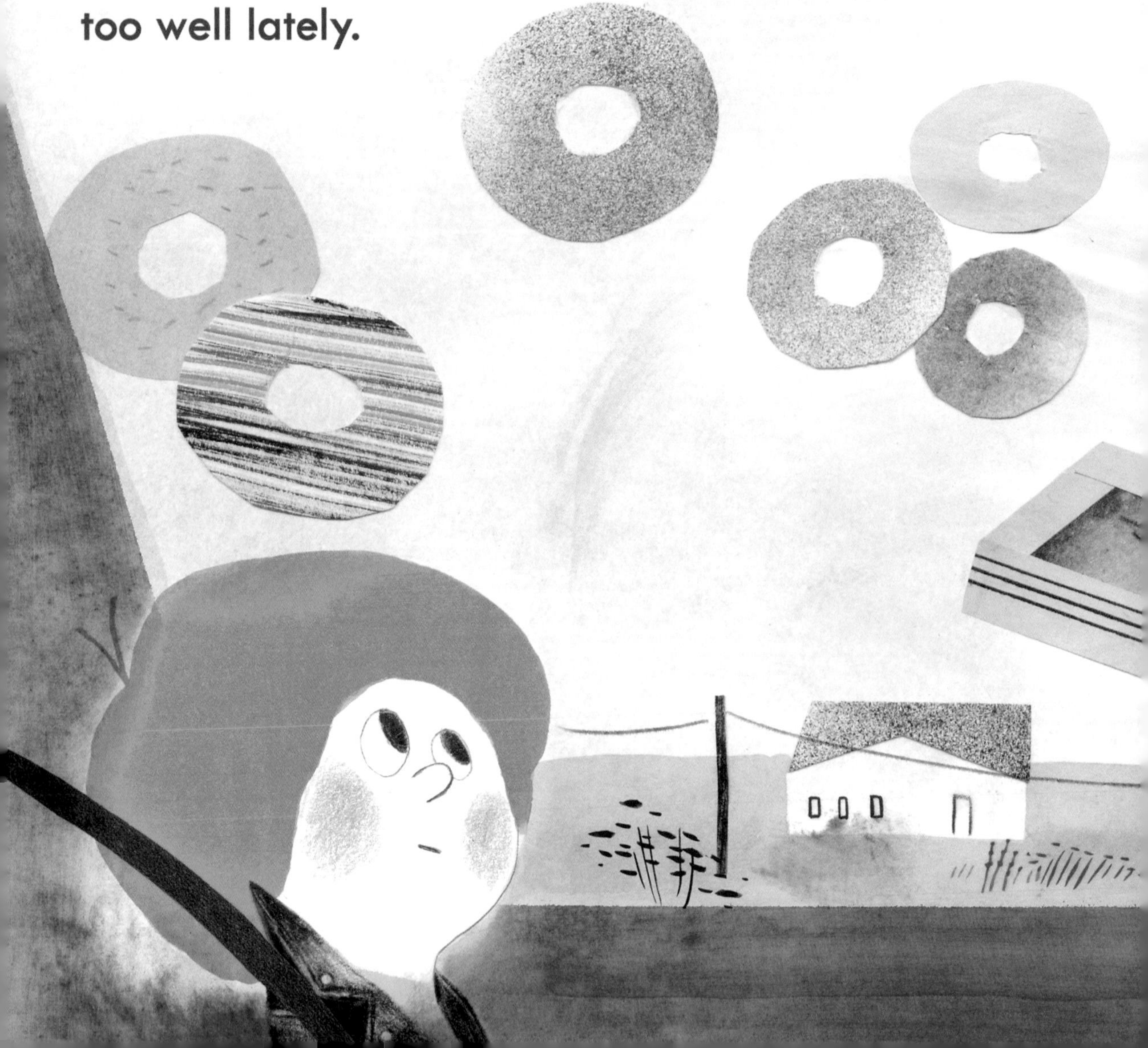

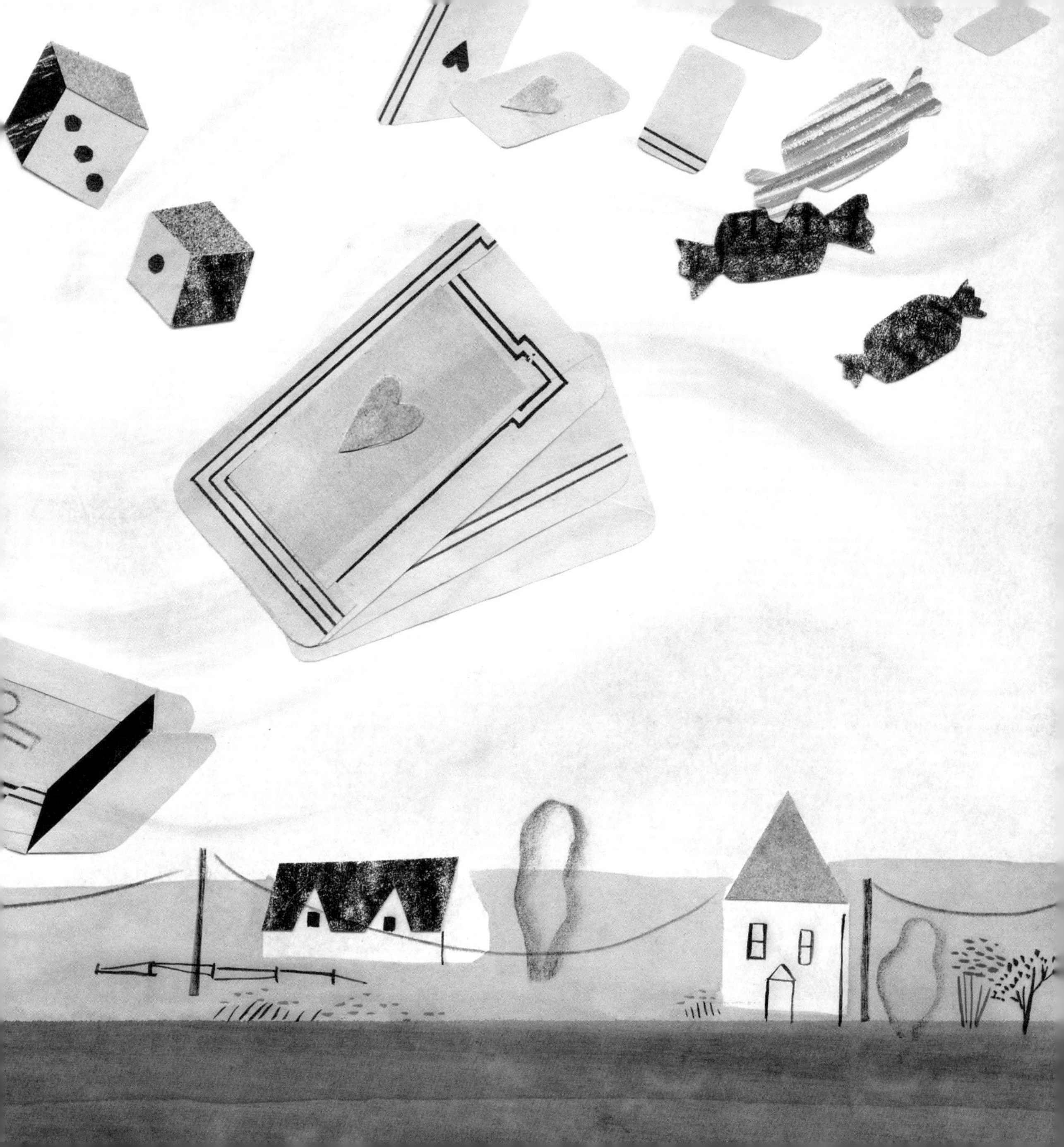

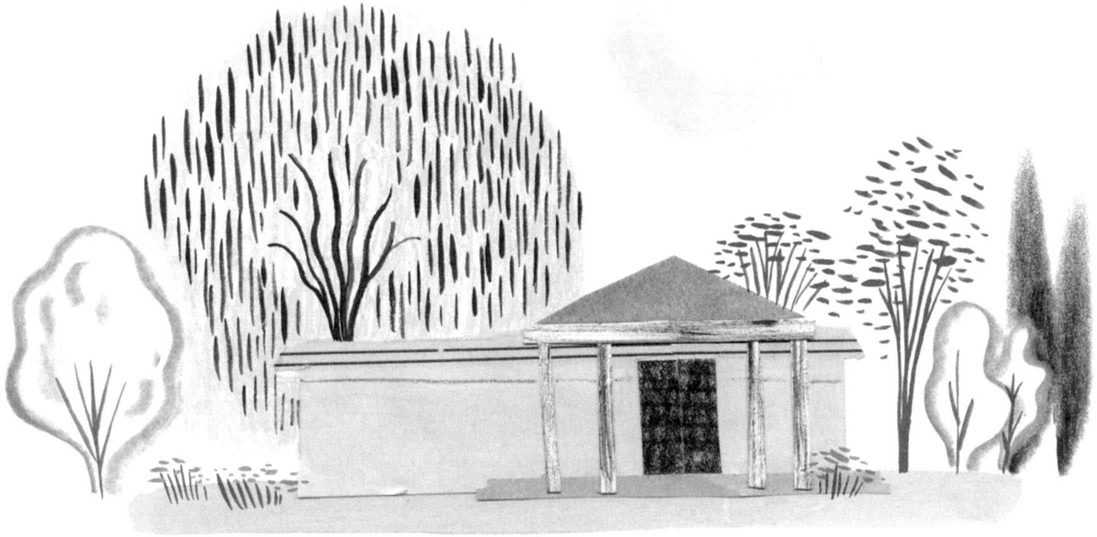

This is Truffle's first time in a funeral parlor.

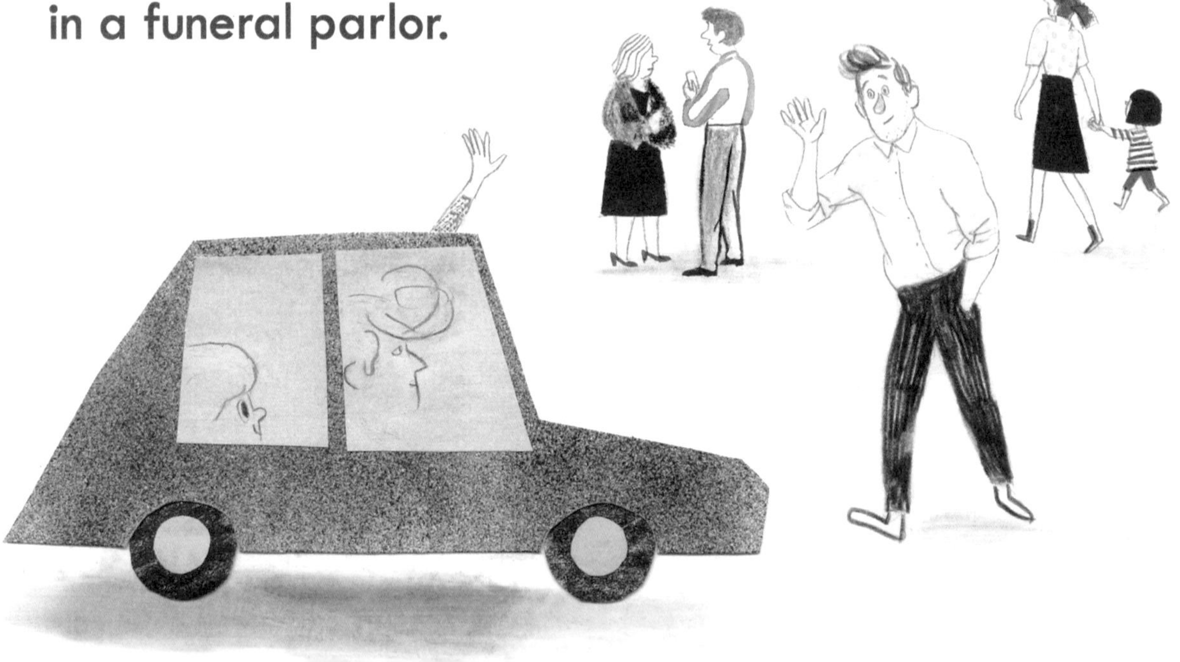

Glad to see you, Hélène.

Truffle's parents are divorced. But every time they see each other, they hug for such a long time Truffle thinks they'll be getting back together soon.

They're not getting back together, Truffle.

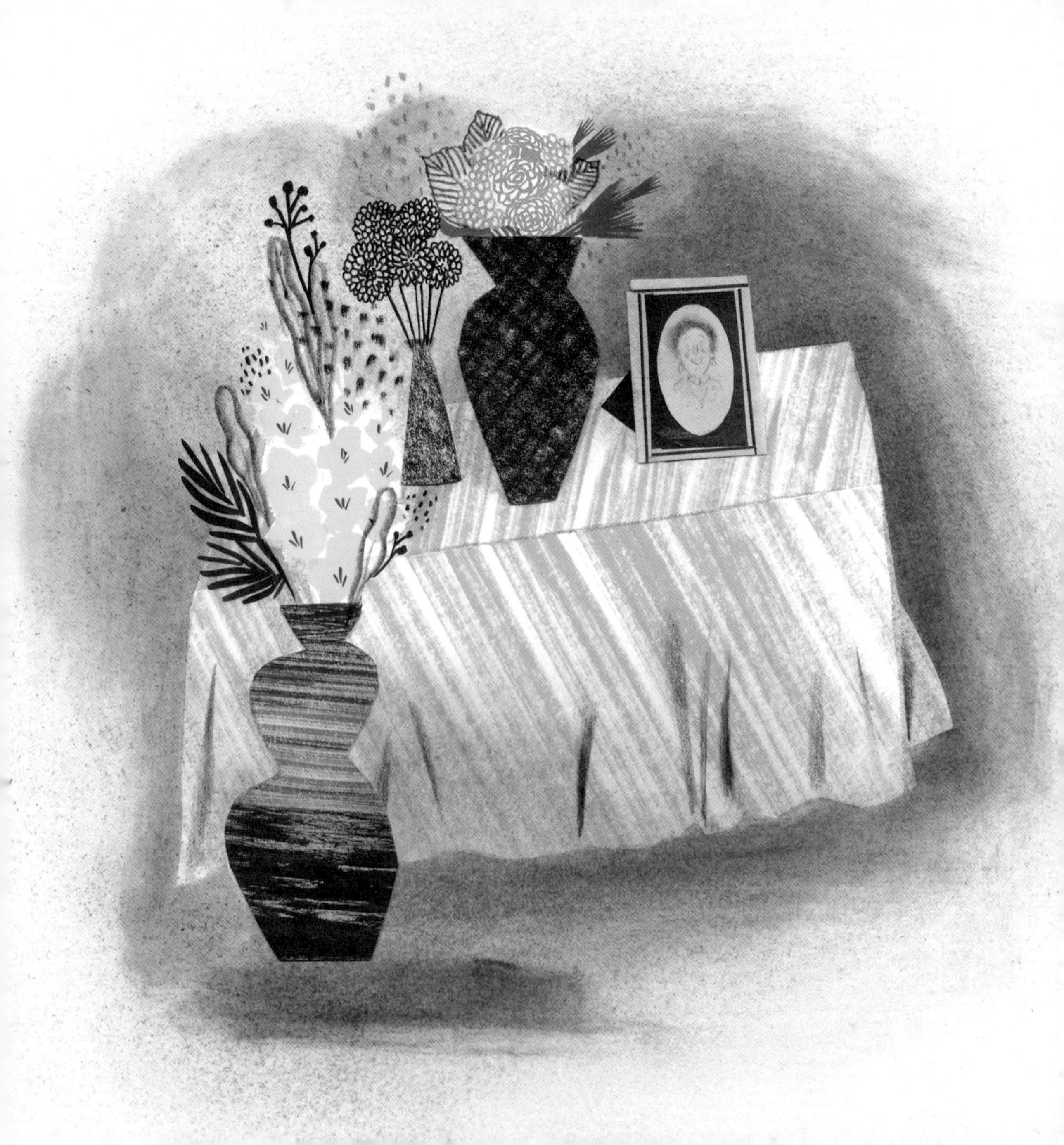

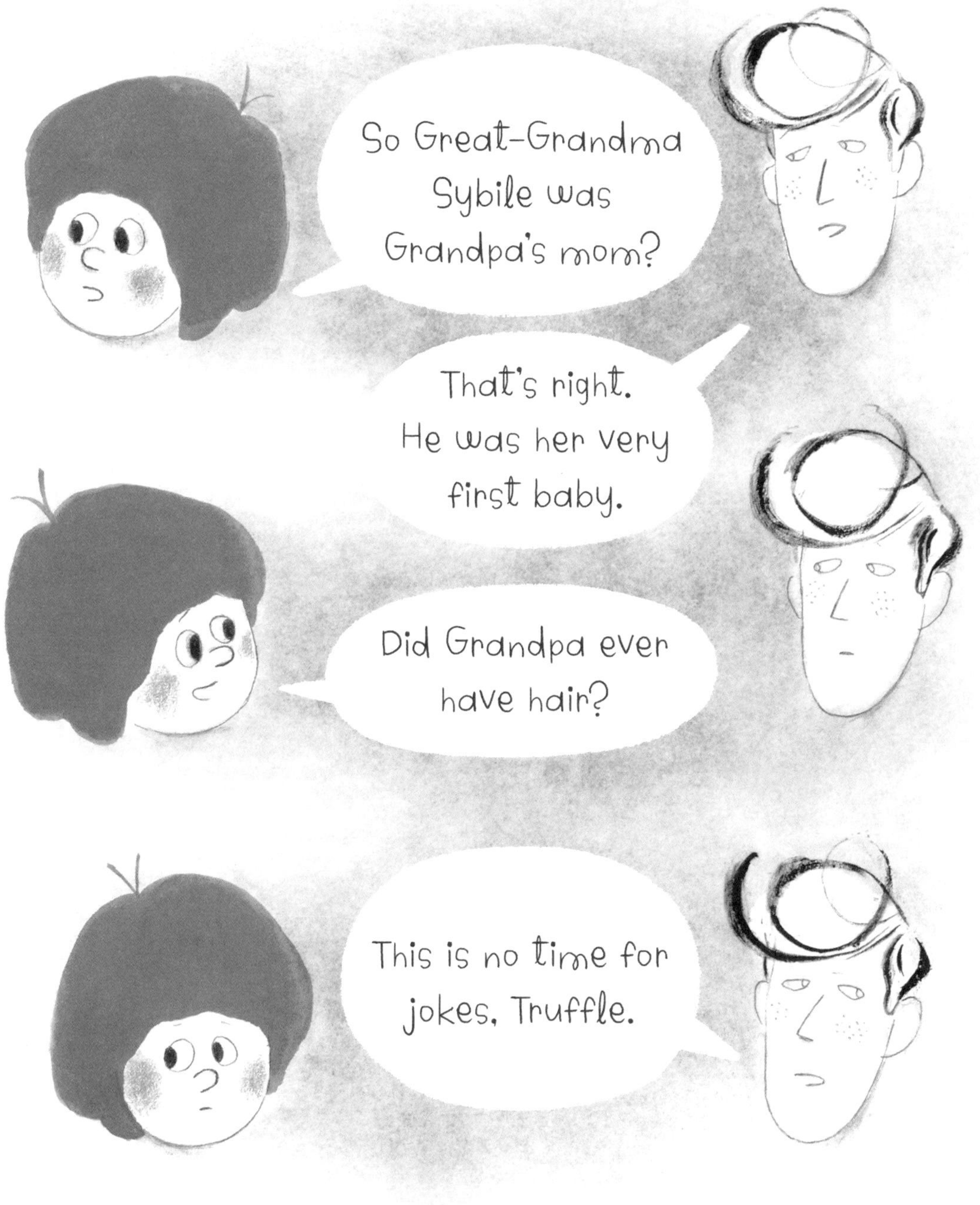
So Great-Grandma Sybile was Grandpa's mom?
That's right. He was her very first baby.
Did Grandpa ever have hair?
This is no time for jokes, Truffle.

I think she might
need a little walk.

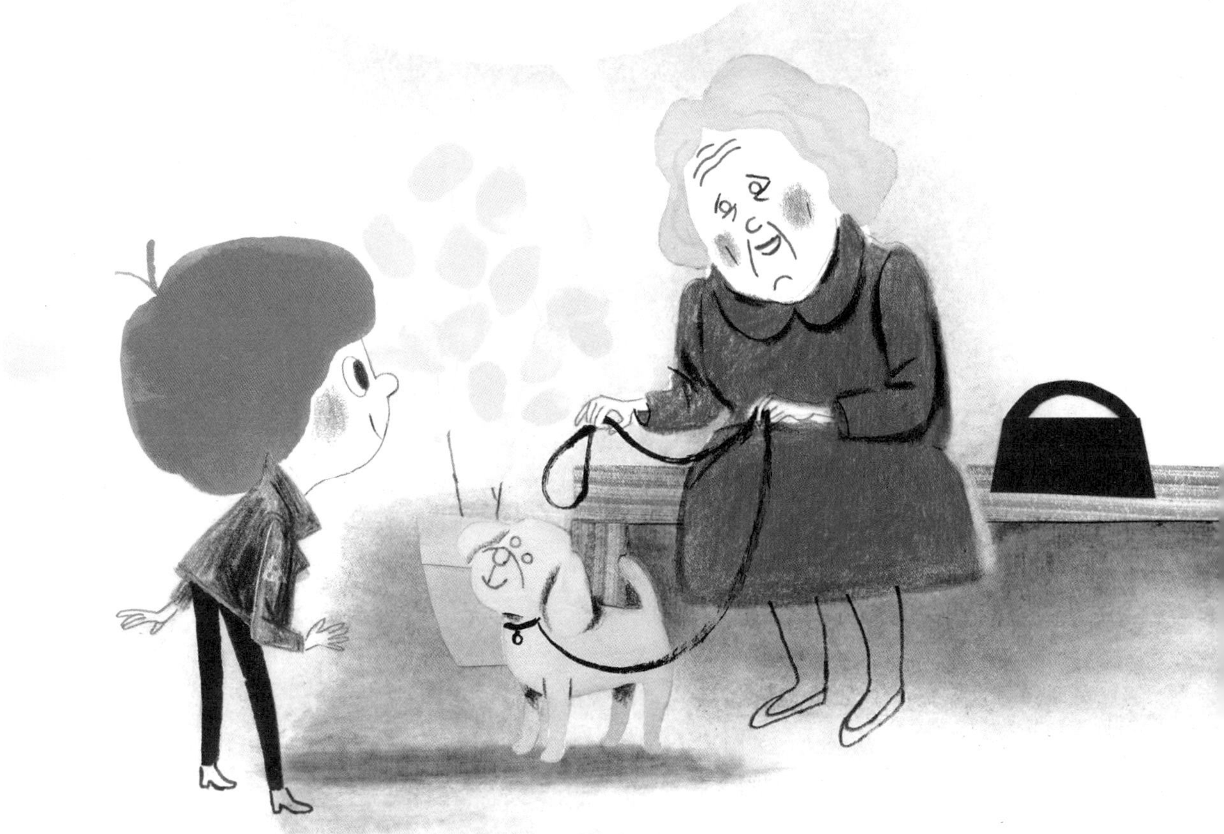

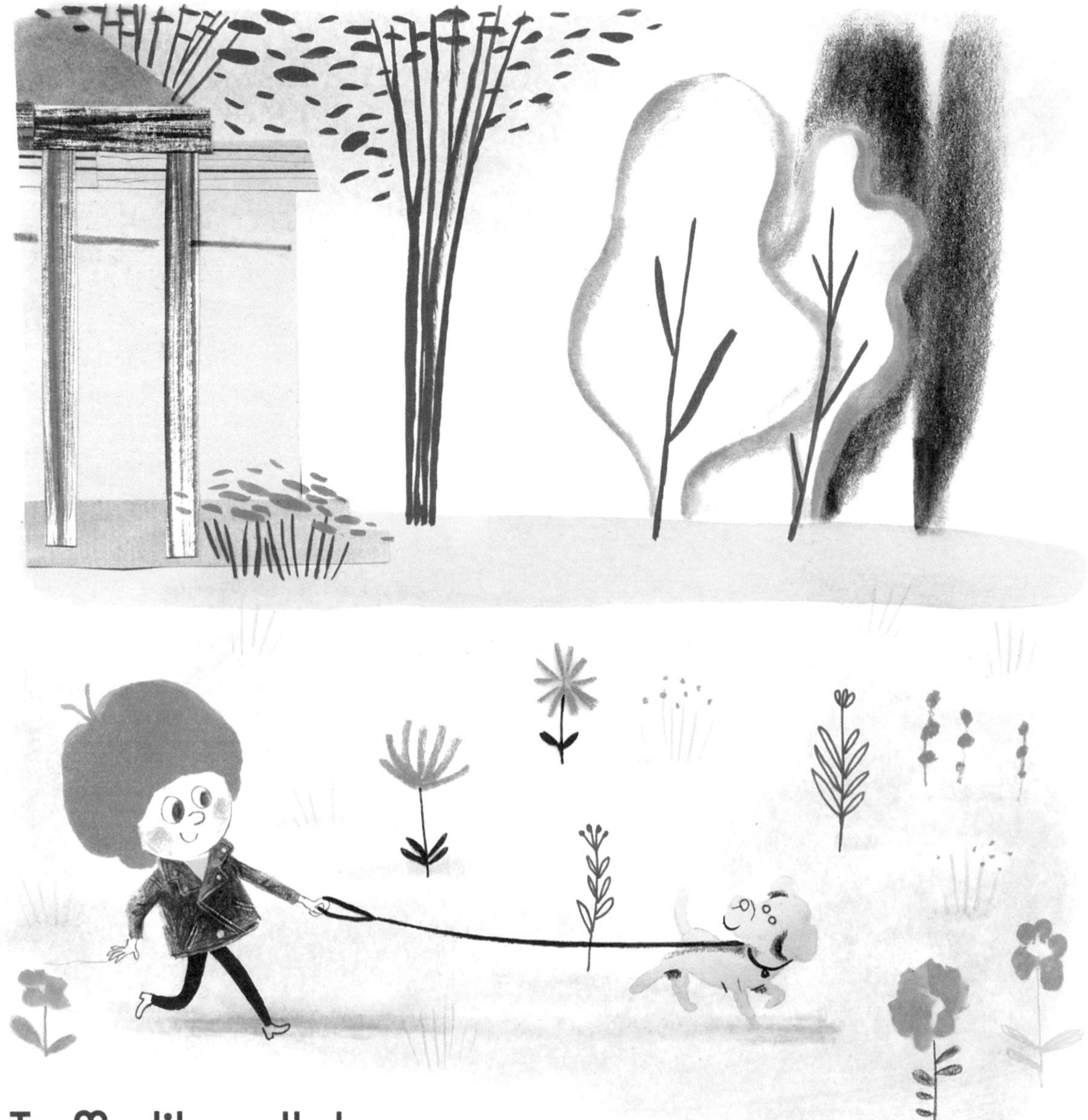

Truffle likes all dogs.

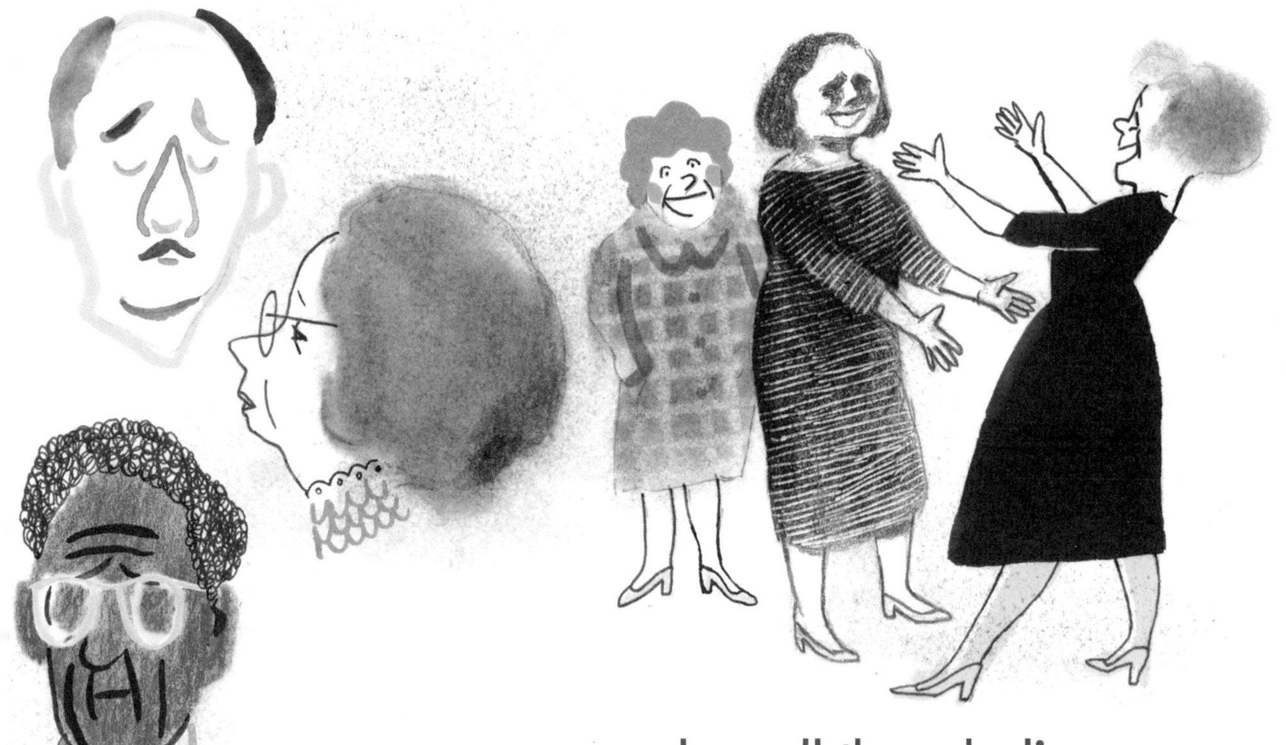

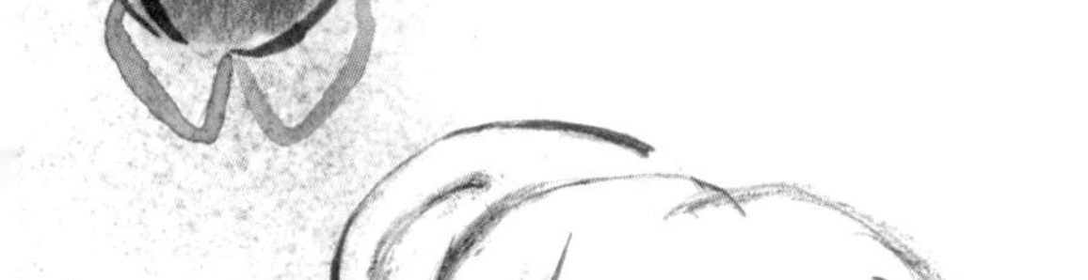

...when all those ladies over
there are laughing?

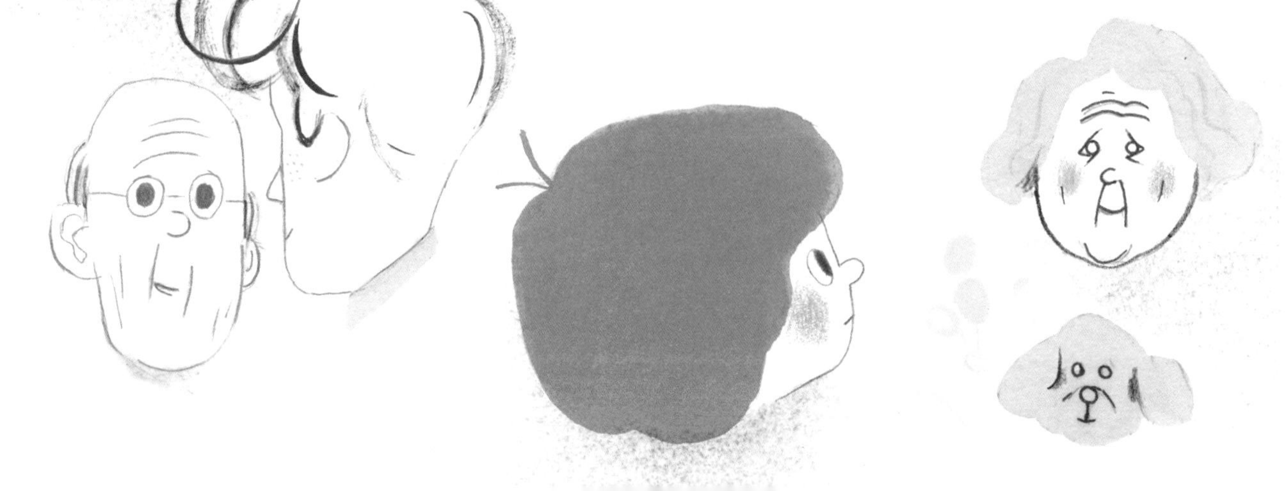

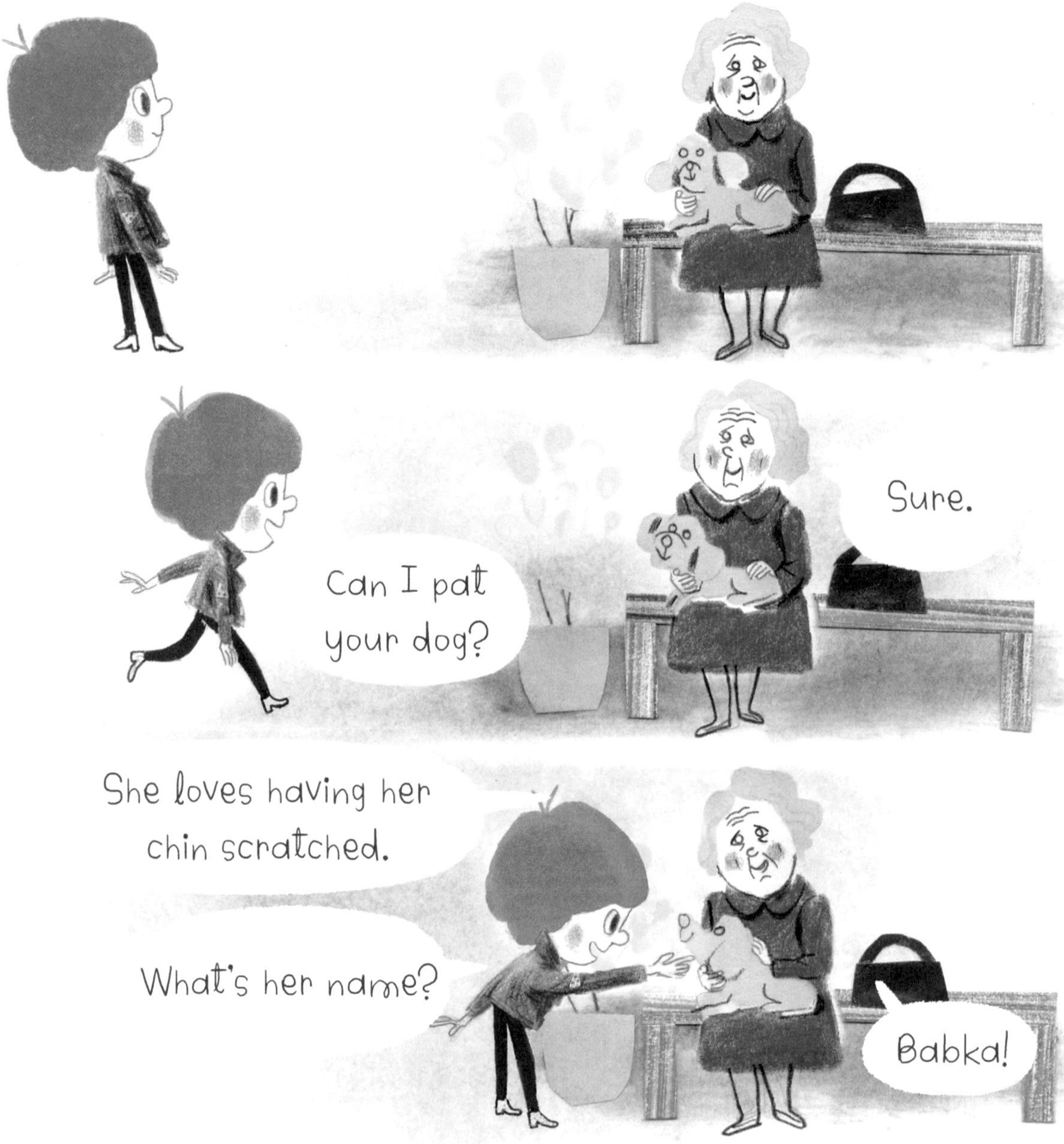
Can I pat your dog?
Sure.
She loves having her chin scratched.
What's her name?
Babka!

The kind with wrinkled skin.

The kind that drool
on the carpet.

The kind that lick your ears.

Once he almost got a dog of his own. A dog with a red coat.

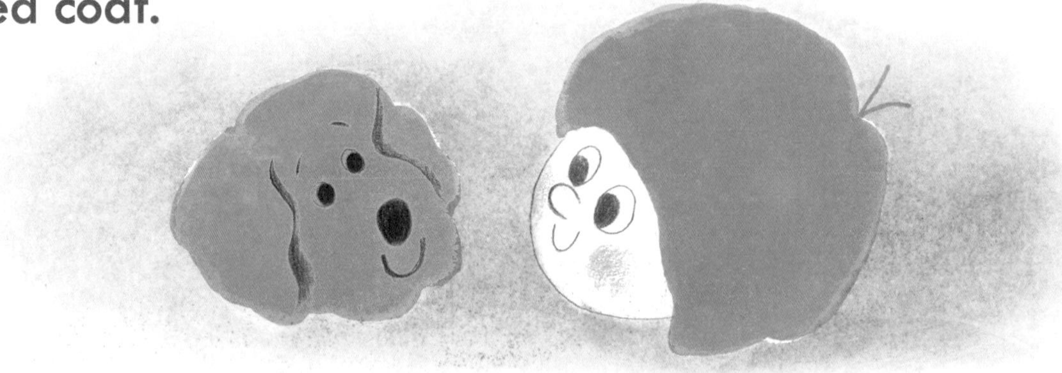

Truffle had already started to imagine all the great things he and Rocket would do together. (That was the name he was going to give him.)

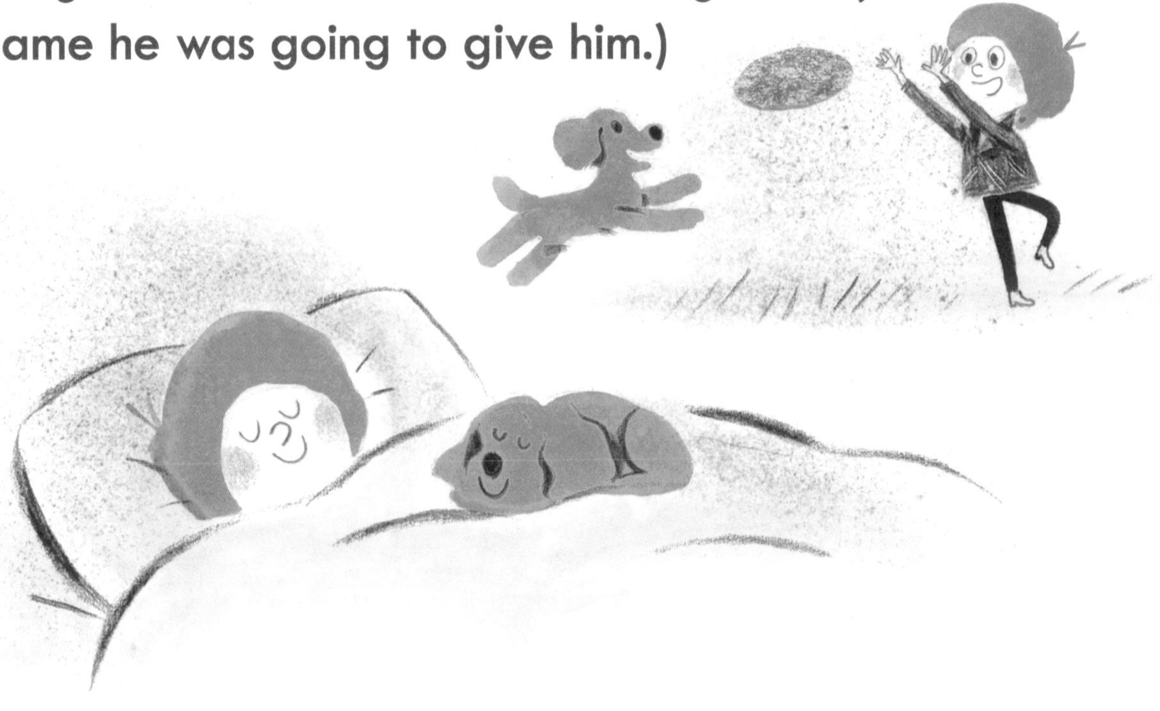

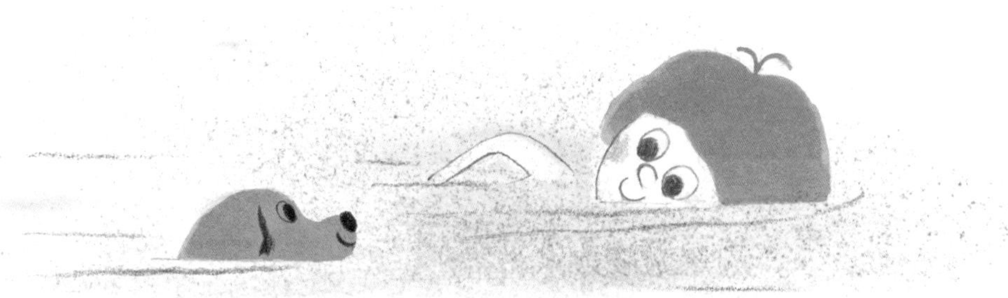

But after just one weekend with the dog, his mother said it would be too hard looking after a puppy and a family and her job all at once.

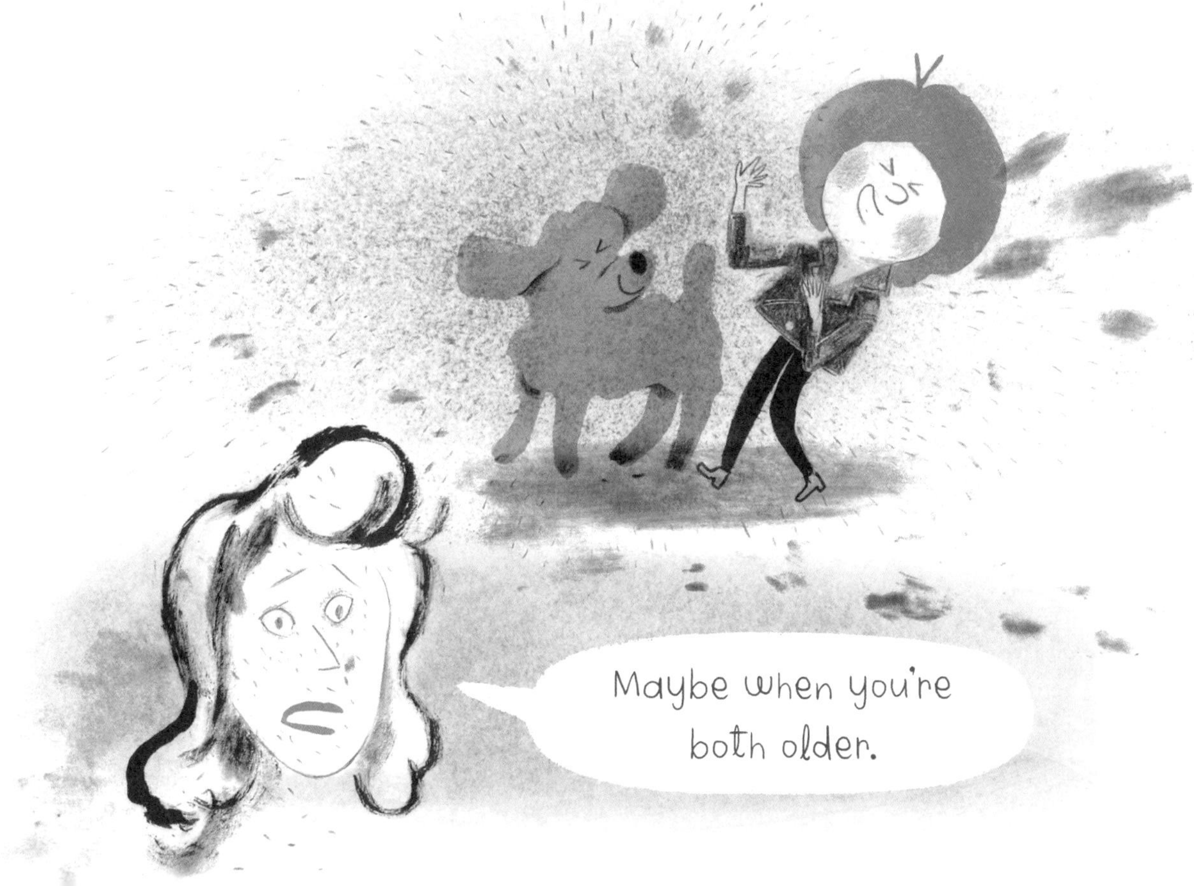
Maybe when you're both older.

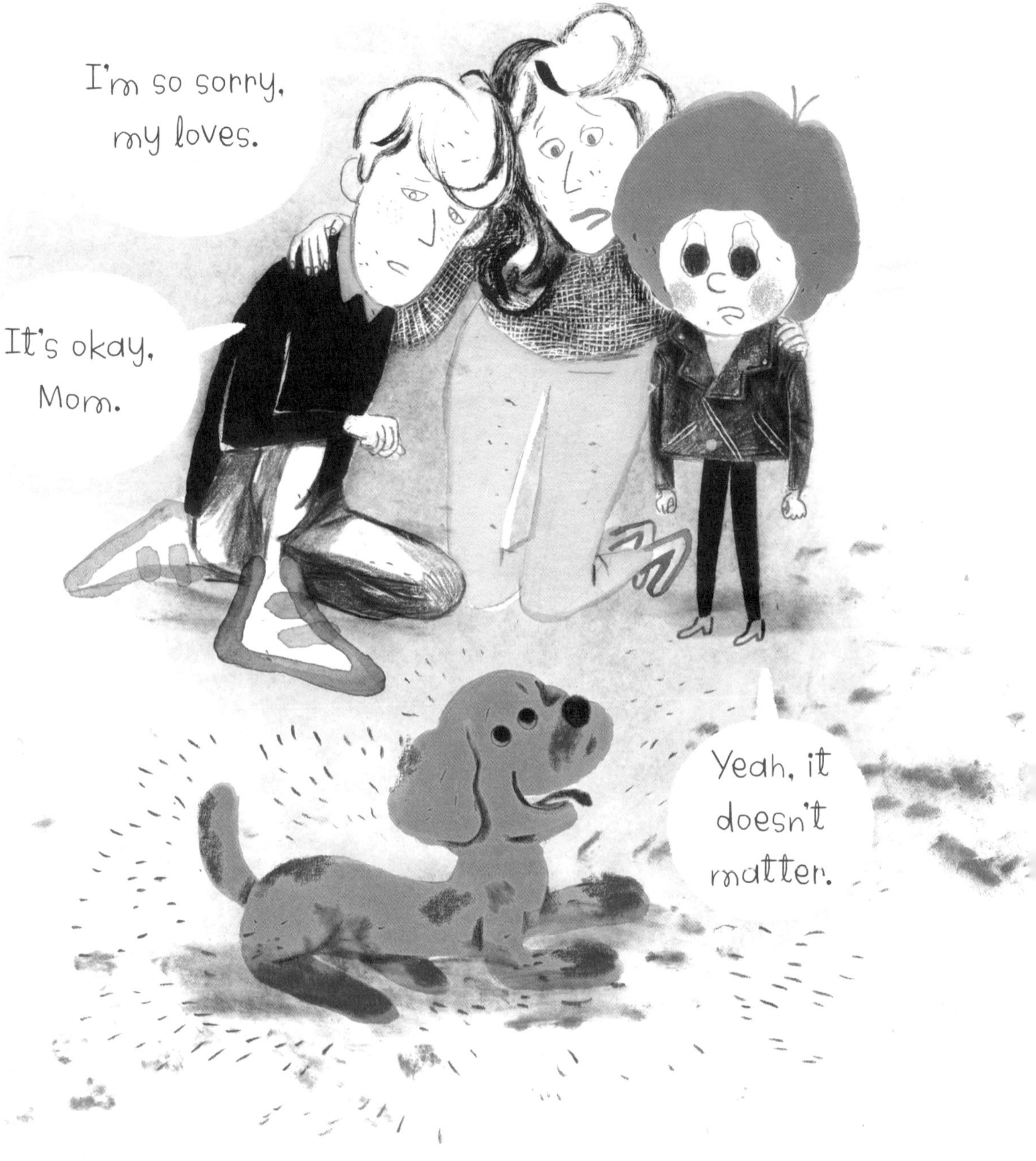
I'm so sorry, my loves.
It's okay, Mom.
Yeah, it doesn't matter.

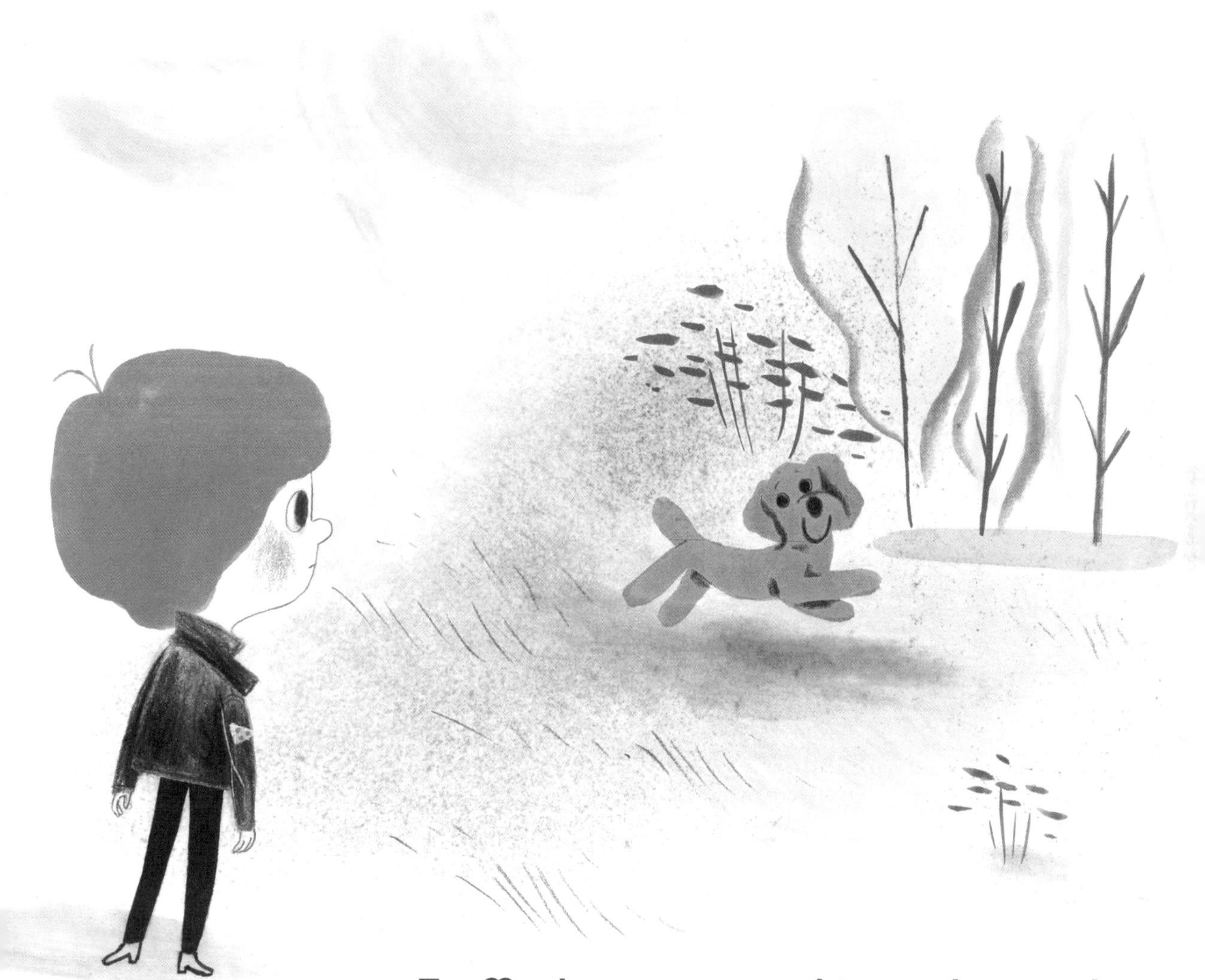

Truffle hates to see his mother sad.
But if someone forced him to drink a truth serum the way they do in the movies, he'd have to confess it does still matter a little that she said no.

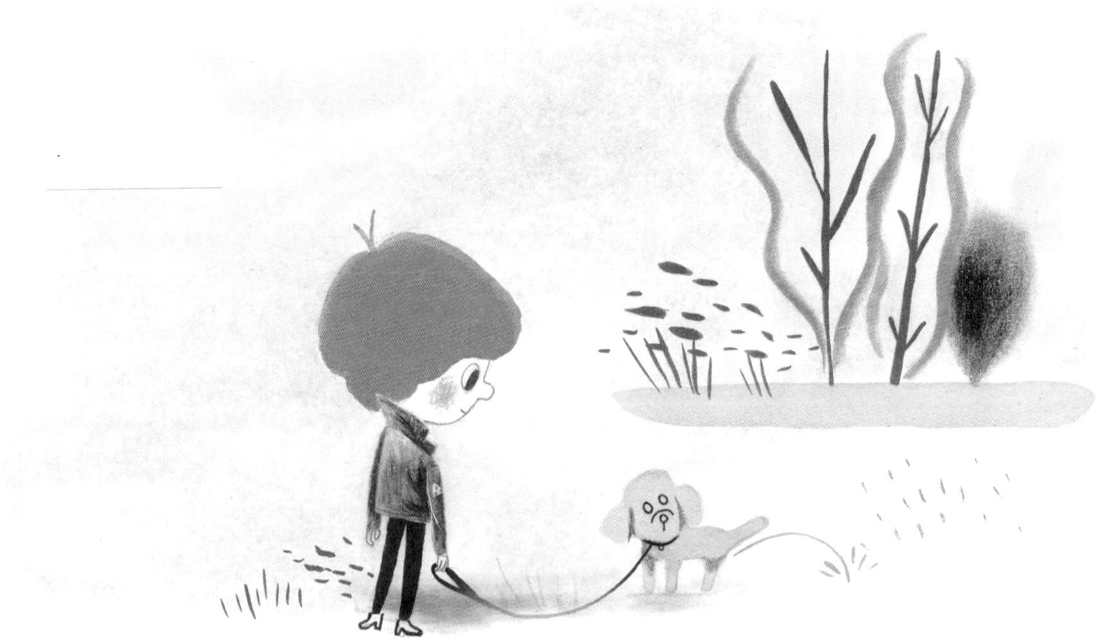

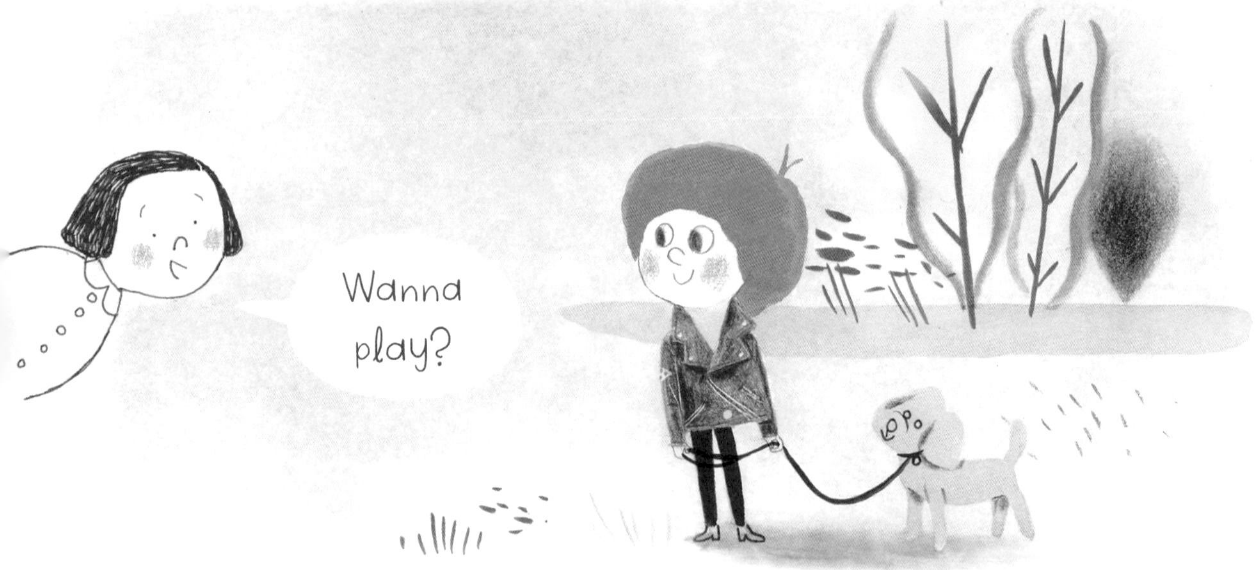
Wanna play?

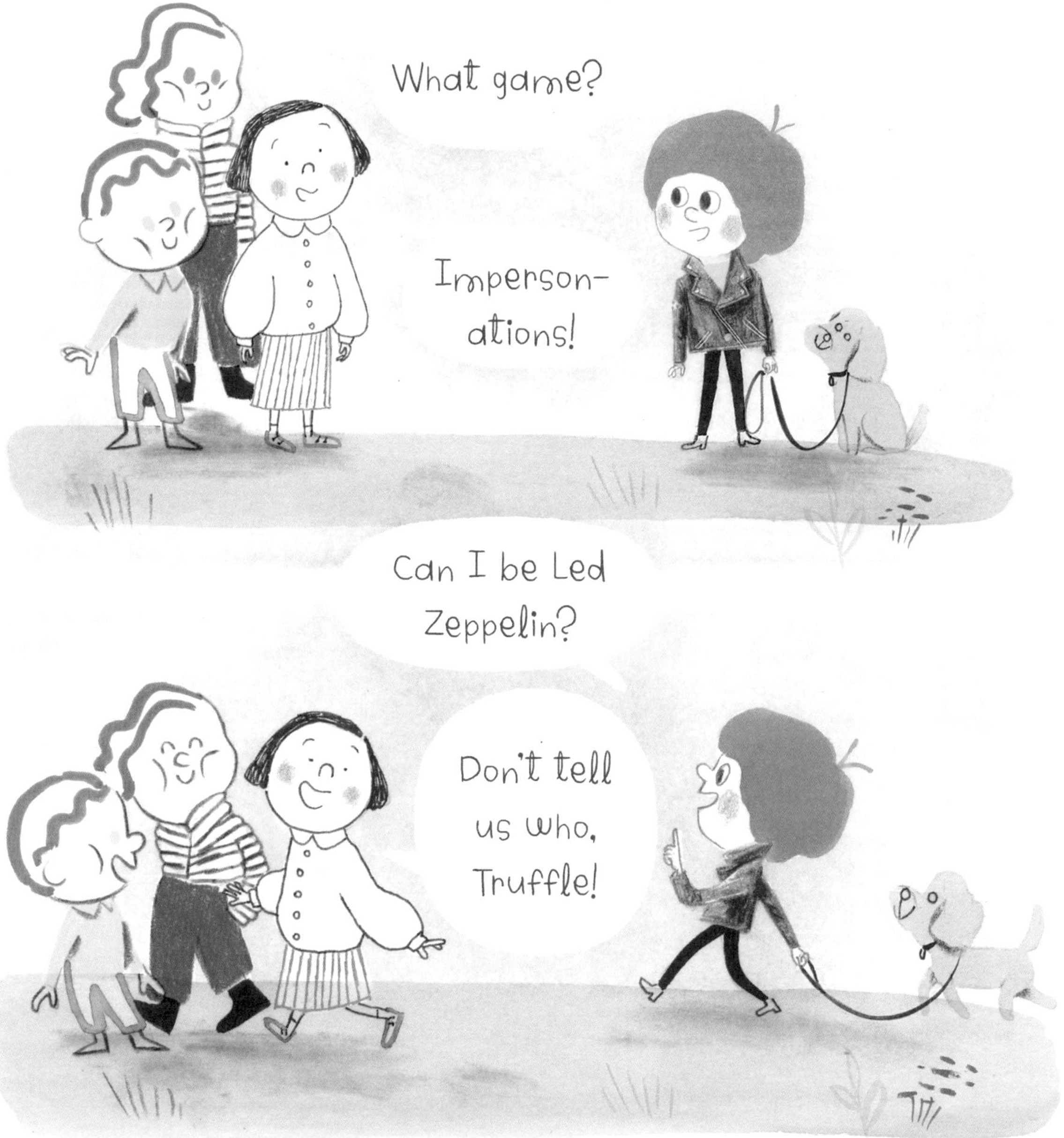
What game?
Imperson-ations!
Can I be Led Zeppelin?
Don't tell us who, Truffle!

Sonoyo is Truffle's favorite cousin. She goes to Japanese class on Saturdays because it's her mother's language. She wants to be sure her other cousins get all her jokes when she goes to visit them in Japan next summer.

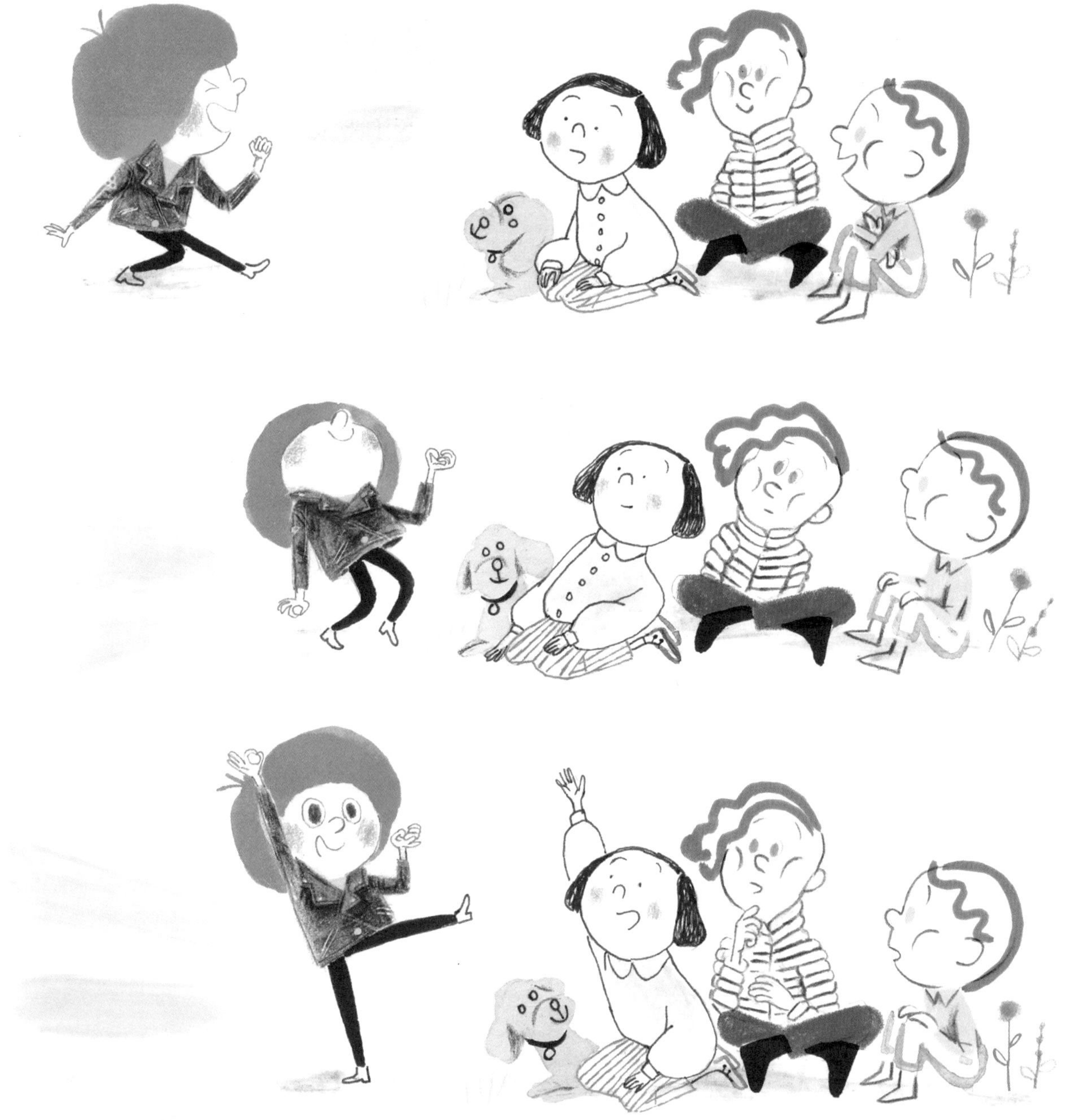

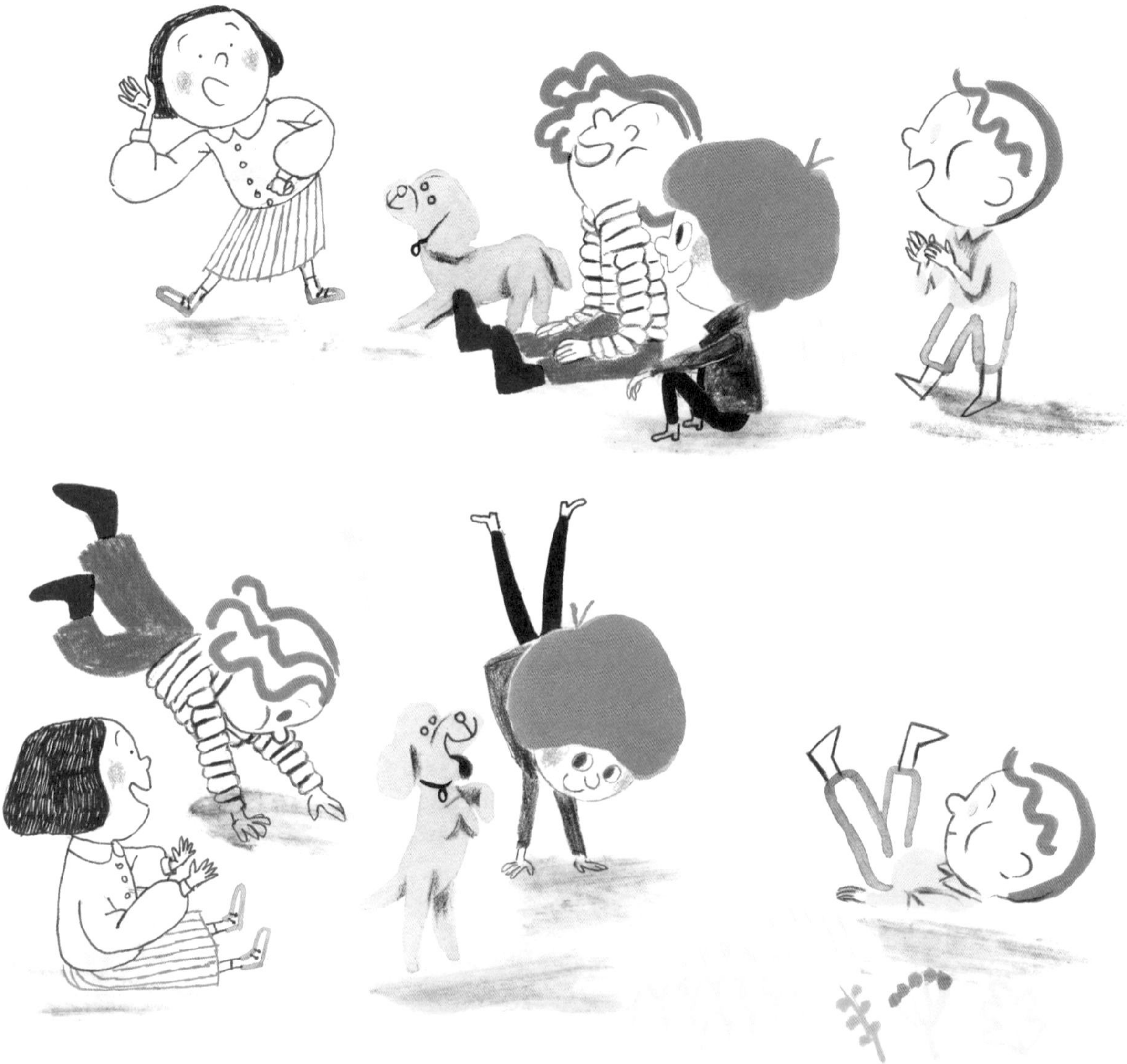

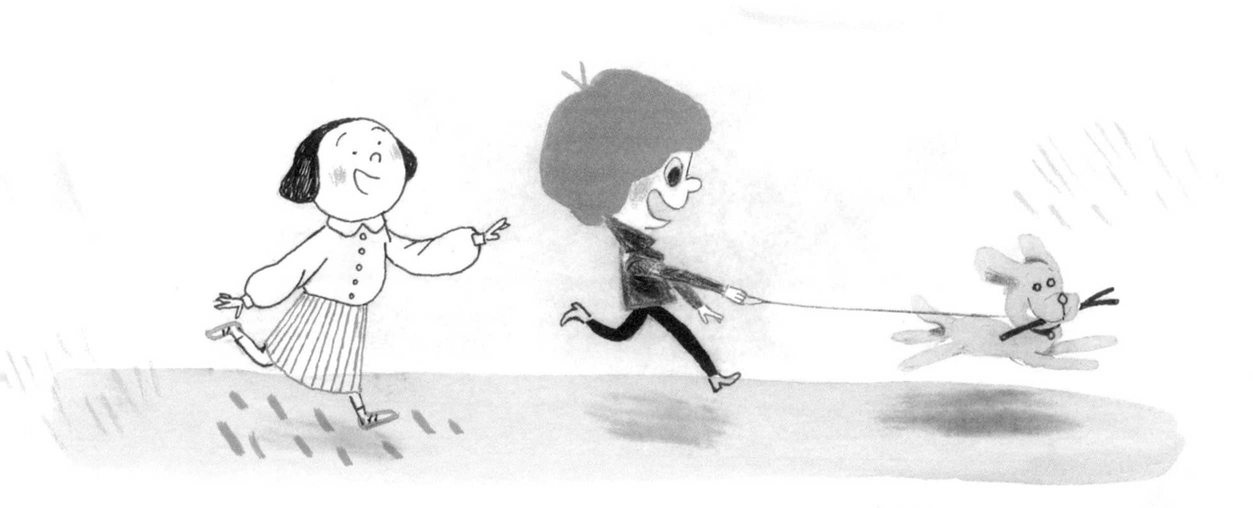

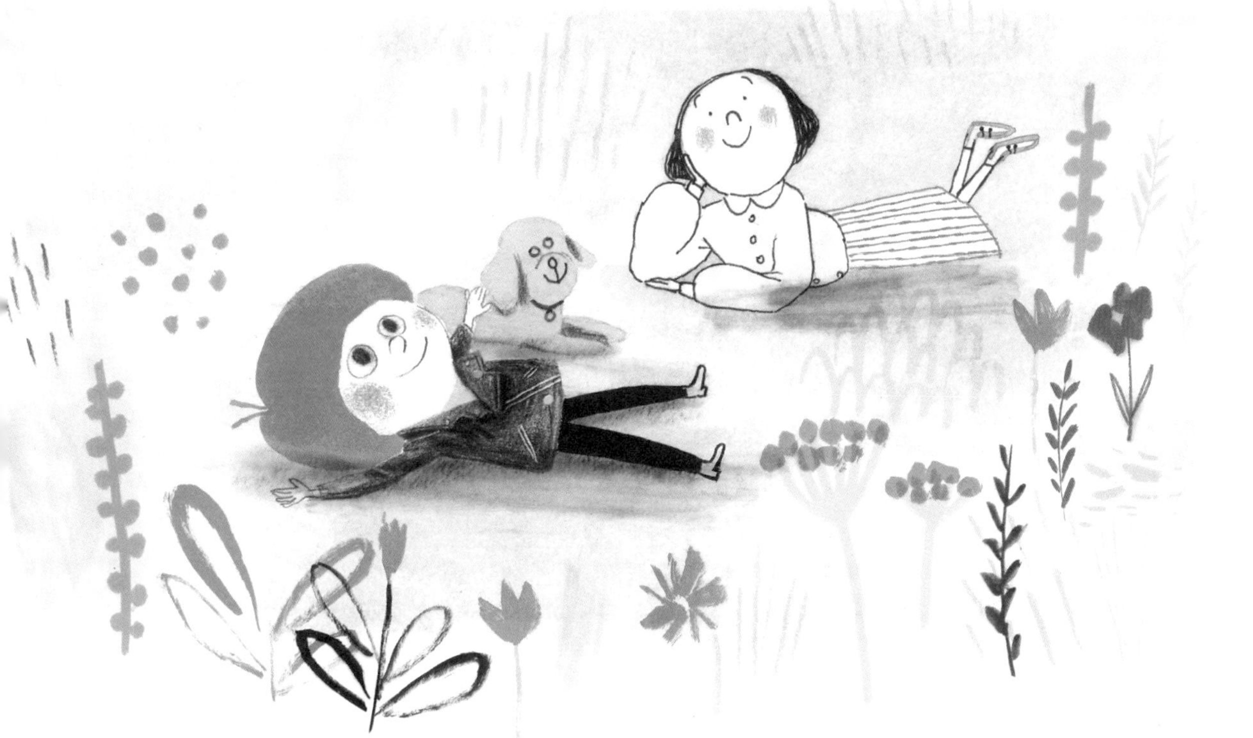

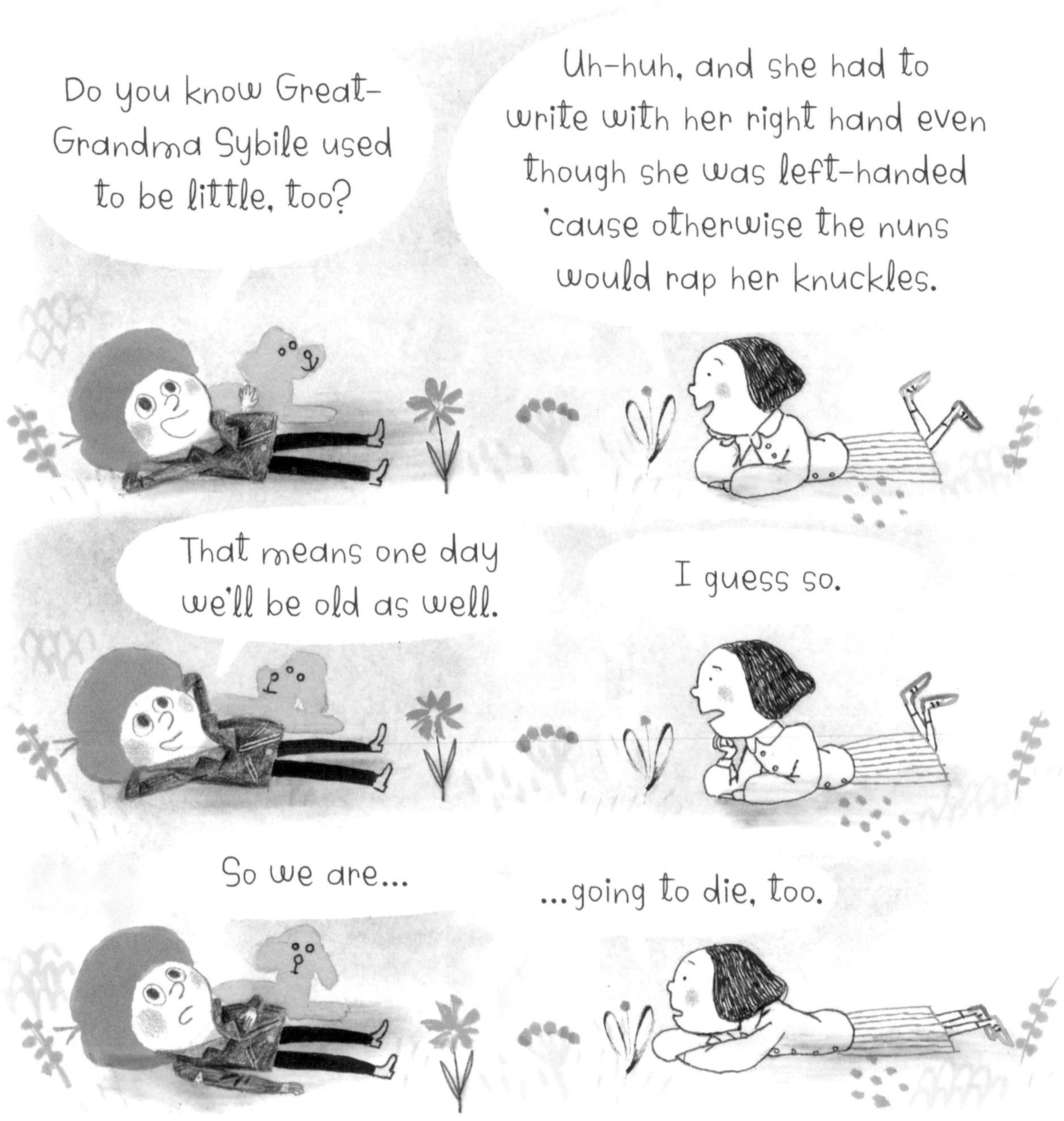
Do you know Great-Grandma Sybile used to be little, too?
Uh-huh, and she had to write with her right hand even though she was left-handed 'cause otherwise the nuns would rap her knuckles.
That means one day we'll be old as well.
I guess so.
So we are...
...going to die, too.

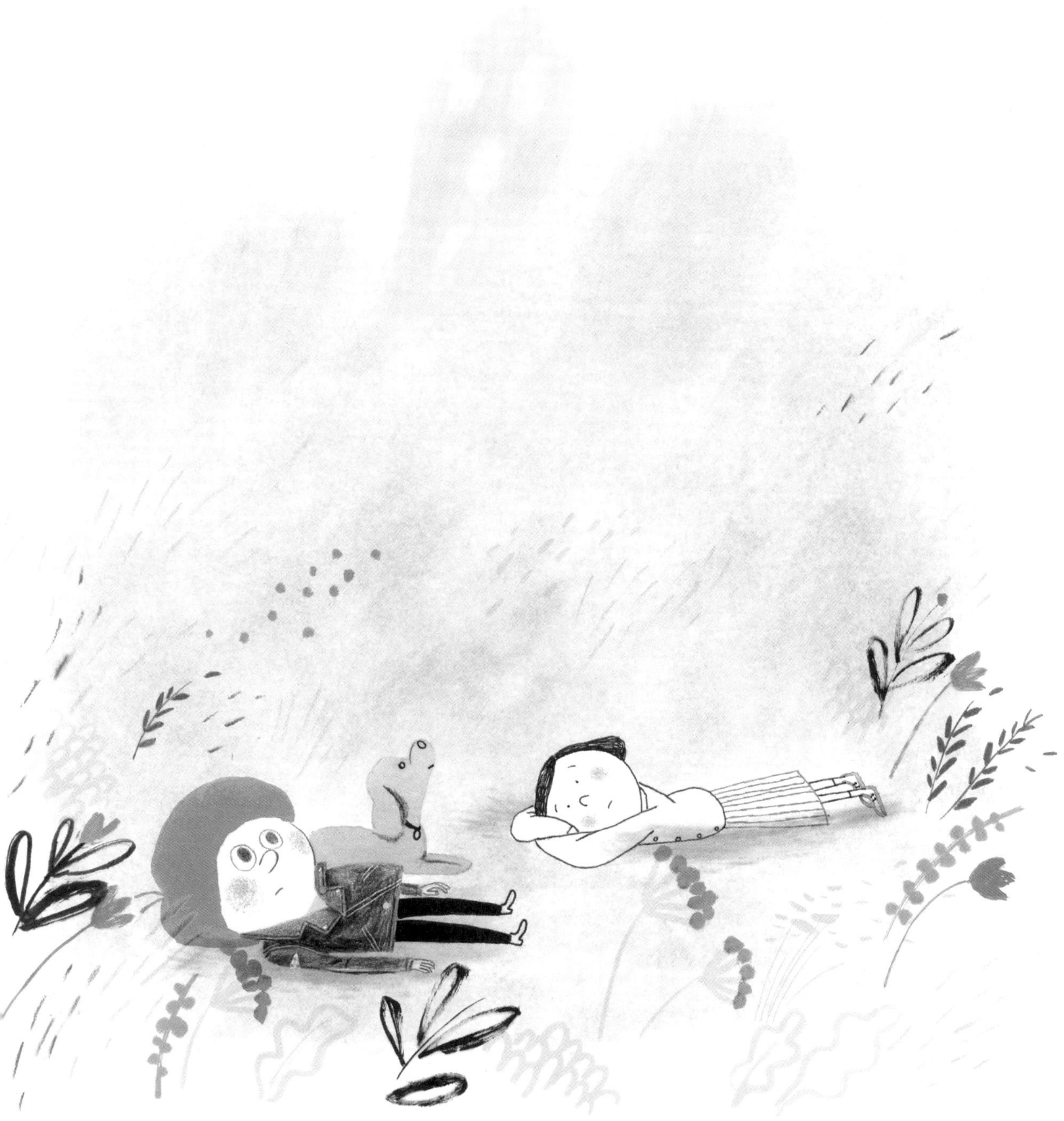

Truffle?
Time to go!

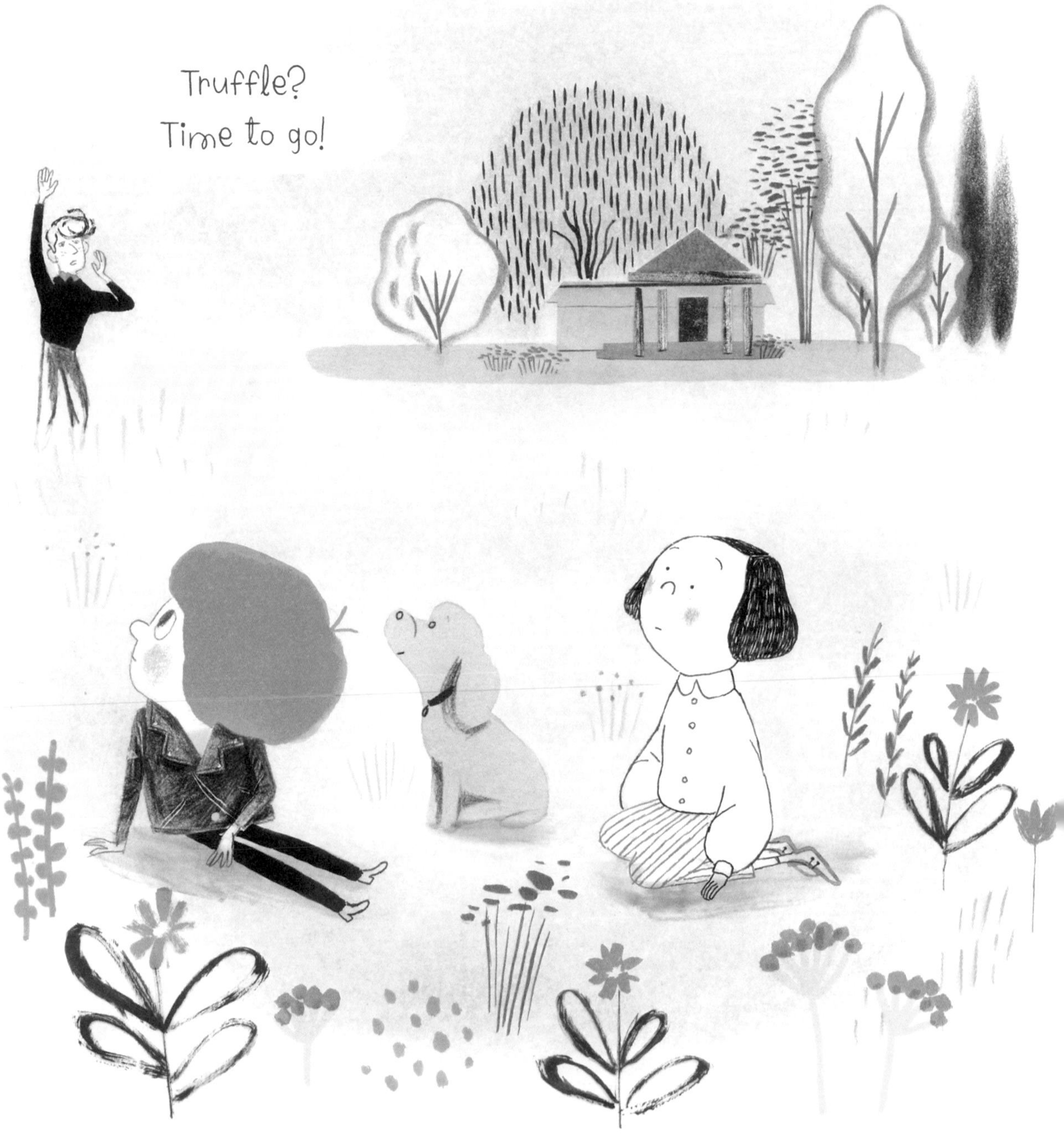

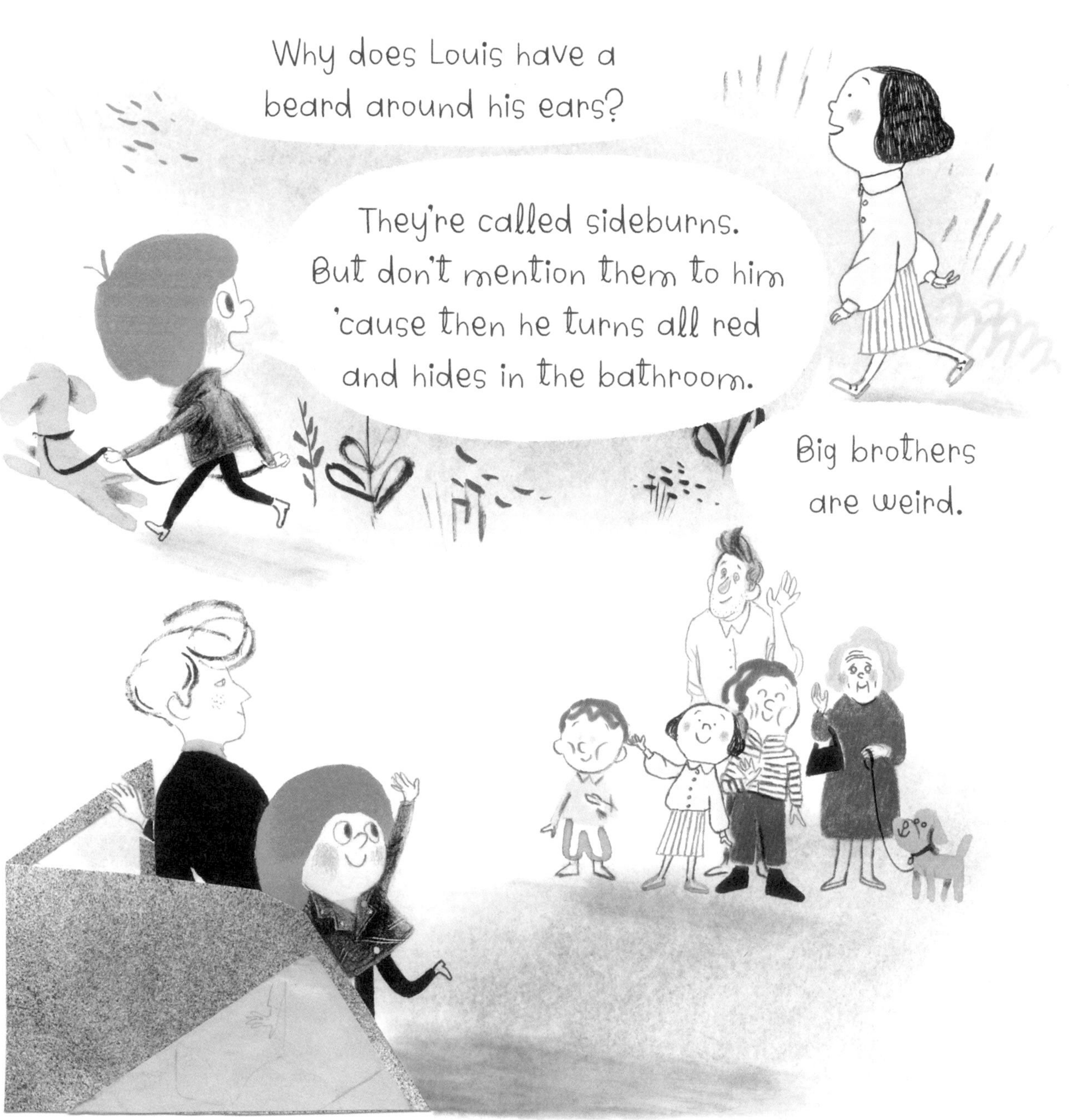
Why does Louis have a beard around his ears?
They're called sideburns. But don't mention them to him 'cause then he turns all red and hides in the bathroom.
Big brothers are weird.

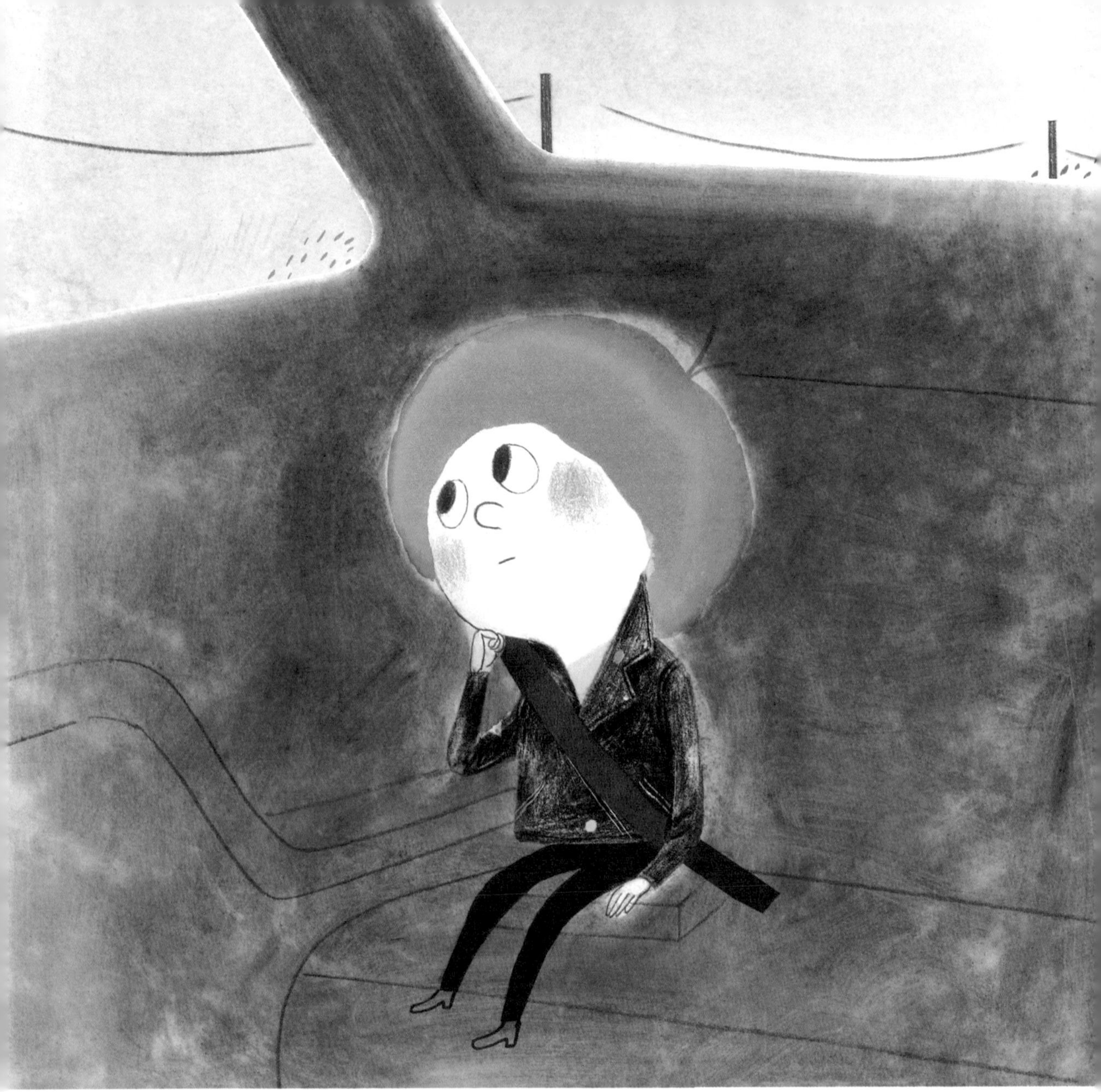

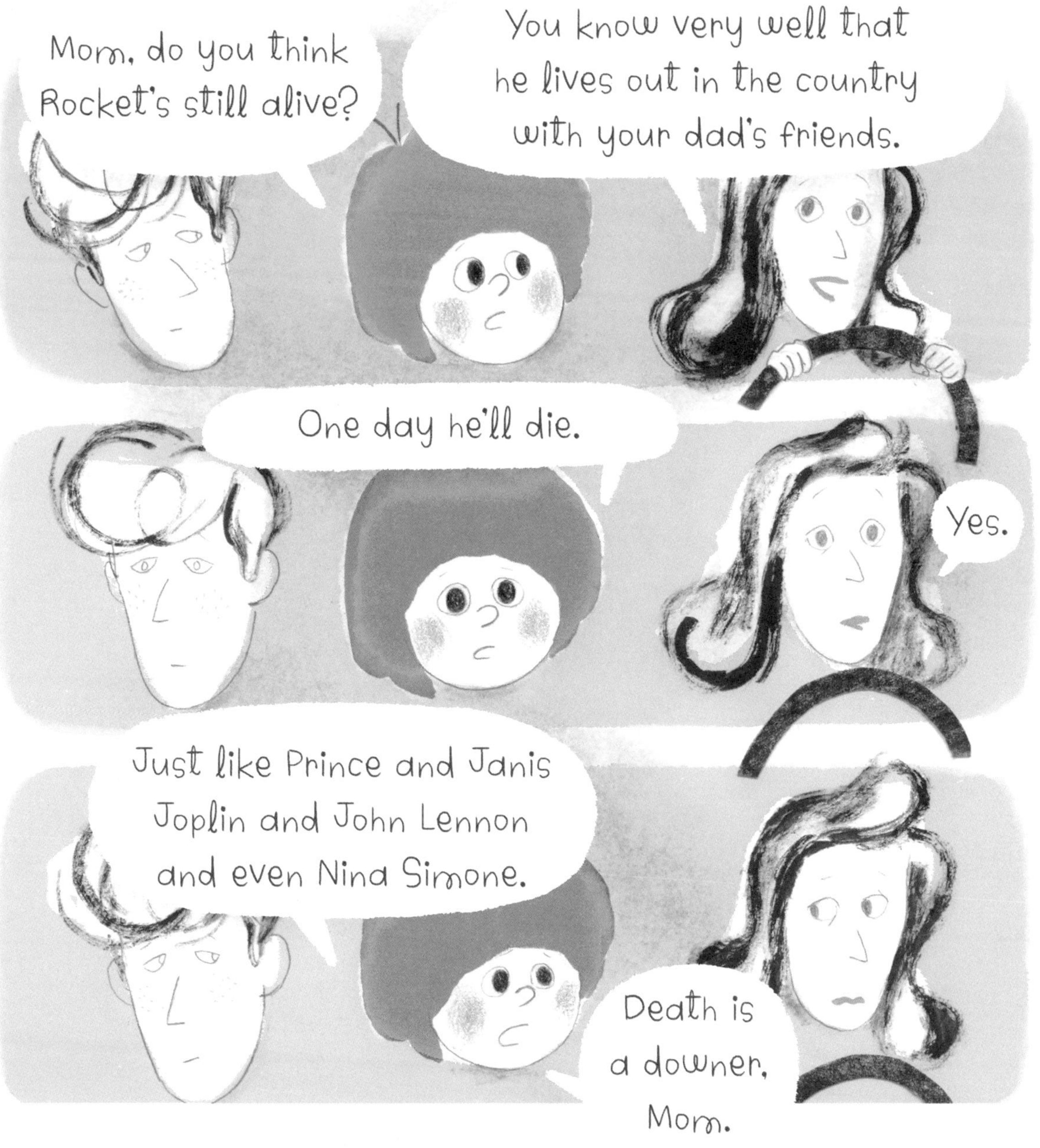
Mom, do you think Rocket's still alive?
You know very well that he lives out in the country with your dad's friends.
One day he'll die.
Yes.
Just like Prince and Janis Joplin and John Lennon and even Nina Simone.
Death is a downer, Mom.

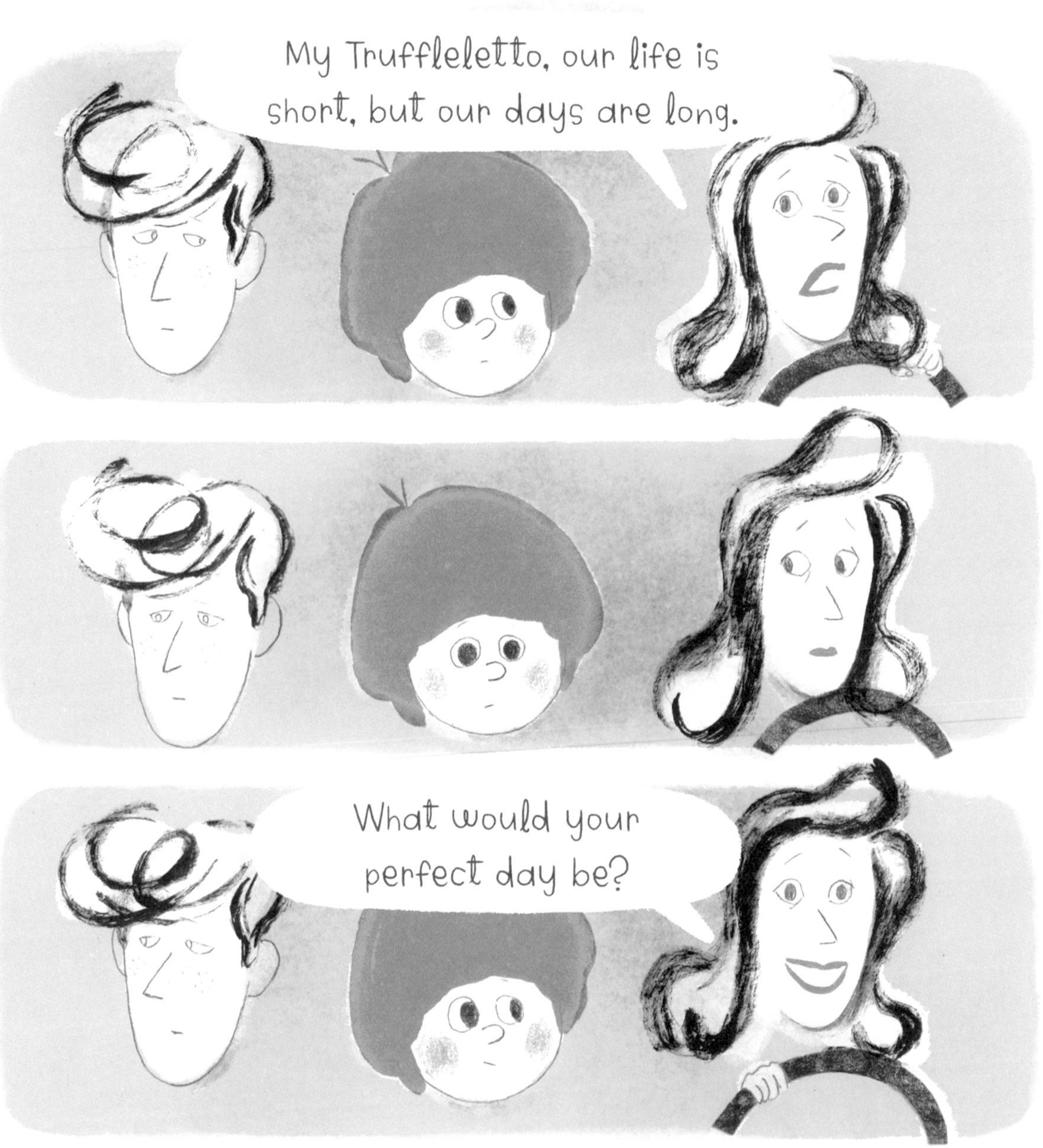
My Truffleletto, our life is short, but our days are long.
What would your perfect day be?

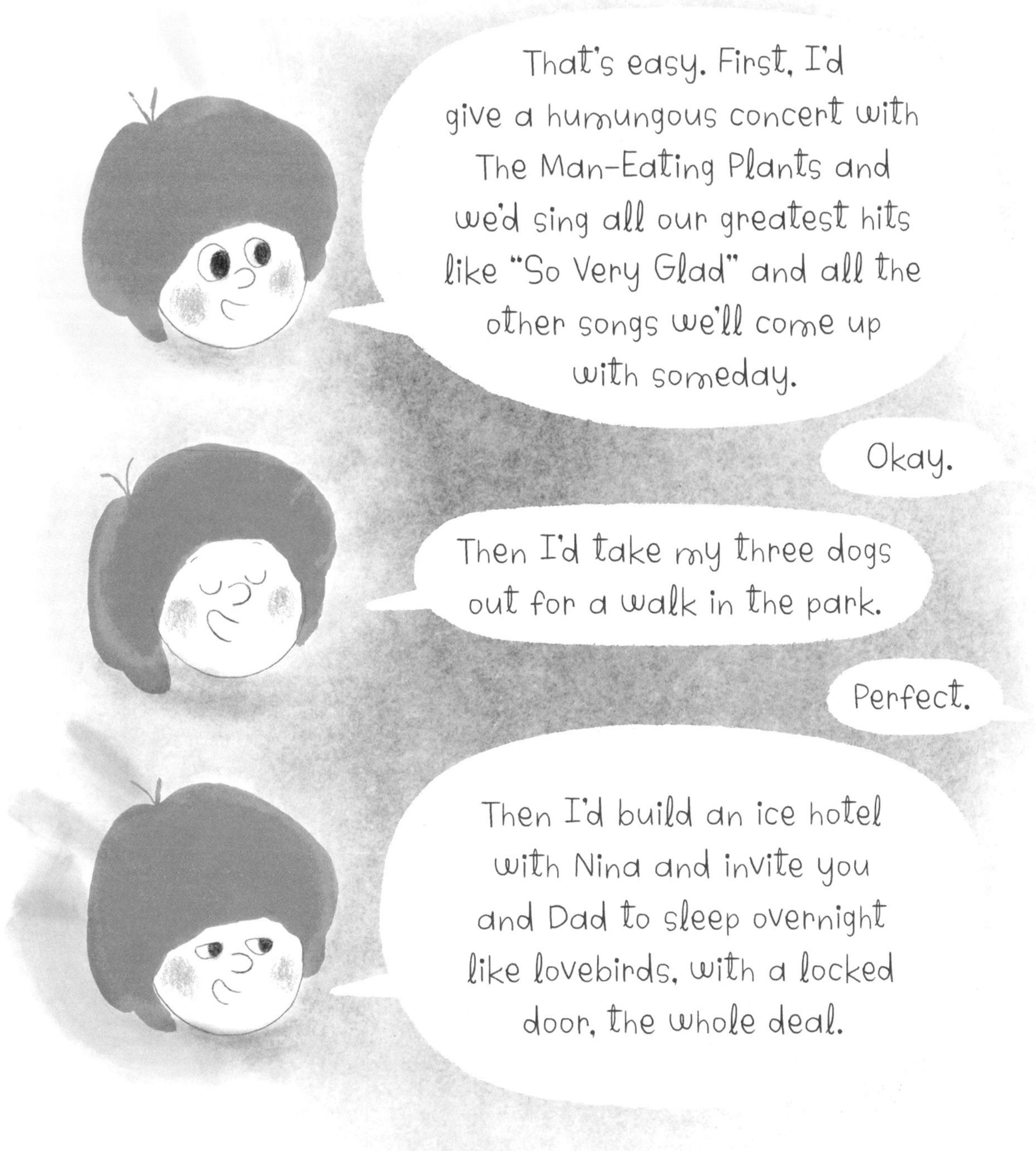
That's easy. First, I'd give a humungous concert with The Man-Eating Plants and we'd sing all our greatest hits like "So Very Glad" and all the other songs we'll come up with someday.
Okay.
Then I'd take my three dogs out for a walk in the park.
Perfect.
Then I'd build an ice hotel with Nina and invite you and Dad to sleep overnight like lovebirds, with a locked door, the whole deal.

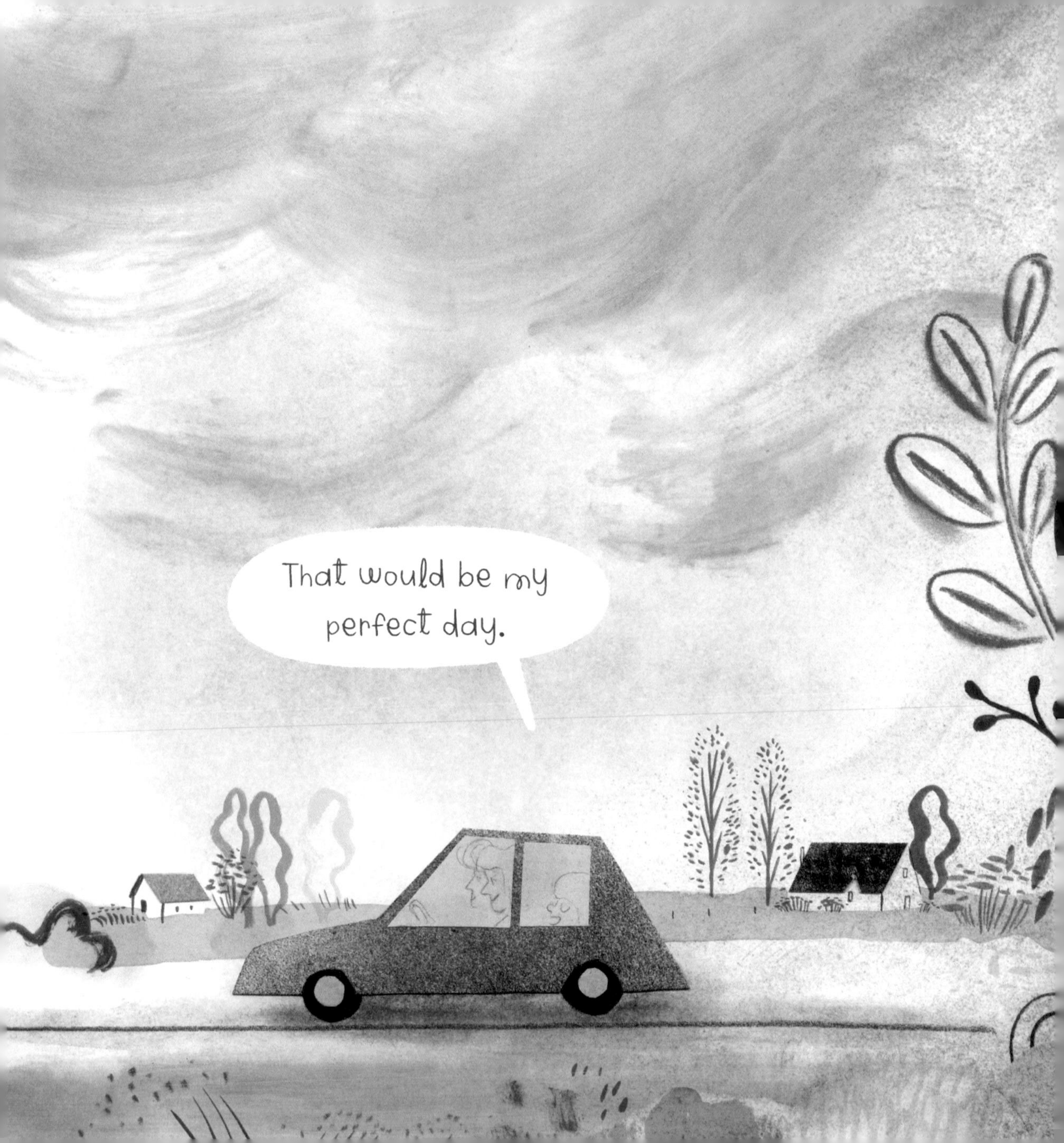
That would be my perfect day.

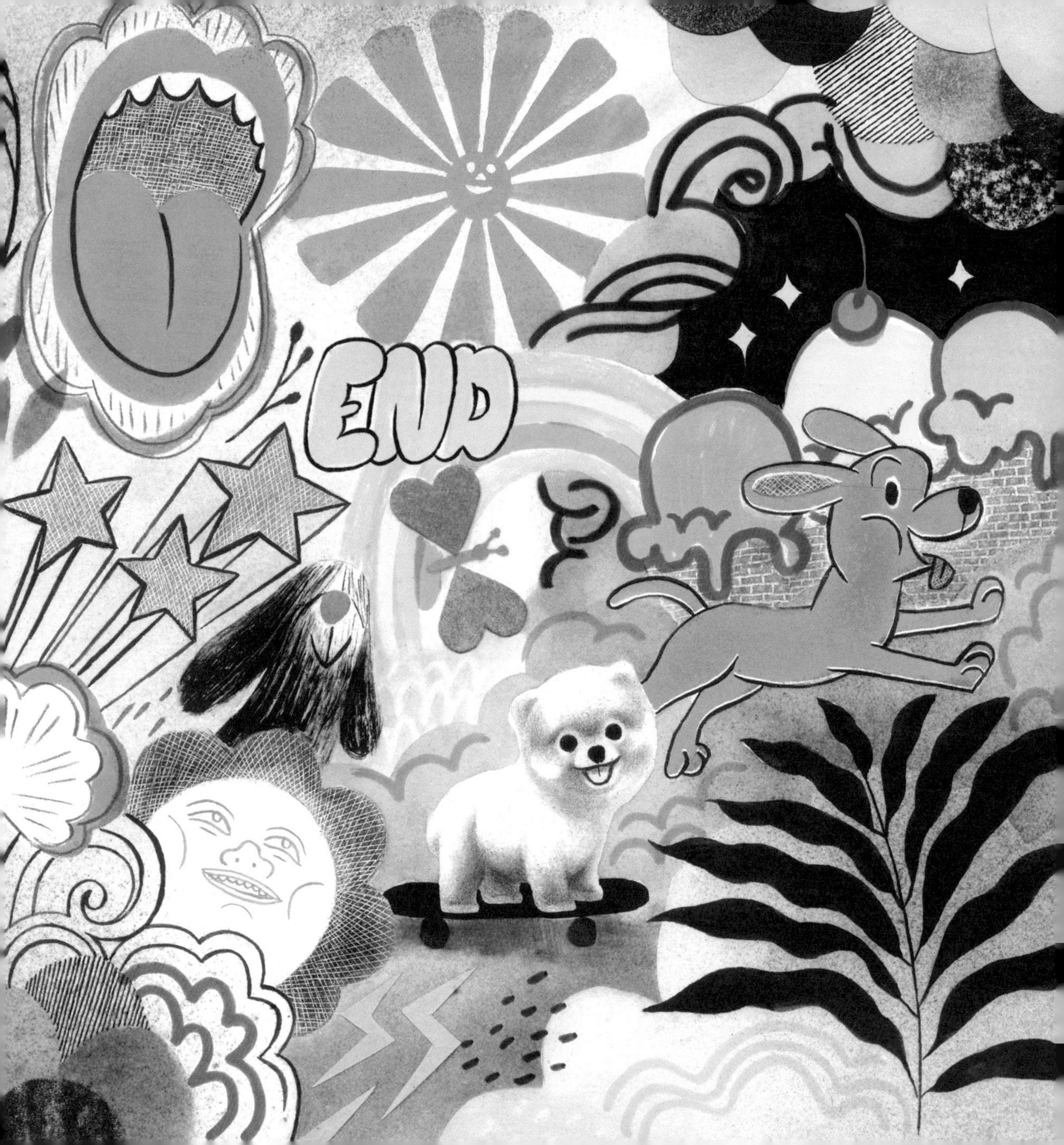
END

Other graphic novels by Fanny Britt and Isabelle Arsenault

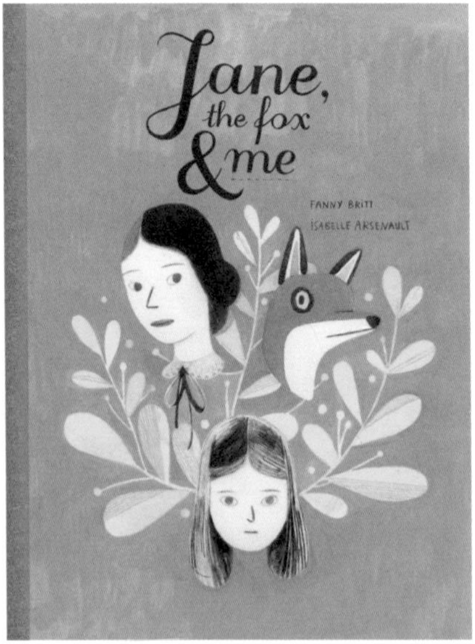

Jane, the fox & me
FANNY BRITT
ISABELLE ARSENAULT

Hélène has been inexplicably ostracized by the girls who were once her friends. She finds solace in Charlotte Brontë's *Jane Eyre*, but when Hélène is humiliated on a class trip in front of her entire grade, she needs more than a fictional character to see herself as a person deserving of laughter and friendship.

Hardcover • ISBN 978-1-55498-360-5
EPUB • ISBN 978-1-55498-361-2

Winner of the Governor General's Literary Award for French Language Children's Illustration
A New York Times Best Children's Illustrated Book
A Bank Street College of Education Best Children's Book of the Year

★ "Britt's poetic prose captures Hélène's heartbreaking isolation . . . [A] brutally beautiful story."
—*Horn Book*, starred review

★ "Readers will be delighted to see Hélène's world change as she grows up, learning to ignore the mean girls and realizing that, like Jane, she is worthy of friendship and love."
—*School Library Journal*, starred review

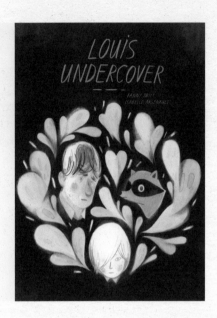

Louis's dad cries—Louis knows this because he spies on him. His dad misses the happy times when their family was together, just as Louis does. But as it is, he and his little brother, Truffle, have to travel back and forth between their dad's country house and their mom's city apartment, where she tries to hide her own tears.

Hardcover • ISBN 978-1-55498-859-4
EPUB • ISBN 978-1-55498-860-0

A Bank Street College of Education Best Children's Book of the Year

★ "Arsenault's symbolic use of color and animated illustrations breathe life into Britt's quirky, beautiful story, which emphasizes that love is the bravest act of all."
—*School Library Journal*, starred review

★ "This nuanced tale of an observant, sensitive boy finding his own brand of strength is bittersweet and beautifully composed." —*Booklist*, starred review